GETTING EVEN

ALSO BY SARAH RAYNER

GETTING EVEN

Sarah Rayner

 ST. MARTIN'S GRIFFIN ≋ NEW YORK

GETTING EVEN. Copyright © 2014 by Sarah Rayner. All rights reserved. Printed in the United States of America. For information, address St. Martin's Press, 175 Fifth Avenue, New York, N.Y. 10010.

www.stmartins.com

Designed by Anna Gorovoy

The Library of Congress Cataloging-in-Publication Data is available upon request.

ISBN 978-1-250-04211-8 (trade paperback)
ISBN 978-1-250-05873-7 (hardcover)
ISBN 978-1-250-03471-7 (e-book)

St. Martin's Griffin books may be purchased for educational, business, or promotional use. For information on bulk purchases, please contact Macmillan Corporate and Premium Sales Department at 1-800-221-7945, extension 5442, or write specialmarkets@macmillan.com.

A different version of this title was published in the United Kingdom by Orion in 2002.

First St. Martin's Griffin Edition: September 2014

10 9 8 7 6 5 4 3 2 1

GETTING EVEN

1. Friends all

"We'll be late," said Dan.

"Aw . . . Five more minutes?" said Orianna, snuggling up to him.

With her head on his chest, she could feel his breath come and go. She gazed absentmindedly past the geraniums on the windowsill and into the distance; she was in that soporific state after making love when nothing else matters. Even the presentation she was due to give that morning seemed less important, although the new business could be worth thousands to the ad agency where she worked.

If I were to die this minute, she thought, I'd die happy. If a bomb were to land *slap bang* on the apartment and snuff us out in an instant, it would be a good time to go.

Her eyes came to rest on the window box. There was something about the zinging red petals against the dusty bright green of the leaves she found beautiful. Even on a gray day like today, they were brimming with life, determined to bloom, defiant.

This was how Dan made her feel—the world seemed heightened,

her senses ablaze. Ordinary experiences were more intense; she noticed things that might otherwise pass her by.

Orianna patted his belly. "You realize this is one of my favorite bits of you?"

Dan breathed in and tensed his lower abdomen. "Look—you can almost see the outline of my muscles."

Much as she loved his body, Orianna was skeptical. Thanks to the amount of sex they'd been having, she'd got to know every inch of him over the last few months and it seemed unlikely she'd have missed such a delicious sign of masculinity. "Where?"

Dan extricated himself from their embrace and sat up. "Here."

Indeed, there were the oh-so-faint contours of a six-pack.

"Ooh yes!"

"I've worked hard for them. I've been doing extra sit-ups with Rob at the gym."

"Because I said I liked your little tummy?"

Dan's voice was gruff. "I've always been a bit conscious of it."

"I didn't mean it as a criticism . . ."

"No, I know . . ." He paused. "You see, I didn't used to be like this."

"Oh?"

"I was quite chubby, when I was little."

She couldn't imagine it. Dan might not be Michelangelo's *David,* but he was in pretty good shape for an ad man with several years' drinking and debauchery under his belt.

He scratched his head, then muttered, "My brother used to call me *Dough Boy.*"

"No!" She couldn't resist poking a finger into Dan's midriff. "Because of this?"

Dan jumped. "Stop! That tickles!"

"What did you say?" She tickled him some more.

Dan laughed, helpless, but preventing further humiliation seemed the incentive he needed to precipitate him out of bed and into the shower. Minutes later he emerged, rubbing his hair dry with a towel so it stood up in haphazard spikes.

"It'd be great to celebrate getting the pitch over with," she said. "What are you doing tonight?" She awaited his response, apprehensive. Although they'd been seeing each other a while and he'd never given her cause to worry, Orianna wasn't confident when it came to men. Moments of uncertainty when she feared he might say he had something better to do still gave her butterflies.

"I've got an appointment with Rob at seven thirty."

"Oh." She turned away so he wouldn't see how disappointed she was. She'd fallen for Dan big-time and couldn't get enough of him. Although perhaps she ought to be grateful—these grueling sessions with his personal trainer seemed to be keeping him trim.

He added, "I'm free afterwards."

Inside she skipped with delight. "I thought you guys sometimes went for a drink, when you have an evening session?"

"Yeah, we do—only a quick one."

"Don't let me stop you."

"No, no, you won't."

Hmm, she pondered, I do so want to see Dan later, and it's about time we began socializing openly . . . Rob would be a good place to start. Besides, it could be worth getting to know him. All this talk of tummies—now I'm in a regular sexual relationship, I might benefit from a little personal training myself. He could help me stave off those Italian curves to which I seem genetically disposed if Mum is anything to go by.

"How about I hook up with you both somewhere? I'd like to meet him."

"Actually, that may not be a bad idea."

"Yeah?"

"I'm a bit worried about Rob."

"Oh?" Dan's *such* a sweetheart, thought Orianna. How touching he's so concerned.

"Having you there might help."

"D'you reckon?" Even though she'd never met Rob, she was flattered by the idea he could need her advice.

"I think he might, er . . ." Dan scratched his scalp again, a habit she'd noticed suggested he was about to reveal something.

What could it be? Perhaps Rob had girlfriend problems, and Orianna, with her female perspective, could help him. She was good at being a sympathetic ear. And maybe, when he met Orianna, he'd realize what a great girl *she* was, and appreciating there were other lovely women out there would ease his pain . . . Not that she'd do anything about it, of course. No, she was in love with Dan (though she hadn't told him yet), but still, it was nice to be admired. She smiled, relishing the prospect of having two men to herself for the evening. "Mm?"

"I think he might fancy me," muttered Dan.

Across London, in Battersea, Rob slept on under his duvet, oblivious to the fact his sexual proclivities were an early morning talking point in Holloway. He'd no client till lunchtime today (thank God) so could indulge in sleeping in, with Potato, the cat, snuggled up at his feet. The revving engines and beeping horns of rush hour had evolved into the soft *schwoom, schwoom* of regular traffic, and his roommate had banged the front door shut long before Rob began to stir. His friends often commented on his ability to sleep through anything; today was no exception.

Eventually, after eleven, Potato made his starvation clear with determined padding of paws on his pillow. Rob rubbed his eyes, looked crossly at Potato and then the alarm clock, admitted the cat was within his rights, and hauled himself blearily into the kitchen. He liked to maintain it was because his job was so *physical* he needed more rest than most, though in truth he would sleep just as long even when he'd been slobbing in front of the television all day.

"You miss our Chloë, don't you?" he said to Potato and scooped an extra spoonful of Whiskas into his bowl to make up for it. Chloë was Rob's old roommate, and a few weeks before she'd gone to work in New York, leaving him in charge of the cat. Rob missed Chloë too, but at least he could regularly correspond with her by instant messenger.

Texting and phoning the US was expensive, but messaging was free, so he would contact Chloë several times a day, keeping her abreast of the minutiae of his life. He'd even written once to tell her the state of his bowels after a rather unsuccessful attempt at a new Indian recipe. It was only when she'd replied tetchily that this was TMI (and Chloë was no prude), especially as she had Important Things To Do (and Chloë tended to welcome distraction), he realized he'd better curb his transatlantic correspondence.

At last he was dressed, propelled by the need to pay his direct debits and keep himself in designer shirts and the occasional designer drug. Armed with numerous toiletries and a post-workout change of clothes, he headed into the West End. He'd do a quick bit of food shopping in Chinatown, then go to the gym and meet his first client. She was from Green Integrated, the Soho agency whose staff provided a sizeable chunk of his business: a woman he'd not met before.

Ivy.

"Perfect weather for *That Sunshine Feeling*," quipped Ivy, throwing her bag and raincoat onto the sofa.

Orianna had been hard at work for almost an hour, nosed pressed to the screen of her computer. She turned to look out of the window. It was raining buckets. "Isn't it?"

"So, sweetie." Ivy's tone was brisk. "How we doing?"

"Nearly sorted. I'm running out captions for the boards."

"You're a star. When do we have to leave?"

"Nine thirty."

"Just time for a coffee."

"You mean you're not going to start the day with a glass of *That Sunshine Feeling*?" Orianna laughed.

"Am I hell," said Ivy, and headed off to the drinks machine.

While her copywriter was gone, Orianna thumbed through their creative work, checking everything was in order. *That Sunshine Feeling*, a new soft drink, could be a very exciting piece of business. Press ads, posters, direct mail, promotions—the lot. She and Ivy had been slaving on the product all week, staying late several nights on the trot.

As she was sticking a caption on the last board, her phone rang.

"Oh, Orianna, hi." It was Esme, the production assistant. "I know you're about to leave, so I'm sorry to bother you."

She was a good deal younger than Orianna and she sounded anxious. Orianna's heart went out to her. "It's OK. What's the matter?"

"I wondered what time you think you'll be back."

"Midday-ish, I guess."

"It's only an urgent brief's come in . . ."

Orianna's heart sank.

"On *Burroso*, the olive oil spread, and I was hoping you and Ivy would have the chance to take a look at it."

Orianna was drained. She'd been planning to take it easier for the rest of the day—catch up on some admin. She was sure Ivy wouldn't relish the prospect either. Yet she liked Esme and wanted to help. "When's it needed by?"

Esme hesitated. "Tomorrow, first thing."

"What is it?"

"The July mailer."

"Ah, yes." Compared to a pitch, this was simple. Orianna and Ivy knew the brand inside out—they should be able to sort it fast. And she was still basking in the glow of that morning's lovemaking with Dan, so well-disposed toward the world. "We'll look at it when we're back."

"Are you sure?"

"Yes." It would mean working through lunch again. But tonight she was going out with Dan and Rob—at least *then* she'd have the chance to unwind.

"Taxi's here," said Clare.

Damn, thought Ivy, I could do with a coffee. Oh well, we're bound to be offered one by the client. She pulled on her coat again, picked up her bag, and followed Orianna and Clare into the elevator and out of the building.

But when they entered the meeting room at Bellings Scott Inc., Ivy was dismayed to see that there were four clients sitting around a large glass-topped table, and all of them appeared to be drinking *That Sunshine Feeling*. Not a drop of coffee in sight.

Bugger! she thought, scanning the room.

They sat down; Clare at the head of the table—as the new business director it was her role to take the lead—Ivy and Orianna together so they could present their creative work in tandem.

"Have a glass of our finest?" offered the guy nearest to them, holding out a jug of near-luminous orange liquid. The other three clients smiled and nodded, as if *That Sunshine Feeling* were the best thing on earth.

Creeps, thought Ivy.

"Yes, please," said Orianna. She gently pressed her foot against Ivy's to signal she should follow her lead.

"Thanks," muttered Ivy.

Clare opened the meeting with an introduction to Green Integrated. As she did so, Ivy, who'd heard the spiel before, found herself contemplating how Clare's mouse-like appearance belied her tenacity. Once Clare got her claws into a new business prospect she was ferocious in her pursuit; she was one of Green's greatest assets, the only woman on the board. Then, as Clare recapped on the brief, Ivy couldn't resist the temptation to typecast each client. It was a game she often played to amuse herself in presentations. The one who'd served their drinks was an East End barrow boy (wider than wide). There was a used-car dealer (fat, balding, probably the boss). Next to him, a department store assistant (a dire case of mutton-dressed-as-lamb), and finally the token female totty (a frizzy-haired twentysomething).

At last it was time to present the creative work. Orianna rose to her feet.

"I'm not surprised you're all drinking *That Sunshine Feeling* this morning." She beamed. "Because as Ivy and I discovered when we began working on the brand, it really gets you going first thing."

You liar, thought Ivy. She and Orianna had agreed it was revolting—way too sweet, watery and, according to the list of ingredients, full of preservatives. Still, Ivy had to admire her colleague's diplomacy.

Orianna continued. "Talking of 'getting going' set us thinking—what is the most obvious symbol of stopping and starting, getting going?"

The clients shook their heads, clueless.

"Traffic lights," said Orianna, as if there was no question.

They all nodded.

She turned to Barrow Boy. "And what's your product made of?"

"Fruit."

Doh! thought Ivy.

Orianna was more patient. "What kind of fruit?"

"Oranges," he said.

Not that you can taste them, thought Ivy.

Orianna turned to Used-Car Salesman. "And, I know it may seem obvious, but what color's your product?"

"Orange."

"And traffic lights?" she turned to Mutton-Dressed-As-Lamb. "What color are they?"

"Orange," she said obediently.

What, all three lights? protested Ivy silently.

But Orianna had them eating out of her hand. "Exactly. Red, *orange,* and green."

Credit where it's due, acknowledged Ivy. Orianna's a wow at presentations. I might have come up with the overall concept, but when it comes to talking others through an idea, Orianna is in a class of her own. Her enthusiasm is infectious, her open and friendly manner a real advantage. That she's so damn sweet looking with those wide brown eyes does no harm either . . .

Orianna coughed.

Ivy, prompted, got to her feet. She picked up the first board from the stack she had propped against the legs of her chair and flipped it around. It was a plain piece of card, covered in an amber-colored paper.

"We thought we'd *own* orange," she explained. "But not just any old orange—that's been done before, as I'm sure you all appreciate." She smiled. *Or perhaps the mobile phone company passed you all by.* "No, we'll own the orange of traffic lights. The orange that says, 'Get ready to go.' " She reached for the second board and pointed at the image of traffic lights with a large orange in the center. "So the amber light becomes our icon. And to go with it, our copy line . . ." She read from the caption, " 'Get up and go with *That Sunshine Feeling!* ' " She stopped and waited for them to take it in, then elaborated. "But that's not all. We don't want to just own orange. We don't want to just own 'get up and go.' We want to own *the entire journey to work.*"

Now it was back to Orianna. "And this is where we really begin to have fun," she said, hauling a third, larger board from the floor onto the table. "We have orange buses. Ads at traffic lights. Bus stops. Subway cards. Cross tracks . . ."

"Ads in the morning papers," interjected Ivy, showing a fourth board. "And not just ads but promotions and competitions on breakfast radio shows. We could sponsor the weather . . ."

Orianna raised a fifth board. " 'Come rain or shine—get up and go with *That Sunshine Feeling!*' Traffic reports: 'When you're in a jam—get up and go with *That Sunshine Feeling!*' Or come to that, mailers that arrive in the post before you've even left for work."

But as she was about to reach for their final piece . . .

"And what happens when we introduce a lime version of *That Sunshine Feeling* later this year?" interrupted Used-Car Salesman.

Ivy was stumped. Typical bloody clients, she thought, throwing a wrench in the works. They probably withheld this information deliberately.

"So, you're planning on a lime flavor?" asked Orianna lightly.

"Not *planning,*" said Used-Car Salesman. "It's a definite go."

"When?"

"September," he said. Ivy could swear he sounded smug.

"We could always run this campaign before that," suggested Clare.

Yet Ivy knew they'd be hard-pressed to get everything produced by then—it was only three months away. In a flash it came to her. "I see no problem with a lime version," she said, struggling not to sound smug in return.

"You don't?"

"No. We use the amber for the orange drink. Green for the lime. Green means go, after all."

Orianna added, "It would just be a simple alteration to the visual. We put a giant lime instead of the green light."

"Easy," said Ivy.

"And cheap," said Orianna.

They were good at this: swiftly gauging the client's mind-set. Ivy looked directly at Used-Car-Salesman, held his gaze. Slowly he started nodding. "Hmm . . . Fair enough. I'll buy that."

"So, moving on," said Ivy, thinking, *phew, what a near miss.* "Here's our final item, which we've executed for this orange flavor, but in fact—now that we're talking about it—would work equally well with lime." She reached for a large yellow envelope and handed it to the frizzy-haired girl, aware she was the only client who hadn't yet been involved specifically in the presentation. Ivy read out the line on the outside: " 'Don't be a lemon.' " She paused while the girl removed the contents. Inside was what looked like an enormous birthday card. The girl opened it and— *ping!*—out popped a giant cutout orange on a spring.

"Brilliant!" said Frizzy.

" 'Spring into action,' " Orianna concluded. " 'Get up and go with *That Sunshine Feeling!*' "

"Nice." Mutton-Dressed-As-Lamb nodded.

"Let's have a look," said Barrow Boy, snatching.

"Me first," said Used-Car Salesman, evidently pulling rank. He pinged open the mailer again. "I love it!" he said. Seconds later, "I love it all."

Orianna glanced at Ivy, jubilant. Ivy gave her a surreptitious wink.

If my instinct is right, we've won the business, thought Ivy. Clare's presentation might have warmed the clients up, but ultimately it was our quick thinking and creativity that cracked it. What a great team we are.

2. Embrace together

Back at their partitioned section of the office later that morning, Orianna and Ivy were midway through the *Burroso* mailing, when Ivy said, "You all right if I go out at lunch? I wasn't expecting this brief and I've got an appointment."

"Of course." It was hardly up to Orianna to object. "Doing anything nice?"

"Going to the gym."

"The gym?!"

"Yup." Ivy nodded. "I'm seeing that personal trainer guy—Rob something-or-other. The chap Dan goes to, you know."

Orianna felt herself flush at the mention of Dan's name and tried to control it. "Let me get this straight. *You're* going to see Rob?"

"Indeed I am. Thought it was time for a new regimen. It being well into spring and all."

"But you don't need to," said Orianna. "You're thin enough as it is. And you've already got a man."

"It's not about being thin," Ivy corrected. "It's about being *toned*. And as for having a man, it's even more reason to take care of myself. Ensure he doesn't wander into pastures new."

Orianna wasn't convinced; Ivy's husband, Ed, hardly appeared the wandering type. "*Everyone's* going to the gym. You were my last hope. Pretty soon I won't have anyone left to go shopping with at lunchtime."

"Darling Orianna. Panic not. I am the woman for whom the term *shopaholic* was invented. I will *never* abandon retail therapy." A consummate mimic, Ivy put on her *Ab Fab* voice. "It's just we'll have to cut back a little, sweetie; go maybe three times a week, not five."

Orianna was consoled. "What time are you meeting him?"

"I've got a few minutes."

"Better crack this concept then." Orianna refocused on her layout pad. Thanks to the natural goodness of its Mediterranean ingredients, *Burruso* purported to be an elixir of youth. Now they'd been asked to produce a piece of direct mail designed to woo consumers who preferred to eat butter.

Olive groves, Italy . . . It came to Orianna at once. "I know! Let's give them the chance to win a trip to the Med. Something about leaving it all behind . . ."

Ivy was quick to sharpen up the line. "You mean like 'Take a holiday from butter'?"

Orianna clapped her hands. "Perfect! And we could send them coupons too—that would encourage people to switch."

"Nice one. There's nothing like the old escape-from-your-mundane-life incentive to get all those suburban housewives hurrying along to the supermarket. That's it. Job done." Ivy got to her feet, and with a swish of designer raincoat, was gone.

Rob wasn't sure what to expect of Ivy. She'd phoned and said she'd noticed a transformation in Dan Cohen recently, so Dan had given her his name, but this, and that she worked at Green Integrated, was all Rob knew. He was hoping, however, that if she was a close colleague of Dan's, she'd be able to shed light on his availability. Rob thought Dan was *prob-*

ably straight, but wasn't 100 percent certain. And even if he was, Rob hoped he might be converted. He'd converted a few straight men before, if only short-term—Chloë used to joke that it was his speciality. But sometimes he wondered if it was really because he feared commitment, and his love life would be more rewarding if he went for more available guys.

Ivy was sitting on the sofa in reception, waiting. He guessed which one she was at once. Long, straight red hair with subtle blond streaks that appeared expensively dyed, scarlet lipstick, emerald eyes with a dash of expertly applied eyeliner—she had Agency Type written all over her. And unless he was mistaken, she was a creative. In a sharply cut, mint-green raincoat, suede hipster trousers, and an exquisite pair of strappy beaded sandals, she was more luxuriously dressed than most of his other creative clients, but her style was a tad too eclectic for her to be an account handler.

"Ivy?"

"Rob?" Ivy flashed him a smile and stood up. "I've heard so much about you."

"You have?" What had Dan been saying?

She squeezed his bicep mischievously. "Dear man, your ability to harden muscles is legendary."

That was it; he was hooked. Rob might not be attracted to the opposite sex, but when it came to a well-groomed woman with whom he could enjoy witty banter, he was a pushover.

Alone in the department, Orianna was free to concentrate on drawing up the mail pack uninterrupted. If she hurried, she might just have enough time to indulge in a chapter of the romantic novel she was devouring before Ivy returned. Five minutes of that and a huge mozzarella on ciabatta were the reward she deserved after all her hard work . . .

The markers squeaked on her pad, the familiar scent hypnotizing her as she drew stick figures to illustrate her idea. Soon she was caught up in a world where planning paper folds, type, and photography were all that mattered. There was no doubt she could work swiftly when she set her mind to it. Ten years' experience of art directing meant she knew her stuff.

After she'd been scribbling for half an hour, Dan put his head around the partition that separated her and Ivy from the other creative teams.

"Psst!"

Orianna looked up, pushed aside her dark fringe.

"Having a good day?"

"OK. You?"

He rolled his eyes. "Frantic." He examined the pile of concepts she'd produced. "And it looks like you'll be keeping me busy this afternoon."

"Sorry." She smiled at him persuasively. "I need costs by tomorrow first thing. Can Ivy and I go through these with you when she's back from the gym?"

"Ivy's gone to the *gym*?"

"Yeah. Weird, I agree, but she's on some health kick. She's seeing your Rob fellow." She lowered her voice. "I hope he won't let slip about us."

"He doesn't know yet," said Dan. "I thought we agreed that until we were ready, the fewer people who do, the better. Though I guess he'll find out tonight."

Orianna nodded, recollecting their pact.

It still made her tingle to remember the night when they'd gotten together. She'd fancied Dan from the moment he'd joined as head of production several months before. He had the dark looks she loved—strong features, with large eyes, a broad grin, and frankly, a big nose. She'd never had much time for snub-nosed types—boyish men left her wondering when they'd eventually grow up. Moreover, although Dan was good-looking—he was over six feet and pretty well-built too—he didn't seem markedly vain or arrogant. Little surprise every other girl at Green seemed to fancy him too; Orianna hadn't believed she stood a chance. Until the Christmas party at the Groucho Club.

It was after dessert and an awful lot of wine. Orianna was sitting at Dan's table along with six other coworkers and, well past tipsy, they were playing an agency party favorite—"Who would you shag, who would you marry, who would you push off a cliff?"—when Dan's turn came.

"I know who I'd shove off a cliff," he said, draining his glass.

"Who?" asked Orianna. The rule was it had to be a colleague.

He checked to see he wasn't going to be overheard. "Russell." There was a sharp intake of breath that Dan would dare be so bold. Russell was only feet away and a powerful figure at Green. He was their financial director—a tough call for anyone—but nonetheless ruthlessly tight-fisted.

Orianna dropped her voice and nodded. "Good choice."

"And marry?" urged Esme.

"Not sure there's anyone I'd *marry*. Not right now . . ."

"He's more interested in shagging!" joshed Earl, the art buyer.

Dan didn't deny it.

"So, who *would* you shag, then?" Esme, opposite, was eager.

"Actually . . ." Dan paused, tantalizing. "Someone at this table."

"Who, who?" Esme leaned forward.

"I'm not telling." He sat back maddeningly.

"You've *got* to tell!" protested Earl.

"Who says? Might ruin my chances."

"Aw, go on," wheedled Esme.

Dan shook his head. "Nope." He folded his arms.

"Spoil sport!" But Dan was her boss, and she wouldn't push him.

He laughed. "It's you, my little munchkin," and he reached across the table to ruffle Esme's elfin-cropped hair.

"Pah!" Esme shrugged him off, sure it wasn't.

But then, when no one else was watching, Dan caught Orianna's eye.

At first Orianna wasn't sure if she'd understood him. Yet as he held her gaze for just that bit too long, she realized she had. She felt herself turn scarlet, her heart begin to race, her palms go clammy. She took a large gulp of wine and looked away, pretending to focus on the adjacent table, where another group of eight were pulling party poppers and exchanging cracker jokes. Presently she felt Dan take his eyes off her. It was only then the realization fully sank in.

Dan fancies *me*! Could it really be true?

She glanced up at him and smiled shyly. He smiled back, that wonderful lopsided grin, and her heart flipped.

Later, she'd found herself allocated to share his taxi home.

"Good job it was down to production to organize the transportation," he said once they were alone in the minicab speeding up Tottenham Court Road.

His place was in Camden, so arguably he lived en route to her place, but by now she was intoxicated enough to be more bold. "You arranged this?"

"Perhaps . . ." Then he chuckled and turned to her. "Arranged the seating plan too." And when he leaned over and kissed her tentatively, softly, she melted.

Since then, their love affair had taken off fast. And although Dan was known as something of an agency heartthrob, there had been little of the does-he-like-me? angst that had caused Orianna many sleepless nights over boyfriends before. As their post-party passion swiftly evolved into sleepless nights of a different order, there simply hadn't been a moment to worry. It wasn't until they'd got together a few times that she'd stopped to consider the longer-term implications.

They were getting dressed in Dan's apartment one morning when a photo on the wall had caught her eye. "What's going on here?"

"My bar mitzvah."

The little black yarmulke led her to wonder. "Do you think it would bother your parents, you seeing a Catholic girl?"

Dan stopped rummaging in a drawer and turned to her. "Honestly?"

"Yes."

"I guess I do. It's silly, they're not especially religious and hardly ever go to the synagogue. My mum knows I've gone out with girls that aren't Jewish before—and I don't think that *particularly* bothers her. But my brother's wife is Jewish and I guess if I was to get really serious with someone that wasn't, she wouldn't be happy. I don't think she'd try and stop me exactly, but I'd get these kind of pursed lips and a frown." He imitated her expression. " 'Ach, sweetheart, she's a very nice girl and all, still, I'm not so sure . . .' " He raised his eyebrows. "How about you?"

"Similar. Though in the long run I reckon they'd be OK—they'd probably decide my own happiness is more important." She laughed. "Anyway, they've had to cope with it before. Seems I've got a thing for Jewish men—my first boyfriend was too."

"That's because we're so irresistibly sexy."

"Of course. Once you've had one they say you can never go back." She watched him pulling on his underpants, admiring his nicely rounded buttocks.

"I'm delighted to hear you picked me for such highbrow reasons."

"You didn't think I liked your mind?"

Dan chuckled. "I don't kid myself."

"But seriously. Do you think it's a problem?"

"Not for me it isn't." Dan unhooked a black shirt from a hanger. "Though when you meet my mum, you'll probably get the vibe of silent disapproval."

However uncomfortable the notion of meeting his parents might be, Orianna was delighted. This intimated he thought they could have a future. She didn't want to push it, so suggested, "Perhaps we'd better not mention it to them yet."

"I probably wouldn't tell them anyway—I tend to keep things like that to myself."

Typical man, though Orianna, but saw his point. Perhaps it would be wise not to inform her parents until they were on a more secure footing either.

She pulled on her knickers and scooped her breasts into the C cups of her bra. As she reached for her lacy top, she was suddenly conscious of the fact she was putting on the same clothes as the day before. I wonder if people at work will notice? she thought. It brought home another worry; that she and Dan were mixing the private and professional. "Ooh. Actually, do you have something I could borrow?"

Dan looked surprised. "What kind of thing?"

"A T-shirt. So no one can tell I've not changed since yesterday."

"Would that bother you?"

"I'm not sure I want everyone at work to know. We're lucky no one suspected after the party."

"Oh. Why? Ashamed of me now?" But his tone was confident.

"No, not at all." Far from it, but Orianna was wary. Although her natural inclination was to tell all, she had been stung by gossip about an office affair in the past. "You know what they say about shagging the payroll."

"Fucking fun?" Dan gave her bottom a playful smack.

"Perhaps we should keep quiet at work for a bit too. After all, given our roles, we could be accused of giving each other preferential treatment."

"Perhaps we shouldn't tell *anyone* at Green."

Orianna hadn't thought it through. "Not even Ivy?" Truth be told, if Ivy hadn't gone away skiing just before the Christmas party, Orianna would have already confided in her.

"Once you tell one person, they tell someone else—it's how things get out."

"But I always tell Ivy everything!"

"I can imagine."

"And we can trust Ivy. I've known her almost half my life—if I asked her, she wouldn't breathe a word."

"Up to you. You wanted to keep it hush-hush."

"Mm." Orianna was torn. She appreciated his point—she enjoyed gossip as much as the next person, but it did amaze her how fast word spread around the agency. Yet in her experience Ivy was exceptionally discreet. It had taken Orianna years of self-revelation to get Ivy to disclose the merest snippets about herself in return, and this was a rare achievement—to most people the intimate details of Ivy's personal life were off-limits.

As Dan reached under the bed for his shoes he continued, voice muffled by the duvet, "I'm only saying, keeping it between the two of us is the best way to be a hundred percent certain."

"I suppose . . ."

"So, business as usual at work." Dan emerged. "No telling *anyone*."

In the end it was the strength of her feelings for him that persuaded her. If things went wrong with Dan, Orianna didn't want the whole agency knowing about her broken heart again. "OK. We'll keep this strictly outside office hours."

Dan grinned. "So you wouldn't be up for a quickie in the stationery cupboard later then?"

3. Tush, never tell me!

Rob peered at the pulse monitor on the cross-country ski machine. "You're very fit for someone who says they don't exercise. If I didn't know better, I'd have guessed you'd been at this for years." He glanced at his new client. Ivy was barely sweating.

"I've a naturally low heart rate. Or so my GP once told me. It has its disadvantages, but my husband always says I wouldn't survive in my industry otherwise."

Rob wasn't sure why, but he was surprised Ivy was married—she didn't seem the kind. "Oh?"

"Advertising, marketing, being creative—it pays not to get easily stressed, you can imagine."

"You're an art director?"

"Copywriter."

"Who's your art director? Would I know him?"

"Her. Doubt it; she's not into exercise. Her name's Orianna."

"Unusual name."

"It's Italian—aristocratic, so she insists. Her family is from Venice and she was named after a Renaissance noblewoman or something. Though they've lived here for years." Ivy paused for a moment to focus. Rob noted she was pushing herself, determined to achieve a perfect rhythm.

"You been working together long?" He was keen to learn more about Ivy—he found it helped gain an understanding of a client's physical requirements if there was a strong mental connection. This seemed a safe place to start.

"Yes, years. We met on a Design and Art Direction course over a decade ago. The tutors team you up and they put us together." She frowned, recollecting. "I think the guy running it thought I'd knock a few spots off her."

Rob nodded. He could already tell Ivy wouldn't suffer fools.

"Orianna was straight out of high school whereas I'd been to college and studied copywriting so was more clued in about the industry."

Rob said nothing. His tactics appeared to be working; if he kept quiet she might divulge more—most new clients had a tendency to gab to fill awkward silences. Not Ivy, however; she was silent then deflected: "Anyway, enough about me and Orianna. Tell me about you. Have you been doing this a long time?"

"Around five years. I used to teach aerobics classes, but got sick of it."

"I bet this pays more."

She's quick, thought Rob, so countered, "Not as much as you chaps get, I'm sure."

"Ah yes, though we have to prostitute our souls."

Rob raised an eyebrow. "I hadn't seen advertising like that."

"Oh, I love it." Ivy gave him another dazzling smile. "Damn the morality; take the money and run, that's what I say." She strode on wordlessly again. After a while, the machine mastered, she seemed to grow bored. "Can I stop now?"

Rob, mesmerized merely by watching her, had been contemplating what dramatic coloring she had. How her flaming hair contrasted with her pale and delicately freckled skin. He was brought back to the assessment with a jolt. "Yeah, yeah, of course. I need to take your measurements next. We'd better stretch a bit, first."

Shortly Ivy was standing in one of the staff rooms, arms lifted while Rob pinched what was definitely less than an inch with an evil pair of callipers. He checked the dial. "I just need your age."

"Thirty-four," said Ivy, rather fast.

Rob did some calculations. "Not bad, not bad," he muttered. Privately he was incredulous. He had clients he'd been training for eons who would give their eyeteeth to have results like this. "Eighteen per cent fat. Do you *really* never exercise at all?"

"Only sex." Ivy winked. "And shopping."

Rob laughed. He liked this woman. All of a sudden, he was inclined to take her into his confidence. There was something he was dying to find out, and Chloë's departure had created a vacancy for a confidante. "Talking of sex . . . How well do you know Dan?"

"Dan?" Ivy sounded surprised. "What do you mean? Goodness! You didn't think anything was going on between *us*, did you?"

"No, no. It's just you said you know him, and I wondered . . . we've been out for a few drinks together, yet he's never talked about seeing anyone."

"Really?"

"I mean, I'm meeting him later, for instance."

"He invited you out?"

"Well . . ." In truth Rob had asked Dan, but was loath to admit being so keen.

"Are you asking if I believe Dan Cohen is gay?"

"Er . . . I suppose so." Rob knew his own sexuality was so transparent Ivy would take it for granted, and wasn't perturbed by her assumption. He was more concerned he shouldn't look like a lovesick puppy in front of someone he wished to impress.

Ivy's face registered understanding. "Do you *fancy* him?"

Rob was longing to confess. "I think he's *lovely*."

"Well I never!"

Is it that surprising I'd fancy him? thought Rob. He's very attractive, and seems a really genuine guy. Perhaps the notion he's gay—or at least persuadable—hasn't occurred to Ivy. Dan is pretty macho, in an understated way.

"It's only I reckon he *might* like me," he said. "He's always so friendly it's hard to tell. Normally I know if someone's interested or not, but he's quite elusive—whenever I mention his love life he changes the subject. He certainly *never* talks about having a girlfriend—he's not even mentioned fancying anyone in all the months I've been seeing him."

"Mm. How strange." Ivy examined her well-manicured nails, checking she'd not broken any during her workout. "What an intriguing thought. I wonder if he's not out of the closet yet . . . I've never really seen him around enough gay men to tell."

"That's what I wondered." Rob danced a little jig inside. Maybe there was hope. Impulsively, he asked, "You doing anything later?"

Ivy hesitated, plainly unwilling to commit until she knew what to. "Why?"

"Perhaps you could join us."

"Oh?"

"We'll be at Lucifer's on Dean Street from about nine." Rob grew excited at the thought. "After all, you work with Dan—"

"True."

"—and Dan recommended me to you, so it wouldn't seem odd, all hooking up. Then you could see how he behaves with me. Watch, and—if you don't mind—tell me what you think."

"Sure," said Ivy. "If it's just a quick drink later on, why not? I've got to meet someone straight after work, but that shouldn't take the whole evening. I'll get there as soon as I can."

"Hi, sweetie." That Orianna whisked her book out of sight under the desk the moment Ivy returned didn't escape her notice. "What are you reading *now*?"

Sheepishly Orianna lifted the paperback.

"*The Betrothal,*" said Ivy, peering at the title. She leaned forward and squinted at the back cover. " '*Amy and Saul. Forced to wed by cruel circumstance. Will it turn out to be a marriage in name only? Sexual passion that quickly burns out? Or could it actually be love?*' Orianna, honestly!"

"What?"

"That looks dreadful!"

"I like it!"

"Oh well. Each to their own." Ivy knew there would be no stopping Orianna—her appetite for romantic fiction was voracious. The only prerequisite was she had to be confident the story had a happy ending. Ivy had witnessed a few occasions when Orianna had been duped into reading something more downbeat; tragic endings could upset her for days.

"How was the gym?" asked Orianna.

"Fine."

"What's Rob like?"

Ivy was inclined to be fulsome with her praise. "Seems a total sweetie. Not your typical all-brawn, no-brain gym instructor."

"Fit though?"

"Yeah, nice looking in a fresh-faced, trendy kind of way. Gay, of course."

"*Che sorpresa.* So, we need to run through these ideas with Dan. I said we'd go and see him. Is now OK?"

"Sure."

Together they made their way to production. As head of the department, Dan was in much in demand. Tasked with having to juggle the needs of both creative and account handling, his desk was chock-full. There was a pile of transparencies he'd been asked to deal with because the photo library was screaming to have them returned and the art director who'd been in charge of them couldn't face confessing he'd lost one, several urgent pieces of artwork due for immediate signature, a jiffy bag of T-shirt samples, and a half-eaten sandwich. Yet the man himself was not to be seen.

Orianna jumped up to look over the walls dividing the large, open-plan office. Each partition was painted a complementary shade—lime, olive, apple, teal—to reflect the agency's name.

Dan came charging around the corner. "Sorry, sorry."

"No worries, we've only just got here."

Dan grabbed his lunch and they headed for a group of bottle-green sofas in the center of the room designed for informal meetings. They sat down, Orianna and Ivy together, Dan at a right angle to them.

"Remind me." Dan munched as he spoke, egg mayonnaise spilling onto his napkin. "This is the July mailer?"

"Yeah." Orianna straightened the pile of marker-drawn ideas and turned to Ivy. "Do you want to go through them, or shall I?"

"Feel free," said Ivy, pleased to settle back and observe. She suspected Rob's theory about Dan was wishful thinking, because for a while she'd had a hunch Dan fancied Orianna, and that the attraction was mutual. Take their body language right now; although they were sitting on adjacent sofas, Orianna's knees were almost touching his, and Dan seemed to be looking at her in a way that was decidedly sexual. It made Ivy, who was used to being the focus of male attention, feel a little ignored.

Well, they can't actually be *shagging,* Ivy concluded. Orianna always confided everything (including, occasionally, things that slightly bored Ivy). It was part of their unspoken deal: Ivy was witty, aloof; Orianna impulsive, vocal. Since the outset it had been this way, and it suited them professionally and personally. Not only had it earned them the respect of their peers and a clutch of prestigious industry awards; it meant that as best friends, each acted as a foil to the other.

After a while, Ivy decided she'd better contribute. "And because we're aiming this at older consumers, we thought we'd have very poetic copy." She pointed at the black lines Orianna had used to indicate type. "Something quite old-fashioned and lyrical to appeal to the sensibilities of our more mature audience."

This was Orianna's cue to lean forward. "So it would be good if we could print it on beautiful paper stock—something slightly textured."

"You'll be lucky, with budgets this tight," said Dan.

"See what you can do? Just for your favorite team?" Orianna widened her dark eyes at him; again this wasn't lost on Ivy.

But then they were interrupted by Ursula, the account director in charge of the account.

"Ivy-I'm-terribly-sorry-but-I've-got-to-leave-in five minutes-for-an-urgent-meeting-with-the-client." She panted at twice her normal one-thousand-words-per-minute speed. "I've-got-some-comments-on-your-copy-and-I'd-like-to-go through them with-you-if-that's-all-right."

Ivy winced to herself. Ursula's copy comments tended to be more valid than most, but she disliked being told her words needed improvement. Still, she knew better than to say so—years of feedback had made her resistant; now she could compromise without betraying how criticism grated. Ursula hopped from foot to foot; clearly she wouldn't take no for an answer.

Ivy stood up. "Sorry, folks, duty calls. Can I leave you two to finish?"

"Of course," said Orianna and Dan in unison.

4. You rise to play and go to bed to work

Not wanting to seem too vain or obvious, Rob only spruced himself up minimally for his date with Dan. In the privacy of the staff changing room, he showered, gelled his peroxide hair (though not in a way that might preclude someone running their hands through it), and swapped his shorts, T-shirt, and trainers for a freshly laundered shirt and jeans and his favorite shoes. A discreet dash of aftershave and he was ready.

Considering how much he fancied Dan, Rob was surprisingly relaxed — that he was used to dealing with him in an advisory capacity meant he felt he had the upper hand. But there was a downside: their relationship was already established on a friendly but formal footing, which would make it hard to talk about anything personal, let alone their love lives. Broadening the conversation would involve courage on Rob's part, especially as Dan was a client and might spurn him. Rob was no coward but didn't enjoy rejection any more than the next person; if anything, he tended to take it particularly to heart. When he'd first come out at the tender age of sixteen, he'd fallen heavily for a succession of older men who hadn't treated him well, and as a result, for the last few years had developed a tendency for casual sex and unrequited crushes. He gleaned much emotional sustenance from his friendships and working relationships, and was rarely short of company and camaraderie. But Dan . . . Rob fancied Dan more than was good for him. In addition, he really *liked* him. He felt at ease with him in a way he seldom did with men he was so attracted to—yet he was also worried that things were getting too comfortable, and if he didn't say something soon, the opportunity for shifting gears would disappear.

Perhaps tonight's the night, he prayed to himself, checking his appearance one last time in the reception mirror. And as Dan emerged from the customer changing room and clapped him on the back to announce he was ready to go, Rob's heart skipped a beat.

Orianna was waiting at the bar in Lucifer's, clutching a much-needed glass of Pinot Grigio. She was early—being good at deadlines—but on edge. She'd been wrapped up in meetings all afternoon so hadn't even had time to touch base with Ivy, and on top of that, pubs always made her feel like a spare part. Perhaps it was the Italian in her; they just weren't her domain. Besides, she was impatient to meet Rob. Not that she thought Dan might reciprocate Rob's interest, but it was intriguing, indeed a compliment, to have her partner sought after by someone else.

She was all the keener because she'd not yet met any of Dan's friends, nor he hers, because of their pact. Initially she hadn't minded the secrecy—that would have been hypocritical given she'd suggested they keep quiet—but now that they'd been together for several months she believed they were ready to dip a toe in the water of going public. Meeting Rob indicated Dan was coming around to the idea.

Orianna shifted on her stool, excitement mounting. She was proud of Dan, and the prospect of being introduced as his girlfriend for the first time was thrilling.

Ivy, on the other hand, was a long way from Lucifer's. She was in Chelsea Harbour, with Green's financial director, Russell. And she wasn't just with him in the professional sense; they were in his apartment—a penthouse with a stupendous view over the River Thames and huge wrought-iron four-poster bed, Ivy on her hands and knees, Russell behind her holding her hips, making the beast with two backs with a vengeance.

"Aaaaaah!" he cried, climaxing.

"Oooooooooh," she responded in kind, as his orgasm also tipped her over the edge. "Hold it . . . right there . . ." She writhed against him, prolonging the pleasure.

"That was bloody amazing." Russell collapsed on the bed.

"Mm," said Ivy. "Incredible." As indeed it was: when it came to sheer, unadulterated, caution-to-the-wind, dirty sex, each was in their element. How much easier it was to let rip like this with one another than with their spouses! Both their partners were—obviously, conveniently—elsewhere. Ivy's husband, Ed, worked in the oil industry, a profession that took him off to Aberdeen for weeks on end, where he remained unsuspectingly faithful to Ivy day in, day out; and Russell's wife and three children lived in a huge house in Herefordshire, just too far away from London for it to be worth commuting on a daily basis.

Ivy looked at her watch. "Hell! I've got to go."

"What, so soon?"

"I'm meeting someone." She started pulling on her clothes. It was one of the benefits of not undressing fully; she was still in her stockings, shoes, and bra.

"Who?" With long, bony fingers Russell reached for a cigarette; inhaling only enhanced his perfect cheekbones.

"No one you know," Ivy tantalized, stealing a drag. She exhaled, blowing smoke away from them both, up in the air. "Just a couple of boys."

She grabbed her handbag and car keys from the bedside table, and presently she was in her silver BMW cabriolet, speeding back into town.

"I hope you don't mind," said Dan, as he and Rob strolled down Old Compton Street, sports bags bouncing against their buttocks in a way that seemed to attract the attention of many of the locals. "I've asked a friend to join us."

"Oh." Rob's first reaction was disappointment. If Dan reciprocated my interest, he thought, surely he'd rather share a drink alone? Perhaps Dan's shy and wants to protect himself—I do that sometimes. Or maybe, just maybe, he wants to introduce me to a third party to get a second opinion, like I want from Ivy . . .

Rob recalled he'd not mentioned Ivy would be joining them either. He was poised to say so when Dan pushed open the door of Lucifer's. At once they were caught up in the hustle and bustle.

"Back in a sec," shouted Dan.

Rob scanned the room. Antique pine furniture, a ceramic-tiled floor, and aged terra-cotta walls lent the place a Tuscan rustic charm which contrasted with the clientele. There was the usual mix: girls giggling because they'd been in the pub since six and were well away, straight men bonding and gay men flirting, media couples enjoying a pre-dinner drink or three.

Moments later Dan was back. And here, unless Rob was much mistaken, was cause for consternation. Because Dan had someone with him. And not any old someone: a girl. A pretty girl, with very dark, shoulder-length hair and big brown eyes.

Her arm was linked through Dan's.

Rob's heart jumped a beat again. Was it possible their arms were linked so Dan could guide this girl through the throng, or because they were great friends? Rob was astute when it came to body language and as the girl smiled up at Dan as they halted before him, he concluded it was more than chemistry; it was genuine affection. It could even— horrors!—be love. Was this a *girlfriend* then, and a serious one at that?

Rob was too much of a gent and too proud to show his upset. He held out a palm. "I'm Rob. And you are . . . ?"

The girl dropped Dan's arm to shake his hand. Rob noted that her grip was firm, assured. "Orianna." Her beam was broad.

What a coincidence, he thought, there can't be more than one of those about. "Pardon me—did you say *Orianna?*"

"Yeah. Why?" She looked puzzled.

"I've heard of you."

Orianna turned to Dan. "I thought you hadn't told him about me?"

"I haven't." Dan frowned.

Rob elaborated. "Aren't you at Green Integrated?"

Orianna nodded.

"Ivy's partner?"

"Yes."

"She mentioned you to me earlier, at her fitness assessment."

"Hey," Dan interrupted. "Looks like that group is leaving. Let's nab their seats."

They moved fast. Orianna threw her jacket over the wrought-iron banister; Rob chucked his sports bag on the velour sofa.

"I'll go to the bar," offered Dan. "What can I get you?"

"Another dry white, please."

Rob and Orianna sat down, Rob on a leather stool facing the door, Orianna on the sofa opposite.

Aware there now seemed little hope with Dan and wishing to be sure exactly how little, Rob cut straight to the point. "Are you two . . . ?"

"Going out? Er, yeah."

"I see." Rob disguised his disappointment. "So, have you been together a while?"

"Not that long. Since just before Christmas."

Rob nodded. "He's a very nice guy."

Orianna colored. "I know."

Blast, thought Rob, she really likes him. I wonder if he likes her as much? "Do you see a lot of each other?"

"Well, we work together, so we see each other a lot there . . . But aside from that, yes, I suppose. A couple of nights during the week and then on weekends."

So it was mutual then.

Then Orianna added, looking worried, "We haven't told anyone yet though—you're the first."

Rob was surprised. "Why not?"

"We wanted to be sure it wasn't just a passing thing. What with working closely together, it can get awkward if it goes wrong. I've seen it happen so often—lots of people in agencies have flings or affairs. And it's fine while it lasts, but when it's over, it can make things tough." She frowned. "It happened to me once . . . and when this guy—Clive— went off with someone else at work and we split up, everyone knew." She shuddered. "It was awful."

Rob nodded. Despite his attraction to Dan, he couldn't resist warming to Orianna. Not in the same way he'd liked Ivy instantly; from what he'd seen so far Ivy was the kind of woman he'd like to party with. She'd be fun to gossip and bitch with, whereas Orianna was a Sunday-papers-on-a-wet-afternoon-lounging-on-the-sofa type. He suspected Ivy would rather stick pins in her eyes than do anything so domestic. But Orianna seemed vulnerable, approachable. That she'd been hurt meant he identified with her.

He kicked himself. Don't be such a softy—this woman's shagging your man! How are you ever going to end up with a partner if you can't be a bit more aggressive? Malice wasn't in Rob's nature, however, whereas curiosity was. "Does *no* one know?"

Just then Dan came back from the bar. "No," he said. "Not yet. You're the honored first." He put down the drinks carefully and took a seat next to Orianna. Rob noticed he rested his arm on the sofa behind her—a gesture that was both casual and protective.

Despite his letdown, Rob was delighted they'd chosen him as their first public encounter. "It must have been ever so difficult to keep quiet," he said, impressed. He couldn't imagine being discreet; he loved to share almost every moment of his own experiences.

Orianna bit her lip and nodded. "Most people, it's fine—I wouldn't go into all the details of my love life with them anyway. But with Ivy it's been hard. I normally tell her everything. Though I guess, maybe"—she hesitated and glanced at Dan for approval—"I might let her know soon."

Mention of Ivy brought her front of mind. "Oh my God!" Rob clapped his hands over his mouth theatrically. "I forgot to say . . ."

"Forgot what?" said Orianna and Dan in unison.

Before he had time to reply, Rob saw a tall, slim figure with red hair and a chic, mint-green raincoat come through the door and head directly to their table.

5. Ha! I like not that

"Ah, Rob! There you are." Given the position of the sofa, it wasn't until Ivy came around to the head of the table that she saw his companion: "Dan!"

Then her jaw dropped.

Beside him was Orianna—she'd been hidden from view by the jacket slung over the banister behind her. Moreover, unless Ivy was hallucinating, Dan's arm was resting around Orianna's shoulders. Immediately Ivy gleaned the body language was not platonic. For once she didn't mask her consternation.

"*Orianna?* What are you doing here?"

"Er . . ." Orianna went scarlet.

Dan came to her rescue. "I invited her. How come you're here?"

"He invited me." Ivy pointed at Rob. She turned to him. "You didn't say Orianna was coming."

Rob shrugged. "I didn't know."

"Oh." Lips pink and glossy, eyes wide with mascara, hair brushed and fluffed . . . Orianna had redone her makeup since Ivy had seen her just after lunch. She spoke her mind at once. "So are you guys seeing each other, or what?"

A pause. Eventually: "Yes," they admitted simultaneously.

"How long has it been going on?"

"Since Christmas," said Dan.

"I was going to tell you very soon," added Orianna.

"Hmph." Ivy was intensely displeased at being caught unawares, but was damned if she'd admit it. "I sussed there was something between you." She addressed Rob. "Guess that answers your question."

Rob nodded.

"What question?" asked Dan and Orianna, again in unison.

"Oh nothing." She shook her head, elusive in retaliation. "Well," she turned toward the bar, "I'm going to get a drink. Anyone else?"

They all muttered they were fine.

Waiting to order a gin and diet tonic, Ivy had moments to appraise. So Orianna and Dan have been going out since Christmas, she thought. Bloody hell; I've been kept in the dark for months—it seems even Rob knew before me! Orianna is *my* partner, *my* ally. Through takeovers and promotions, we've been loyal to one another over our bosses, colleagues, and clients . . .

Ivy drummed her fingers on the wooden countertop, upset mounting. The bartender evidently thought the signal was aimed at him, and came to serve her at once.

Yes, she thought, Orianna's such a romantic, her relationship with Dan is sure to take precedence—doesn't the fact they've been going out on the sly signal a shift already? Years before, when she fell for that dreadful Clive in the design studio, she told me *everything*. So this new-found secrecy is a sign she's moving away from me. Worse, whatever I share with her might get passed on . . .

Ivy shuddered. Imagine Dan being Orianna's chief confidante! She hated the prospect she might be replaced, that she was, in effect, expendable. Of course, she herself was married, and if she chose to, could share similar intimacies with her husband, Ed. But he didn't work with them, so she didn't see it as the same, and as it was she rarely confided in him.

It was also true that she was having an affair with a colleague herself. Some might have said she was hiding great swathes of her private life from Orianna; certainly she'd not told her friend about her own three-year liaison. But she figured her relationship with Russell was hardly one she *could* be public about, not without upsetting a very big apple cart. And Ivy had no wish to do that; relations with the financial director suited her just fine the way they were. He was good-looking, sharp, and as cofounder of the company, had a lot of influence.

Anyway, she reasoned, I'm not in love with Russell. I'm way more detached than Orianna will ever be. I might be having sex with a colleague on the board, but our needs come first. Besides, I've an opt-out clause—my marriage, whereas Orianna is in danger of putting all her eggs in the rather dodgy basket of Green Integrated. Not a wise move at all . . .

Carts and baskets, apples and eggs—Ivy's mind was sprinting even faster than normal. It was a relief when her thoughts were interrupted by the bartender with her drink, and she could slow them with the mellowing effects of her second favorite drug.

"Oh, Lord," Orianna whispered. "I wish I'd had the chance to tell her myself."

Dan checked Ivy was out of earshot. Yes; her back was turned and the general hubbub would act as a buffer. "Me too."

"Still, she doesn't seem to have taken it *too* badly." Orianna sounded hopeful.

"No," agreed Rob.

But you don't know Ivy like we do, thought Dan. The last thing he wanted was to upset Orianna, yet Ivy's response made him hesitant. Dan wasn't easily intimidated—he liked to believe the best of people—but he'd long been wary of Ivy. Although he'd never fallen victim to her

sharp tongue, he'd seen her censure Esme, and noted she was not someone to rub the wrong way.

Sure enough, when she returned to the table and pulled up a stool,
Ivy's tone was curt. "So who else is in on your little secret?"

"No one," said Orianna.

"And we'd rather you didn't tell anyone else just yet." Perhaps he
could smooth things over. "Orianna was desperate to tell you."

"Oh yeah?"

"Though I encouraged her to wait."

Ivy's lips were tight. "Why?"

"You know what agencies are like."

"Mm?"

"We thought it best kept to ourselves initially. This is the first time
we've been out together."

"It's true. They've literally only just told me," said Rob.

"Really," said Ivy.

"Yes, really," protested Orianna.

"But you could have trusted me!"

"Blame me," offered Dan.

"If you say so," muttered Ivy.

Dan was tempted to argue. He'd a hunch Ivy was quite capable of
harboring dark secrets of her own if it suited her. But he knew that Orianna adored her, and they made a fine creative team—one of the best in
the agency, if not *the* best. He took a swig of his beer and resisted, shifting
to news he was confident would refocus their interest. "I heard Neil's
resigning."

Ivy leaned forward. "You *what?*"

"Neil's leaving."

"No!" exclaimed Orianna. She gave him a friendly punch. "Why
didn't you tell me before?"

"I've only just heard," he explained. "One of the joys of working late.
You get all the news. Now if you girls would just stay beyond five thirty
sometimes, who knows what you might find out?"

"Cheeky bugger." Orianna laughed.

Ivy got straight to the point. "Where's he going?"

Orianna added, "Who told you?"

"He did. He said I'd find out shortly, but wanted to tell me himself. He felt as head of production I deserved to know."

Rob coughed. "Who's Neil?"

"Our creative director," said Ivy brusquely and repeated, "Where's he going?"

"To Manchester."

"*Manchester?*" Ivy scoffed.

"Why?" asked Orianna.

"Apparently he's sick of the rat race." Dan shrugged. "He's bought a house in the Peak District and he and his wife are moving back up north. He's going to freelance at some agency run by a friend of his or something—"

"Good God!" Ivy was agog.

"—and take up fine-art painting."

Ivy snorted. "Has the man no style?" She paused to take a sip of G&T, then delivered her verdict. "Well, well. Though I always said he couldn't cut it. Downsizing? How dreadfully passé."

The next morning, Ivy went straight to Russell's office.

"Got a moment?" she asked, shutting the door and taking a seat opposite him before he could answer. "What are you doing?" He appeared to be counting out pens of some description.

"UV markers," said Russell. "I'll be handing them out later. I want you all to label your PCs, Macs, printers—anything valuable—with Green's postcode. The ink's invisible to the naked eye, but it shows up florescent under ultraviolet light. Helps the police track stolen goods."

"Sounds like something from a bad detective novel. Can't Green afford anything more state-of-the-art?"

"Sometimes you don't have to spend heaps—so long as it does the job."

"Yeah, right." At times Russell was so tight it was laughable. He was exacting too: papers stacked in trays, files sorted by date, books stored alphabetically—it was a wonder he could create the mess necessary to work. Everything had its place; *I'm in control*, it said, doubtless why he was such a good FD. But she wanted his attention so came straight to the point. "I gather our beloved creative director's resigning."

Russell turned to face her. "News travels fast." He appeared unfazed.

"Indeed."

"Who told you?"

"Dan." Ivy was dammed if she owed Dan her discretion now. "When does Neil go?"

"Sooner the better, far as I'm concerned. He hasn't been pulling his weight for quite a while."

"Any idea of who'll replace him?"

Russell shrugged. "Not yet. I suppose we'll begin the usual trawl using headhunters at some point." He removed his reading glasses to focus on her. "Why?" His pale blue eyes narrowed. "Got someone in mind?"

"Oh no. Just wondered, that's all."

"Whoever it is, I'm sure you'll be able to wind them around your little finger."

Ivy smiled. "Maybe." She paused. She didn't fancy resuming her writerly duties yet; she was still preoccupied with the revelations of the evening before. The prospect of umpteen letter variants was boring— far more stimulating to bait her lover, and it made her feel better to show she got to hear agency gossip first. "Yeah, I met up with Dan for a drink last night—that's where he told me about Neil."

"Oh?"

"And guess what?"

"What? He fancy you or something? Make a pass?"

"No. In fact . . ." She spiraled a string of her hair provocatively. "He's already seeing someone in the agency."

"Oh yeah? Who?"

"Guess."

"Jeez, I don't know . . . He's a good-looking man, or so I gather. Can't see it myself. Could be anyone. Wasn't he having a fling with that blonde in accounts?"

"Lara?"

"Yeah, that was her. Cute little thing."

Ivy bristled. She didn't like Russell finding another girl attractive, however patronizing his appreciation. "You're way out of date. That was months ago—he soon tired of her. No, this is altogether more serious, been going on a while."

Russell frowned, then admitted, "You've got me. Who?"

"It's off the record."

"Of course. You can trust me."

Ivy hesitated. On one hand her loyalty to Orianna remained; she wouldn't want Russell to know. On the other, both she and Dan had irritated Ivy the night before; that Dan had jumped to Orianna's defense had made Ivy feel more excluded. Besides, Russell was a master of concealment. It was this that swayed her. "OK . . ." She paused for effect. "It's Orianna."

"Orianna!?"

Ah! The joy of revelation. "What do you think of that?"

Russell raised an eyebrow, impressed. "Well, I'll be damned." He chuckled to himself. "Never would have put those two together. How sweet."

"Mm."

"It'll be very interesting to see how long that lasts."

"Yes." She got to her feet. "It will indeed."

As she reached to open the door, Russell remarked, "Have you only just found out?"

She didn't like to be reminded. "I've had my suspicions for a long while."

"But you didn't know for sure?"

"No."

"I'm surprised she didn't tell you."

"Yes, well, she didn't." Ivy left his office abruptly. Pointing out she'd been kept in the dark made her feel stupid, even—anathema—naïve.

She hated being seen as less than 100 percent knowing, especially by the ever-worldly Russell. She headed back to her desk, resentment mounting.

Yes, she concluded, I'm far from ready to forgive Orianna yet . . .

6. A constant, loving, noble nature

Sunday afternoon, a fortnight later, Orianna was gardening. She had a gift with plants, and nurturing her small patio supplied a broader canvas on which to express her artistic talents. Over countless weekends she'd lovingly created a verdant haven, albeit overlooked by Victorian terraces. It provided her with a sanctuary away from the cut and thrust of work—within its four whitewashed walls there were no briefs, deadlines, or client demands.

A pair of carefully trimmed box trees on either side of the back door paid lip service to the formal gardens of her classical heritage, but otherwise it was a pleasing hodgepodge. She'd stuck a variety of antique tiles willy-nilly on one wall because they seemed "meant" to go there, painstakingly decorated a cheap garden table with a huge mosaic daisy because daisies made her happy, and commissioned an eccentric potter friend to make her a fountain which would not be to everyone's taste, but which she appreciated.

After five years of planting, pricking out, and pruning, the garden was to some extent looking after itself, and a mix of perennials had grown to fill gaps that had once needed weeding constantly. This was fortunate, as now that Dan was on the scene she'd slacked off, preferring to spend time in bed with him than on her beds and borders.

Nevertheless, by the end of May she was reaping the rewards of a morning spent sowing seeds two months previously, and all that was required this afternoon was to fill a few small remaining spaces. This Orianna was doing with her favorite scarlet geraniums, while Dan emptied ash from the barbecue. For Orianna had made clear—in as diplomatic a fashion as possible—that this was her room of her own, and Dan was only permitted a walk-on part.

She pressed the bottom of a plastic container to dislodge a plant. "Have you heard any more about a replacement for Neil?"

"No, have you?"

"Apparently they've problems finding someone."

"Do you know why?"

"We do such a mixture of stuff. It's been hard to find a candidate with a broad enough background."

Dan finished shoveling the ash into a bucket, stood up, and dusted himself down. Then he said, "You should apply."

Orianna was stunned. "Me?"

"There's no one else in the garden, is there?" Dan lifted a pot and peeked under it with mock seriousness.

"I hadn't thought of it . . ." She assimilated. "Do you think I'd be any good?"

"I wouldn't suggest it otherwise. I reckon you'd be brilliant."

She put down the tray of plants, focusing on him. "*Really?*"

"Yes. I do."

"Why?"

"Well, you've shed-loads of experience, for starters. How long have you been in this industry?"

"Eleven years."

"And at Green?"

"Four."

"You're a group head, right, so you and Ivy are responsible for overseeing several juniors?"

Orianna nodded.

"It goes without saying you've knowledge of the whole marketing mix."

"Mm."

"You've won lots of creative awards."

"About ten." Orianna smiled. She was beginning to see what he meant.

"Plus you work extremely hard and everyone likes you. You're one of the most popular people in the agency."

"*Am* I?" Orianna hadn't seen herself that way at all.

"Of course you are." He came over, took her hands in his, and squeezed them.

"You're biased."

He kissed the top of her head. "Yup. Still, you know I'd never say these things if I didn't believe they were true."

Orianna frowned. Surely Dan wouldn't raise my expectations needlessly, she thought. He's been managing juniors a while, and is aware of the troubles it can cause. Moreover, thanks to his role, he's a hub of the agency, so often gets to know how people feel about each other ... Suppose he's right?

But he had forgotten one thing. She pulled away. "What about Ivy?"

"What about her?"

"I couldn't put myself forward without her. We'll apply as a team."

"I'm not sure the company would go for it," said Dan, taking a seat on a low wall edging a flower bed.

"Why not?"

Dan paused, as if thinking how he should put it. "You'd be quite expensive as a duo, wouldn't you? Be too costly for them."

"Bet it would be cheaper than getting someone new. They're paying us already so could get away with giving us a raise rather than shelling out an additional six-figure salary for some high-flyer."

"I suppose . . . But you know how sacrosanct they consider the board to be. They won't put me on it, and it could upset the balance to have *two* creatives join them at the top."

"Not as much as having a brand new CD wanting to stamp their mark. Imagine what upheaval that might cause."

"True." He paused again. "I don't think Ivy would be as good a creative director as you, though."

Orianna was taken aback. "Really?"

"No." He held her gaze, and said gently, "Ivy isn't as dedicated as you."

"She works bloody hard!" Orianna protested. "And lots of copywriters don't work such long hours as art directors—the writing often gets finished first."

"Agreed." Again Dan hesitated. He seemed unsure whether to be frank. "I just don't think she'd be quite as popular as you, that's all."

"Lots of people love Ivy!"

"Mm . . . they do, and I agree, she's very good—"

"She's won almost as many awards as me!"

"I know, I know." Dan held up a hand to slow her. "Though people like her in a different way; she's ever so clever, but she's not as good a people-manager."

"Oh." Orianna could sense her face fall on behalf of her friend.

"You know what it's like, I get to see a lot, and some account handlers—Ivy rubs them the wrong way. She can be a bit uncompromising, compared to you, and they find her abrasive sometimes, sharp. And as for the juniors . . . She can be rather intimidating."

"But that's not such a bad thing, surely?"

"By and large it doesn't matter, and I think the two of you work well together. She benefits from the way you handle things, I suppose."

Orianna had always seen their partnership as mutually beneficial. It hadn't crossed her mind Ivy might be profiting from her own more softly-softly approach. She mulled it over for a while, silent. It was true Ivy hadn't been as friendly of late—she hadn't asked Orianna much about Dan, a sign she was miffed. But Orianna hoped it would pass once Ivy got used to their relationship.

Just think of all the years we've worked together, she reminded herself. What fun we've had, building our reputations, developing our roles and earning extra responsibilities as a team. Surely nothing could seriously come between us? She remembered their joint success at winning new business as well as awards. No, she decided, I really value the part Ivy has played in my career, and I'm not going to jeopardize it.

"Wherever I go, Ivy goes with me," she said, turning to resume her planting. "I'm not applying on my own. So the board will have to take us as a team. Or not at all."

The following morning Orianna and Ivy were bouncing around ideas for a new hair-care product, when Ivy said, "There goes the power lunch," as a catering trolley was wheeled by.

Orianna swiveled her chair. From where she was sitting, she could see that it was laden with high-class canapés—crackers and caviar, salmon vol-au-vents, prawns in batter, chicken satay, even quails' eggs. All that food made her hungry.

"I can't believe it's a month since the last board meeting."

"Notice they don't get the boring sandwiches we have to suffer at our lowly meetings," said Ivy. "No wonder they're all so bloody fat."

Suddenly Orianna felt rather plump. "They're not *that* bad. Russell's quite slim."

"Well, aside from Russell."

"And Neil's not that overweight either."

"Evidently he doesn't have the fat cat mentality, does he? Going to live up north."

"There are fat cats up north too," said Orianna. She knew Ivy in this mood; there would be no shifting her cynicism.

"Anyway." Ivy checked the clock. "That's persuaded me. I'm off to the gym."

"What, *again?*"

"I haven't been since Friday. If I go now I'll catch a class." She nodded toward the boardroom. "Last thing I want is to end up like that lot." And with that she picked up her sports bag and was gone.

Orianna was growing accustomed to spending this time alone. Ivy seemed to be spending more lunches away from her and Dan only ever had time to dash out for a sandwich. Besides, she was still cautious about being seen overtly socializing with him, not wanting to expose their relationship to the agency as a whole. Shopping alone wasn't the same, so she decided to explore the ideas she and Ivy had been discussing further on the Internet.

Twenty minutes later there was a cough behind her. She turned around.

It was Russell. He glanced about. "Er . . . Is Ivy around?"

Unless she was mistaken, he looked a little uncomfortable. "She's gone to the gym. Did you want her?" Orianna had noticed that on certain projects Russell worked with Ivy quite closely, in private. She said it was so he could give her insight into their financial clients.

"No, no." Russell seemed in a hurry. "It's you we want to see. Got a second?"

"Mm." Orianna was mystified.

"Could you come and join us in the board meeting, then?"

"Yes, of course." Damn, she thought. I'd have worn something smarter had I known I was meeting them all.

Russell led the way. The room was the largest in the agency, with a ceiling so high it echoed. Its windows looked out across the rooftops of W1, and a sheet of the palest green smoked glass ran the length of the wall facing into the creative department. It was hung with Venetian blinds, which could be pulled down for increased privacy—all but one were lowered now.

"She was free." Russell smiled at his colleagues, and shut the door.

Orianna noticed he appeared relieved to have gotten her out of public earshot. Oh dear, she thought, have I done something wrong?

"Sit down," invited Neil.

She looked at him. He grinned at her; he didn't appear cross at all.

Orianna took at seat opposite Neil, Clare, and Russell and between the other board directors—Gavin, the head of client services, and Stephen, the managing director.

"Have you any idea why we wanted to talk to you?" asked Neil. As her immediate boss, he knew her best. They'd always gotten along rather well.

"No." Orianna's concern mounted.

Neil coughed. "We wondered if you'd be interested in becoming the creative director."

"*Oh!*" Despite the conversation over the weekend, this was a total bombshell. Her mind clicked and whirred. "Did *Dan* say something to you?"

"Dan?" Russell shook his head. "I did hear you two were seeing each other . . ." Orianna flushed. ". . . but no, he's not said anything to us at all. Not to me, at any rate." He turned to the rest of the board. "He said anything to you guys?"

They all shook their heads.

"Oh," said Orianna again. Now their relationship was public whether she liked it or not. Weird, she thought, I wonder how he found out? Dan had asked Ivy to keep it quiet. But she didn't have time to contemplate. "It's just he suggested it, yesterday, and I assumed—"

"He'd put us up to it? No." Neil laughed. "We came up with it all by ourselves."

Orianna was aware the spotlight was on her, but was too astounded to speak.

"It's not *such* a bizarre idea, you know," said Neil.

"You've been with us for years," said Gavin.

"And brought in lots of new business," said Clare. "Your performance at Bellings Scott was a triumph."

"You work on some of the agency's most profitable accounts," said Stephen.

"Plus you've won even more awards than I have," said Neil, a touch sardonically.

"And to be perfectly frank, we can't find anyone better," said Russell.

"Right . . ." Orianna was trying to keep pace.

"So you would seem the obvious choice," concluded Neil.

"Thank you." She paused. So many compliments; a life-changing offer—it was a lot to take in. She was only beginning to digest it all when she remembered Russell had wanted to catch her on her own, without Ivy. "And Ivy? She would be joint CD with me? The Bellings Scott win was as much her work as mine, if not more."

The board members looked at one another. There was no mistaking it; they were awkward.

Eventually, Neil spoke up for the rest of them. "We think it would be better if there was only one creative director. The agency is used to things being run that way, and we're not sure that it would be appropriate to have a team."

"Gosh." Orianna didn't know whether to be flattered or dismayed. Perhaps they couldn't afford them both?

Then Clare said, "Frankly, we think you'd do a better job," which put paid to that.

"As a matter of fact I saw a great art director for lunch last week whom you might like to bring in to team up with Ivy," suggested Neil.

"Oh. Right." Yet again a response failed her. Her world was being turned upside down.

Neil prompted, "I leave in six weeks. It would mean a new title, obviously, and a position on the board, maybe not immediately, but within, say, three months. We can discuss money later, if you'd prefer."

Then Russell, clearly impatient, interposed. "Though we need to establish right now—otherwise we'll carry on looking. Are you interested in the role or not?"

7. I grace my cause in speaking for myself

"Yes," said Orianna.

It came out before she could stop it. She might be modest compared to most of her peers, she might be more concerned for Ivy (altruism was hardly the hallmark of agency employees), but one trait overrode them all.

Ambition.

Without ambition, Orianna would never have flourished in an industry where ruthlessness and drive counted as much as talent, often more.

Swiftly, silently, she reasoned. Modesty aside, I'm talented. Deep down I'm sure I'm as good as—if not better than—the next man. I've worked under enough ineffectual bosses to know I can do the job, and do it well. Wasn't it the combination of diplomacy and conceptual skill that set Neil apart? I've learned from him, but he's grown weary of the commercial world, whereas I've fire in my belly regarding work. And people say my enthusiasm is infectious. All good reasons for taking the job . . .

Hmm, Orianna pondered, that still leaves the problem of Ivy . . . Yet, if the situation were reversed, would she do the same for me? Give up promotion, more power, prestige, and money? I'm not sure she would. Ivy's always looked after numero uno—until now that's meant not jeopardizing our relationship. If Ivy were offered this opportunity, wouldn't she take it too?

"Yes," Orianna repeated. "Naturally, I am interested."

"Good." Neil sat back, openly relieved.

He may well be the one who put me forward, she thought. Certainly, as my boss, he'll have given my promotion his blessing. Without his recommendation I wouldn't be here. She continued, her voice restored, "As you mentioned, I have been playing a key role in Green Integrated for the last few years."

"It's hardly a similar level of responsibility," said Russell.

"Obviously a group head only oversees a few people, not a department. But in some ways it will be more of the same."

"How do you mean, *more* of the same?" Russell didn't mask incredulity. "Surely it's a different role entirely?"

He wasn't going to make this easy; he seemed keen to turn the conversation into more of an interview. Well, if need be, she'd argue her case. She said, "You've already said I've helped win new business; as a creative director I'm sure you'd want me to do more." They all nodded, no one more vigorously than Clare. "You've also noted that I work on some of the agency's most profitable accounts"—Gavin nodded—"and I'm sure you'd want me to make them even *more* profitable." Now it was Stephen's turn to give his silent approval. "Plus, you've observed my track record when it comes to awards." Orianna looked directly at Neil, growing increasingly buoyant.

"No need to rub it in." Neil winced.

"I'd like to aim for more golds next year. Though the main thing is—no disrespect to you, Neil, but you'll understand me saying this— hopefully I'd have a free rein. So I'd be able to accomplish these in the way I see fit, rather than deferring to someone else." She turned back to Russell, determined to win him over. "So that's what I mean by delivering more of the same. All this you'd expect from a good CD. In addition, I'd like to make sure that I operate in as sympathetic a fashion as possible. I'd like to be a good manager of people. Something"—she recalled Dan's pep talk—"I believe I've already shown I can do. I've not had to trample on anyone to get where I have today, and I'd rather not start now."

"Very noble." Orianna didn't miss Russell's sarcastic tone. "I'll eat my hat if you manage that."

"Yes what about Ivy?" nudged Clare.

"I'll handle Ivy," said Orianna. Instinct told her now was not the time to abdicate responsibility. Having been offered a senior position, she had to seem worthy, lest it be snatched away before she'd proven herself. Although she'd yet to acknowledge it, she was beginning to see her life differently—her attachments were shifting as a result of her involvement with Dan. "I'd rather none of you mentioned this until I've had the chance to talk to her."

"Fine," they concurred, clearly delighted to be let off the hook.

"And what about Dan?" asked Russell.

"Sorry. *What about Dan?*"

"Well, you're having an affair, aren't you?"

"We're in a relationship, if that's what you mean," Orianna corrected. She wondered again how he knew. Was it Rob? He could have let it slip to someone at the gym, perhaps word had spread from there . . . Oh well, she thought, I could have made the same mistake myself.

"Don't you think being involved with another senior employee might cause the odd problem?"

This riled her. "Such as?"

"Like conflicts of loyalty, giving each other preferential treatment, bringing personal issues and arguments into the workplace, perhaps showing yourself up as unprofessional to your junior colleagues? You know the sort of thing."

"It hasn't caused difficulty so far," said Orianna. What business was it of his?

He forced a nod.

"I truly don't see it as a problem," Clare interjected.

"There are others dating in the agency," Stephen pointed out. "I'm not sure it's relevant, if Orianna thinks she can handle it."

"I didn't know you *were* seeing one another," said Neil. "But now that I do, may I say I think you make a nice couple."

"Thank you." Orianna smiled. What a decent guy Neil is, she thought. I'm going to miss him. Then she saw Ivy flash past the smoked-glass wall. She took the initiative, turned again to her colleagues. "Are you offering me the job?"

Neil glanced at Russell.

Russell nodded.

"Yes," said Neil.

"Then I'd like to accept."

"Great," said Neil.

Orianna continued, "Before we finalize the salary, I'd like to have a deeper think about what I'd plan to do for the agency. It might be good to set aside some time in a few days, and meanwhile I'll gather my thoughts into a short presentation. I'd prefer to leave discussing the package until then. Would that be all right by you?"

"Good thinking." Neil nodded.

Stephen checked the agenda. "We've got quite a lot to crack through."

"I'd be happy to move on," said Clare.

"Then would you mind if I left you to it? I've a meeting shortly."

"That's fine," Russell granted.

Orianna glanced through the smoked glass to verify Ivy was out of sight and surreptitiously left the boardroom.

Dan was in the middle of being shown some uninspiring product shots by a photographer's rep when he noticed Orianna hovering. He could tell from her jigging feet she needed to speak urgently, so while the rep was concentrating on a particularly dull transparency, he mouthed, "Give me ten minutes."

Afterward, he went to find Orianna. She was brainstorming ideas with Ivy. "Did you want me?"

"Er . . . no, it's OK."

But she seemed uncomfortable, even jumpy. "Are you sure?"

"Yeah, yeah. It's nothing. I'll catch up with you later."

"Now you two lovebirds—no secrets in the office," said Ivy. "Actually, Dan," she caught his arm as he turned to leave, "you're a man with a fine head of hair, when all around you are losing theirs. How do you feel about hairspray?"

"What, for *me*?" He shook his head. "Never used it."

"Why not?"

"Hardly a guy thing, is it?"

"Precisely my point." Ivy turned to Orianna. "We've not a hope in hell of getting men to use this product, as long as it's called hairspray. Unless they're drag queens. We'll have to change the name."

Dan returned to his desk—umpteen messages had amassed in his absence—and shortly there was the red flag of a priority mail.

Quick, while Ivy's gone to the loo—you psychic or what? I just got called into the board meeting and they've offered me the job of CD! Can you believe it? Trouble is they want me without Ivy—just as you thought. How spooky is that? Need to discuss where I go from here/what salary to ask for/how to tell Ivy. Over a celebratory drink—where do you fancy? She's coming back. Gotta dash.

O

xxxxx

P.S. Delete this NOW.

"Well, that went well," said Ivy, as she and Orianna returned to their desks later that afternoon. "Shall we celebrate?"

"Er . . . I was going to meet Dan."

"Ooh, ever the doting couple. C'mon, Orianna. You're getting dull in your old age. Get him to join us later. That client's so hard to please—we deserve a reward."

"Oh . . . OK." Orianna chewed her lip. She hated knowing something

Ivy didn't already. It was bad enough having been secretive about seeing Dan, the last thing she wanted was to be professionally underhanded too. She'd badly wanted to talk to Dan about how best to play it but . . .

To hell with it, she thought. I'm a big girl. If I'm going to be creative director, I should be able to deal with this on my own. Perhaps I should tell Ivy now. Who knows, she might not take it so badly. She's never been as openly ambitious as me—she's always so scathing about senior management. If don't put it off Ivy can't accuse me of keeping it from her, and where better to do it than over a drink, with her in a good mood? I'll let her choose the venue too.

"Where shall we go?" she said.

"Cassio's." Ivy didn't hesitate. "Let's get out of here as soon as we can."

While Orianna was in the ladies' room repairing her makeup, Ivy e-mailed Russell.

Off for drink with O. Will cab it to you after—have some vino breathing for me. Expect me around eight.

8. I am worth no worse a place

Minutes later Ivy and Orianna were perched on chocolate-colored leather chairs on either side of a low table in the window of Cassio's bar, sipping a gin and diet tonic and dry white respectively. Ivy liked coming here—the clean, spacious design was exactly the decor she loved, and a stylish clientele made it a good place to people-watch. All around them strangers chatted, and the lack of music meant they didn't have to shout.

"That was a great bit of spontaneous presenting," she congratulated.

"Thanks."

Orianna looked embarrassed, but Ivy was used to her modesty. Occasionally she found it irritating, right now she was feeling magnanimous. "They're not the easiest client in the world."

"Mm." Orianna frowned. There was no doubt her manner was subdued.

"Hey . . ." Ivy leaned over the table toward her friend. "Is something up?"

"No, no," said Orianna, a touch too fast.

"Is it Dan?"

"No!"

"I don't want to see you hurt again. Are you *sure* you two are OK?"

"I promise, we're fine," said Orianna. Though she sighed, and Ivy remained concerned. Orianna's behavior had been strange all afternoon. As if her mind were elsewhere, when normally she was so focused.

Ivy didn't find intimate gestures easy, but appreciated one was called for. She squeezed Orianna's hand. "Whatever happens, you'll always have me."

"Will I?" Orianna's big brown eyes were wide with worry.

Ivy was genuinely touched. To think I was afraid she wouldn't need me anymore. "Of course."

"That's a relief." Orianna sighed again.

"Come on," coaxed Ivy. "You can tell me."

Orianna removed her hand and took a huge sip of wine. And another. "I don't know how to say this . . . But I know you were pissed off when I didn't tell you about Dan, so I don't want to keep this from you too."

Then it clicked. It was inevitable. Some might think Dan quite a catch, and Orianna was thirty-three, impatient to get on with her life . . . She must be anxious about admitting they were taking the next step so soon. Ivy cut to it. "Are you getting married?"

"Goodness, no!"

"Oh." Must be something else. Ivy paused, assessing. Orianna hadn't seemed off her food, but perhaps not even morning sickness would accomplish that. "*Pregnant?*"

"No!"

Ivy was mystified.

"I promise, it's nothing to do with Dan."

Oh my God; worse. "You're not *leaving* Green, are you?"

"No." Another sip of wine.

Although almost all of Ivy's drink remained, Orianna was nearly at the bottom of her glass. Ivy had to get this out of her before another trip to the bar was needed. She tried to disguise her impatience. "What is it then?"

Orianna looked away, glanced at Ivy nervously, and eventually said, "I've been promoted."

It was as if she'd been punched. Ivy sat back in her chair, head spinning. "What do you mean . . ." she said slowly, ". . . *you've* been promoted?"

"I mean just that. I've been promoted. To CD."

Ivy started to shake. "When did you find this out?"

"At lunchtime." Orianna's voice had dropped to a whisper.

Ivy spoke with spiked precision: "*While I was at the gym?*"

"Yes."

"I see . . ." Ivy struggled to control her mounting fury.

"They want me to take over once Neil has gone——"

"They want *you* to take over? Let me be clear. *Just* you?"

"Yes."

"How nice." Ivy spat. "And where precisely does that leave *me?*"

"As group head . . ."

"Like I am now, in other words? But without you?"

"Er . . . yes. Well, we can get you a new art director, obviously. But the board thought it would be better to have just one CD."

"Without a copywriter?"

Orianna looked down. She was purple with embarrassment. "Mm, at least in terms of an official title, yes. They . . . um . . . I think they only want one member of the department on the board."

"I bet they do!"

"Ivy——" This time Orianna tried to squeeze her hand, but Ivy snatched it away.

Ivy was beyond hurt; she felt utterly betrayed. All those years as a duo apparently counted for nothing. "Didn't you tell them where to shove their bloody job without me?"

"I tried, honestly . . . But they wouldn't hear any of it."

"The hell you did. I know what you're like. So fucking wet sometimes." Ivy shook her head in disbelief. "I'm appalled. Absolutely appalled. So you're going to take the job then?"

"Er . . . yes . . . I have," said Orianna softly, then added, "I hoped you'd understand."

"Pah!"

"I thought you didn't want to be CD. You've always said the role stinks; that it involves all the worst, most boring and adminny aspects of our jobs and none of the fun."

"Ri-ight . . ."

"And I'll make sure you get to work with me on things; I'll still need a copywriter some of the time."

"Gee, thanks." Ivy looked down at her glass, and ran her fingers around the edge. Compared to Orianna's, it was still full. There was only one thing for it. For a split second she didn't give a flying fuck that they were in the window, in full view of everyone at the crowded bar and numerous passersby. And Orianna was just sitting there in her sweet little summer dress, her hair so flipping perfect, her girly-girly makeup so recently reapplied.

Instantly, before she had time to reconsider or regain her composure, Ivy picked up her G&T. Then she slung it, with the most fantastic accuracy, ice, lime, and all, over her partner.

And as Orianna sat in shock, her dark locks dripping, makeup running, designer dress clinging to her ample curves like a wet T-shirt in a sordid competition, the lime slice wedged in her cleavage, Ivy picked up her bag and stormed out of the bar.

Rob was on his way to meet a friend at the far end of Dean Street, having finished at the gym, when he saw Ivy several yards ahead of him, exiting Cassio's at breakneck speed. He was about to say hello, but she crossed the road and headed in the opposite direction, not noticing him at all.

Hmm, he thought, I wonder if anyone else from Green is in there? He peered through the floor-to-ceiling window. Good God! Sitting just a few feet away was Orianna. She was completely drenched, as was the table before her. A waiter was struggling to soak up the mess with paper napkins, but Rob could see it was going to take far more than that, so a combination of nosiness and gallantry propelled him up the steps and into the bar.

"Orianna?"

She looked up, distress undisguised. "Oh! Er . . . Rob! Hi."

"What happened?" He unzipped his bag and handed her his sports towel. "Here. It's a bit damp, but . . ."

"Thanks." Orianna seemed mortified to be seen in such a state, and Rob didn't blame her. Cassio's was not a place to show oneself up. After she'd mopped the worst, she said, "I'll go to the ladies' room and sort myself out."

"I'll wait here," said Rob, curiosity increasing.

As Orianna edged through the crowd, people turned to stare. She'll feel worse when she sees herself in the mirror, thought Rob, his heart going out to her. I'd better check she's OK. While he stood waiting, he phoned the private members' club and asked the girl in reception to explain to his friend he'd been delayed. Then he went to order a Diet Coke.

"Wow," said the bartender. "That was fun."

"What happened?"

"Her friend threw a drink at her."

"Really?"

"That's what it looked like."

"Any idea why?"

"Couldn't hear the conversation, but they seemed to be chatting like normal, then suddenly, *wham!* This foxy redhead slings her entire drink at your friend."

"Was it *deliberate*?" Rob knew he should be horrified, but he so loved drama.

"Didn't look like an accident to me."

"Blimey." Rob flinched, imagining. "I wonder what brought that on?"

The bartender jerked his head. "You're about to find out."

Rob turned to see Orianna. Her hair and clothing were still damp, but she'd made herself look reasonably presentable.

"Thanks." She handed him back the towel.

"That's OK." Rob couldn't contain himself. "What happened?"

Orianna glanced at the bartender, obviously realized he must have witnessed it all, and said, "Ivy threw her drink at me."

"Heavens!" Rob feigned surprise. "Why?"

Orianna bit her lip. "I told her I got promoted." She appeared to be expecting further censure.

Rob was perplexed. "Shouldn't she be pleased for you?"

"Perhaps." Orianna nodded. "But I guess Ivy felt she should have been promoted with me."

"Ah, I get it." He remembered Ivy explaining they worked as a team. So now Orianna would be Ivy's boss. Ivy was not someone he'd want to cross; the prospect was scary. "Ouch."

"I thought I ought to tell her. I hate keeping secrets from her and you saw how upset she was about me and Dan. I should have known she'd take this badly."

"Not necessarily," Rob sympathized. "Did she really expect you to turn down the job?" Ivy was his client so he knew his loyalty should be to her, especially as Orianna was dating a man he still fancied. Yet once again he warmed to Orianna's manner. Maybe her desire to be liked echoed his own; certainly he identified with her difficulty in keeping important news to herself. He was sure she'd not meant any malice. And there was no doubt she was the victim of horrible public humiliation—and in these circumstances Rob was cast in his role: he was her knight in shining armor. He gulped down his Diet Coke.

"Look, I'm going to meet a friend at Blacks, so I'd better go, in case she's waiting. But if you fancy joining us you'd be welcome."

Orianna looked around the bar. A number of people quickly turned away, ashamed they'd been caught gawping. "It'd be good to get away." She smiled gratefully. "I'm supposed to be going to dinner with Dan later, but I guess I can call him and say to meet me there. If you're sure?"

"Of course," said Rob, secretly gleeful. Now he'd not only be able to find out the full story, he'd get to see Dan again socially too.

Screw the taxi.

Ivy's Z4 was in the Poland Street parking garage—she'd been planning on leaving it overnight—but now a relaxing drink was the last thing on her mind. She needed to let off steam, big-time, and at least her sleek silver sports car wouldn't let her down. She flew down Wardour Street as fast as her stiletto mules would allow. Even impractical heels could not hamper her, such was her fury. She whisked up the concrete stairs of the multistory building—*tippy tappy*—and, before her BMW was even within sight, aimed her key to flick off the alarm. *Biddle-up, biddle-up,* it beeped, and she was in. She sat down with a *boof* of air escaping leather, threw her bag on the adjacent seat, and *snap! snap!* unclicked the catches to lower the roof. In with a CD, up with the volume. Blast anyone who might object.

"How much?!" Ivy hurled the fee at the poor guy in the kiosk and with a cop-show screech of tires was on her way.

If the horn got used once en route, it got used a dozen times. As for red lights—it was lucky there were no police around to pull her over. The traffic through Soho was maddeningly slow—all those irresponsible couriers, irritating pedestrians, and, worst, *imbecilic* tourists—but once she was on Park Lane she could vent some spleen outstripping any boy-racer who dared take her on.

How could she? *How could she?* HOW COULD SHE? Ivy was so consumed by rage she hadn't the energy to be upset; doubtless that would come in due course, but then she'd keep it to herself. Being seen as vulnerable was something she loathed; tears made her cringe. Yet if there was one person who Ivy *had* allowed to get close, it was Orianna. Over the years coming up with ideas, Ivy had opened up bit by tiny bit. The result was that Orianna had become more than a colleague or friend; she was in many ways Ivy's surrogate partner in life.

For if Ivy were honest with herself (which she preferred not to be), her relationships with men left much to be desired. She couldn't face the implications, so hadn't discussed things with her husband, but for several years her marriage had not been great. Aside from Orianna—to whom she'd moaned occasionally—no one had any inkling how she felt, but although things had been good briefly, now she and Ed tended to go their separate ways.

And as for her lover, Russell was Russell; good for two things—sex and Ivy's ego. She liked sleeping with him—it made her feel attractive and desirable, and the secrecy was thrilling at times. She relished having a powerful, good-looking man in her thrall, someone who'd do his utmost to keep on her right side. Or so she'd believed until now . . .

Her mind raced. My husband wusses out on me—I've long gotten used to that. But my best friend betraying me? My lover selling me down the river? It shows no one's worth trusting. No one!

Twelve minutes later, Ivy was there. She turned off the engine and reversed the actions of the Poland Street parking garage: roof shut, stereo off, bag picked up, alarm on. Then *tippy tappy* up the stairs—she couldn't be bothered to wait for the elevator—and *pring!* on the doorbell.

It seemed to take him an age to answer. She could hear the bolts sliding back, the chain unlocked, then, at last, she was in.

"You're early." Russell was still in his work shirt and trousers, though he'd loosened his tie and there was the noise of water running in the bathroom. Doubtless he'd been poised to take a pre-shag shower.

"Indeed," said Ivy, voice clipped. She led the way into the kitchen. There on the white marble counter, as requested, was a bottle of wine. A particularly fine Cheateauneuf-du-Pape. It was uncorked, glasses at the ready.

"May I?" Without waiting for a reply, Ivy poured them each a glass. She stood back and casually took a sip, resting her bottom against the counter. "Tell me, Russell," she said acidly, "did you have a meeting at lunchtime?"

"You know I did." Russell was unperturbed.

"And who else was in that meeting?"

"The rest of the board, of course."

"Not my art director, perchance?"

"Orianna?" He paled. "Mm . . . I guess she was."

"Now, Russell." Ivy's voice was sickly sweet. "Tell me. Were you party to this *promotion* she seems to think she's been offered? Does her spectacular *solo* rise to creative director have anything to do with you?"

"Er . . ." Russell, who normally had an answer to everything, was clearly caught short. Presumably he hadn't expected her to learn of the move quite so fast.

"Because forgive me if I'm wrong, but it seems to me that as financial director of Green Integrated you had some teeny part to play in all this—ah! Stop!" Seeing his mouth open in protest she held up a palm. "Don't pretend you didn't sanction it in some way. If you didn't, you ought to watch out—for control of this agency seems to be slipping out of your hands. But frankly, I know you, so I wouldn't believe you. My guess is you gave it your tacit approval or certainly didn't have the guts to object. Which, given that you and I have been *fucking*"—she delivered the word as if it were a weapon—"for, ooh, what? Three years? Or is it four? I take to be a rather gross misdemeanor on your part. Don't mess with me, Russell—*I'm* the one you should be looking out for at Green, not Orianna. And if you don't, remember, dearest, I can make things pretty spectacularly embarrassing for you and little Mrs. Russie-pie at home. A little bunny-boiling behavior might become me beautifully. But in the meantime, take *this* as a warning of what might be to come."

And with that she hurled the bloodred contents of her glass straight at him, covering his crisp white shirt in a stain his wife would find impossible to remove.

9. The raven o'er the infected house

"Oh my God! Oh my God! Oh my God!" shrieked Rob.

Orianna had already gleaned he could be theatrical, and knew Blacks was a media haunt where starry behavior was commonplace, but his entrance to the bar seemed OTT all the same. Then, as Rob flung his arms around an hourglass brunette and squeezed her so hard Orianna almost expected her to pop, she realized it was simply a greeting. My goodness, she thought, does he treat *all* his friends this way?

"How are you then?" He held the girl at arm's length like a proud father. "Let me take a look."

His friend stood back, laughing, and Orianna took in an expressive face, an unruly mop of curls, and an outrageous, turquoise, tiger-striped dress.

"Give us a twirl," commanded Rob, and she twirled obligingly, quite unembarrassed that the guy on the door, the bar staff, and Orianna were all watching. "*Love* it. New purchase?"

The girl nodded. "SoHo special, darling." She mimicked his campiness.

"You look pretty happy to me." Rob checked her over again.

She grinned. "I am."

"The city suits you."

"I'm having a *heavenly* time." She had a way of speaking that was particularly sensual, thought Orianna; in fact, with her barely hidden bosom and fishnet tights, she seemed a bit of a sexpot. "Ooh, it's *so* good to see you!"

She hugged Rob again, and Orianna was beginning to feel awkward.

"Oh my Lord, honey, I'm so sorry," he said. "How *rude* of me!" She stepped forward. "Orianna, this is my ex-roommate and dear, dear friend—indeed, far be it from me to mince words—my bestest friend in the whole wide *world*, Chloë Appleton. Chloë, Orianna, a recent acquaintance but one who I am certain is a kindred spirit too."

Orianna smiled. In the face of such exuberance she felt a little shy.

Chloë held out her hand. "Hi," she said. "Been for a swim?"

Dan was at his desk sorting invoices when his mobile rang.

"Hi, Dan? It's me."

"Where are you?"

"That's why I'm calling. I'm on Dean Street. We're at Blacks. I had to come out to phone you—you're not allowed to make calls inside."

"How did you get in there? I didn't know Ivy was a member."

"She's not; Chloë is."

"Chloë?"

"A friend of Rob's."

"But I thought you were with Ivy?"

"It's a long story. Ivy's gone. Rob was meeting a friend of his here and invited me. Why don't you come and I'll explain?" Orianna's voice cracked. "I could do with seeing you actually."

"Are you OK?" As earlier that day, Dan was worried. She should be over the moon following her promotion. What on earth was going on? "Why isn't Ivy with you?"

"Eh?"

"I said, *where's* Ivy?"

"It's no good, I can't hear you." Orianna raised her voice. In the background he could hear the buzz of traffic and people. "This signal's crap."

"You're breaking up. I'm losing you . . ."

"Sorry?"

"OK," he bellowed, feeling silly in the quiet of the agency. "I'll be right down."

"Ask for Chloë at the door," she yelled, and the line cut out.

"Let's go to the lounge," said Chloë, taking Orianna's arm. They left Rob at the bar getting a round and Orianna followed Chloë up several flights of stairs.

At the top, Chloë pushed open a heavy door and led Orianna inside. Orianna had never been to Blacks before, though she'd heard of it, and for all her trauma was intrigued. The room was dark though it was still light outside, but eventually she was able to make out the gothic interior. Vintage prints and contemporary oil paintings hung on olive green walls; there was a vase of fresh flowers on a marble-topped table and candles galore. An assortment of brocade cushions, satin sofas, and armchairs made up the ad hoc seating, with the exception of a small room at the back, which was entirely taken up by a huge bed. On its tapestry covers three people lay talking and laughing. As Chloë guided her to a vacant sofa, Orianna noticed everything looked worn and loved— the antithesis to Cassio's clinical modernism. This was much more her style.

"So, have you been a member long?" she asked.

"I joined when I went abroad. I thought it would be nice to have somewhere to chill now that I'm not based here. It's good for business meetings too."

Orianna could imagine the sort of meetings one might hold here; the place had the air of a den of iniquity, but didn't say so. Yet she didn't wish to be drawn into the Ivy story before Dan arrived either, so steered the conversation elsewhere. "How come you're in London now?"

"I'm here for my brother's wedding."

"How lovely," beamed Orianna.

"Rob's coming as my guest."

So Chloë didn't have a serious boyfriend then. Odd, thought Orianna. A sexy girl like her? It's a reminder nice men are a rarity—I mustn't take Dan for granted.

"Where is it you're living?"

"New York—I moved there in April."

"My, how exciting." Orianna was envious. She and Ivy had often said they'd like to work there for a while, though she was certain she could never live there. She doubted there'd be many of her beloved geraniums in the Big Apple. "So you've gone for work?"

"I'm setting up a magazine."

"*Really?*"

"You might have seen it. It launched here in February."

"Oh?"

"It's called *All Woman.*"

"Ooh, I know that! I love it!"

Chloë clapped her hands. "Honestly?"

"I buy it every month."

"The magazine was my idea, initially. I was the editor here, now I'm launching it in the US."

"That's amazing." Orianna was reverential. She was used to her job sounding impressive; all of a sudden Green Integrated seemed parochial. She wished she'd done more TV ads, which is what seemed to impress those outside the industry.

Sure enough, Chloë asked: "So what do you do?"

"I work in an advertising agency."

"Is that how you met Rob? I know he's got lots of agency clients."

"Yeah, my boyfriend's one of them."

"I see. So, what are you—a creative?" Chloë assessed her. "You must be."

Orianna laughed. "Because it's not everyone who comes to Blacks soaking wet?"

"No. I just meant your style—you know, it's kind of . . ."

"Hippy?" Orianna plucked at her floaty dress.

"It's feminine, yet funky," clarified Chloë. "I like it."

"Thanks." Orianna was pleased. The editor of *All Woman* thought she looked good! After such a horrible encounter with Ivy, this was just what she needed. Self-confidence restored, she was keen to impress Chloë in return. "You're right; I'm an art director. But actually I've just been offered the job of CD."

"Creative director?"

"Yup. Only today as a matter of fact." For the first time that day, she allowed herself to feel properly proud.

"Wow! But that's brilliant!"

"Why thank you." Orianna blushed. Given Chloë worked abroad, she felt able to confide, "I only wish my copywriter, Ivy, thought so. She threw her drink at me when I told her."

"Hence the wetness? Oh dear. A woman upstaged, eh? That's a dangerous thing."

"Precisely."

"Is she a friend?"

"Mm." Orianna had another rush of guilt. "I'm not sure she'll *ever* forgive me."

"She'll come around, if you're nice to her, surely?"

"You don't know Ivy." Orianna grimaced.

At that moment Rob came up to them with a tray of drinks. "See who I've found. They let me sign him in for you." At his shoulder was Dan.

"Sweetheart!" Dan kissed Orianna. "Is everything alright?"

"Oh Dan!" she burst out. "I told Ivy about my promotion—"

"You didn't!"

"I know it was probably silly, but I thought she might understand; she's always said she loves the writing bit of copywriting and hates all the rest that goes with it, she's never that interested in our juniors, and I didn't think she was bothered about becoming CD." Orianna was aware she was being indiscreet, but had to offload. "And I didn't want her to be cross if I didn't tell her, so I decided to let her know at once, but she was furious. I've never seen her more angry." She paused for breath, and the shock of Ivy's reaction hit her again. She gulped back tears, determined not to seem pathetic in front of Chloë and Rob.

"Woah!" said Dan. "Slow up." He took hold of her hand and stroked it. "So, I take it you've accepted the job then? It wasn't clear in your e-mail."

"Yes. I agreed there and then, at the meeting."

Dan hesitated. "It's only that you said yesterday you'd never do it without Ivy."

Had that only been twenty-four hours ago? What a lot had happened since. "I know I did, but then I changed my mind."

"Oh."

"Was that awful of me?"

"You know I sometimes think you're too nice for your own good."

"Not anymore." Orianna sighed. "I feel like the biggest bitch on the planet."

"Honey, if there's one thing you'll never be, it's a bitch. Others can lay claim to that title, not you."

"Ivy thinks I'm one. When I told her, she threw her drink all over me and then Rob came into Cassio's and gave me his towel and rescued me."

"She *what*?"

Orianna recounted the story. When she'd finished she turned to all three of them. "What do you think?"

"I don't know her very well," said Rob, "and she's a client, so I don't want to be disloyal. Actually, I like Ivy but—um—she's not someone I'd want to get on the wrong side of." He was obviously struggling to be generous. "Perhaps I could speak to her? Say you didn't mean to upset her so much and you're really worried? I know you'll see her tomorrow but she's got a session with me before work and it might be good coming from someone else."

Orianna nodded. "It's a thought . . ."

"Frankly, I think she's overstepped the mark," interjected Dan. "Ivy has no right to treat you that way—she's supposed to be your friend. It pisses me off. I'd like to give her a piece of my mind."

"But you can understand why, surely, given our history?"

"Yes, but you asked my opinion, and that's it. I can't say I think very highly of her. It just shows the board was right to promote you, not her." Seeing Orianna's anxious expression, he stopped to consider. "Having said that, there's probably not much point in you getting pissed off with her—I guess it's not your style, and it'll only bring you down to her level. You know what would be very cool, if you want to win her over?"

"No."

"Play *her* a little, for once."

"Such as?"

"Be nice to her."

"You think?" Dan was usually good at diplomacy, he was probably right.

"It might not be what you feel like doing, but I've always found a little buttering up of you sensitive creative types"—he winked—"does a world of good."

"True . . ." Orianna turned to Chloë. She'd just met her, but already valued her opinion. Not only was Chloë a woman, so would understand the nuances of female friendship, but her position as editor of *All Woman* mirrored the role Orianna was about to step into—she was keen to hear her take. "Chloë?"

"My honest opinion?" Chloë frowned; evidently she'd been giving the matter serious thought. "If she threw her drink at you, partner, friend, whatever, it's simple. You'll never be able to work together effectively now. And you're her boss, or soon will be, so have the power to implement changes. I think, once your old CD has gone and you've gotten your feet under the table, you should make life difficult for her, ease her out, so she ends up wanting to leave. And if she won't go of her own accord, then, given her misconduct, fire her. Make her redundant or something. She's trouble, so I'd get rid of her, pronto."

10. The net that shall enmesh them all

"I can't fire her though, can I?" said Orianna. "She hasn't committed a sackable offense, and it's not easy to get rid of people."

She and Dan were at the Leicester Square subway station, waiting for the train. The platform was hot, humid, and heaving. Film credits had rolled, theater curtains fallen, pubs rung the closing bell—everyone was keen to get home.

"I guess. Ivy has been at Green a long time."

"I see why you're pissed off on my behalf"—she kissed him—"but it's complicated. We go back years. I was even her maid of honor, for goodness' sake."

"I'd forgotten that."

"I know she was a cow earlier, but most people don't understand Ivy." Orianna sighed. "She's not had it easy, you know."

"I'm sure she hasn't."

"I'm not exaggerating; she had a difficult childhood."

"Didn't we all?"

"Not like Ivy. Her father walked out when she was ten."

"Really?"

"She doesn't talk about it much, but it always sounded horrid. You mustn't ever tell her I told you this, but he ran off with his wife's best friend, set up house with her and her kids around the corner. His new wife made things tricky, so he virtually dropped his first family altogether. Cruel, if you ask me."

Dan nodded. "That explains a lot."

"It gets worse. When Ivy was a teenager, some other man dumped her mother and her mum fell apart completely, had a kind of breakdown, and Ivy was left to look after her younger brother almost single-handedly. She hardly sees her dad now—the last time was at her wedding, when they were useless, the lot of them. Her stepmother refused to come, her father left after the ceremony—he didn't stay for the meal, let alone speeches, and he should have given one! And her mother was a quivering wreck, sniveling through the whole thing. Dreadful behavior—they were all so bloody wrapped up in themselves."

"When it was supposed to be Ivy's day."

"Exactly."

A train drew into the station. Orianna and Dan made their way to the center of the crowded car. They had to stand, but at least could continue talking.

"Must have been odd, being maid of honor through all that."

"Oh, it was OK. Though Ivy did say she liked my speech especially."

"You gave a speech?"

"An informal one, spontaneously, as her dad had disappeared, I thought it would be nice." She smiled at the recollection. "I remember Ivy saying it showed I knew her better than Ed."

"Her husband?"

Orianna bit her lip. All this only made her feel guiltier. "So I can't simply get rid of her. I'd never live with myself. It's hardly how I want to start out as a boss—firing my best friend."

"No." Dan contemplated, brow furrowed. "Perhaps if you gave Ivy a chance to get used to the idea it might blow over."

"I hope so . . ."

The train arrived at Caledonian Road. They headed up in the elevator, through the barriers, and out of the station. Walking the final stretch, Orianna said, "It was interesting, though, wasn't it, Chloë's perspective?"

Dan took her hand. "Mm."

"And she probably knows what she's talking about. After all, she's done pretty well for herself, hasn't she? I mean, she doesn't even look that old—she can't be as old as me—and she's been the editor of two magazines already."

"She seems quite a go-getter."

"Do you reckon she's doing better than I am?"

"You can't compare yourselves. You don't work in magazines."

"We're both in the media."

"I don't think journalism pays as well as advertising though." Dan seemed keen to look on the bright side. "And now you'll be earning even more."

"I guess so."

Orianna walked in silence, brooding. They'd had a pleasant evening, but the banter was only a temporary distraction. Beneath the surface she remained in turmoil about Ivy. Soon her disquiet emerged. "She's very attractive, isn't she?"

Dan turned to her. "Who, Ivy?"

"Chloë."

"I suppose." Dan agreed. Then added, "Sexy."

Orianna felt a stab of jealousy. "Sexier than me?"

"You're different."

"So she *is* sexier."

"I didn't say that."

"You didn't have to." Orianna grew mournful. "I know I'm not sexy like that." Beside Chloë's hourglass figure, she'd felt plain plump.

"You're being silly. You're really pretty!"

"I don't want to be pretty. I want to be sexy!"

"Of *course* you're sexy." Dan dropped her hand, faced her, and took both her shoulders, giving them a squeeze. "I wouldn't be having sex with you otherwise."

"Now you're being literal." Orianna looked down, determined not to be comforted. Thoughts of Chloë's achievements fired her competitive spirit. "But I don't see why I *should* turn this job down. I deserve it! I've worked hard all these years, and I'm good at what I do! So what if Ivy came up with the Bellings Scott concept? It's not my fault if people like me more."

"No, it's not. This Ivy thing has really got to you, hasn't it?" He held up her chin and smiled gently.

But his sympathy only reactivated her misery. "Oh Dan!" Emotions enhanced by tiredness and wine, Orianna started to cry. "I've a ghastly feeling about all this, I really have . . ." She sniffed. "I don't think Ivy will ever forgive me, I've seen what she's like. But it's hardly as if I can turn the job down—I've already accepted it. Even if I did, she'd know I was prepared to take it, and resent me all the same." She stopped, gulped, then laughed through tears at the ludicrousness of the situation. "I keep things to myself—Ivy's furious. I try to be honest—she hates me more. I turn the job down—I suffer. If I accept it—*she* does. I can't win."

"It'll be weird sleeping on the sofa," said Chloë in a hushed voice as Rob opened the front door. "Is John here?"

"Probably," Rob whispered.

They tiptoed down the hall.

"Gosh, it's so tidy!" said Chloë as they entered the kitchen.

"John loves cleaning."

"How bizarre." When Chloë and Rob had shared the apartment, they'd lived perilously close to chaos. She eyed the bleached sink. "It's a completely different color!" She filled the kettle as if this were still her own home and wandered into the living room. "Ah, Potato!" He was curled up in his favorite spot on the couch. She scooped the cat into her arms.

John wouldn't appreciate that tickling Potato's chin could engender such bliss, Rob thought. "Oh, I do miss you!" he cried, giving Chloë another hug. Potato found the encounter a bit squashed and wriggled out from between them.

"Ditto." Chloë embraced him back, and extricated herself to reach for two mugs. "So . . . Do you still fancy Dan, or what?"

"Am I that transparent?"

"Darling, I've known you for *years*. The way you laughed at his jokes and hung on his every word, how you looked at him, your being desperately *nice* to Orianna . . . It was obvious."

"Ah well." Rob fetched the tea bags. "Some things never change. You and me, we always go for unavailable men, eh?"

"Speak for yourself. I've a date with a *single* banker."

"Atta girl! Where did you meet him?"

"Oh, it'll probably come to nothing. I met him in a bar a couple of weeks ago, and he's really busy and so am I, but we've finally managed to make a date."

"If he's a banker he's bound to be rich." Rob concealed a twinge of envy. Why didn't *he* ever get asked out? In comparison to Chloë, he appeared to inhabit a romantic desert. A recent clearing out of his bedside cabinet had even revealed his stash of condoms to be past their sell-by date. Sighing, he thought of the one man in whom he *was* interested. He needed confirmation he was desirable. "What do you reckon about Dan then?"

"I think he's incredibly nice looking. And he seemed a genuine guy."

"It's just I really like him."

"I know. And I can tell he's very fond of you."

"D'you think?" Rob was pleased.

"Yes."

"Just fond?"

She looked at him squarely and said gently, "I think he's in love with Orianna."

Rob's heart sank.

"I want you to be certain you're not falling for him because you can't have him. We both love a challenge, but hankering after an unavailable guy is often a surefire way to a broken heart, and I don't want to see you hurt." Chloë grinned. "That said, if there's anyone who can convert even the straightest of men, it's you. You're irresistible when in the mood. Never say never, that's my motto."

11. Foul charms

In Chelsea, events were taking a different turn. Russell was most displeased to have an expensive shirt ruined, let alone be told how to behave by Ivy. The moment she put down her wineglass he grabbed her wrists and pinned her to the counter.

"You're being ridiculous," he hissed. "You of all people should appreciate however much clout I have. It takes more than one person to get anything signed off at Green. You know I don't have the power to veto something ratified by the rest of the board. I argued for your joint promotion, but my fighting so keenly on your behalf was beginning to look suspicious. The company simply can't afford you both, either politically or financially." He paused, and as Ivy relaxed her rigid stance, edged his leg between hers. "*Entre nous,* my dear, we're only offering Orianna the job because she's cheaper than other candidates we interviewed. We'll give her a negligible raise to keep her happy and working all hours, but it'll be far less than the crazy amounts they were demanding, trust me. And the agency has hardly had a good year—these are hard times for any enterprise, and it's not as if we've big financial backing. Whatever we shell out in salaries comes straight off the bottom line."

His breath was hot on her neck, the fabric of his trousers rough against her skin; Ivy felt a rush of arousal. She'd long found his power a potent aphrodisiac—never more so than now.

He pressed on. "You'll also recall that I've engineered you a salary substantially higher than Orianna's, although she has no idea. This promotion will merely even up the balance and give her some meaningless little title—she won't be on the board itself for a while, I guarantee, no matter what she's been told. Bear in mind Neil was only granted board director status less than a year ago, and he had to fight Stephen and Gavin tooth and nail to get creative representation at the top. They're hardly going to give that amount of authority away if they can avoid it, are they?"

Ivy had to admit she could see what he meant. And as Russell began to rub her inner thigh, her willpower waned.

"One other thing." His voice was quiet and harsh. "If the agency isn't careful, it's possible there'll be layoffs, so I wouldn't protest too loud. Because you're soon to be a writer without an art director, it could backfire horribly. You're extremely well paid, not to mention your other benefits, and it's tough out there. I don't think you'd find it much fun, job hunting . . . So you should count yourself lucky, or I could end up battling for rather more than your promotion and a position on the board."

Jesus, thought Ivy, what he's saying is *disastrous* career-wise, but what he's doing feels *so* good . . . By now she was powerless to contradict him.

Russell eased up her skirt and slipped his hand into her knickers. "And as for your tittle-tattling, it strikes me that Ed wouldn't be any happier to hear about your industrial relations over the last three years than my wife. Would he?"

"No!" Ivy gasped. He'd hit a nerve.

"Because with that huge pad in Hoxton and that sexy little car . . ." As he pushed his finger deep inside her, he drove his argument home, "I'm not the only one with a lot to lose."

That Ivy knew his game only made her hornier. There was nothing like playing with fire, and when Russell removed his hand and lifted her—legs apart—onto the cool marble work surface, rapidly undid his belt and fly, and penetrated her hard and fast, it brought back that classic scene from *Fatal Attraction*, with a similar mix of pleasure and pain.

At 4 a.m. Ivy woke with a jolt. The situation felt worse with Russell snoring beside her, so she gathered her strewn clothes, dressed in the bathroom so as not to wake him, and left the apartment.

The night air was cool, but she lowered the roof of her BMW anyway, hoping the wind might help blow away the hurt. But as she headed east along the Thames Embankment, the city's emptiness only emphasized her loneliness, and by the time she drew up to the traffic lights of Vauxhall Bridge, there was no getting away from the indelible sense of betrayal.

Ivy pressed the arrow to lower the window and leaned her elbow on the door while she lit a cigarette, inhaling the toxicity deep into her lungs. She could feel its poison burning, burning, and savored the sensation. And as she watched the smoke coil up in a thin gray trail away from the glowing red, dissipate, and finally disappear, she cast her mind back, ancient fury rising again.

It still made her spit how she and her brother had been forced to live after their father had run off with *her*. Ivy's mother had been strapped for cash; Ivy had never had the clothes, cosmetics, LPs, and books she craved. But her father had argued—persuaded by *her* Ivy was sure—he couldn't afford child support, and their standard of living had crumbled. The walls of their mock Tudor had seemed to grow increasingly closed in, and as Ivy had passed the huge house where her father had lived with his new family on her walk to school, it had made the injustice feel more acute.

Yet despite her unhappy adolescence—or perhaps because of it—Ivy had been determined to be no put-upon Cinderella. Instead she vowed she'd never lack for anything, and chose a career that enabled her to claw a comfortable lifestyle as swiftly and painlessly as possible. Once

through the indignities of training, copywriting proved the perfect ve-
hicle for her cynical, sharp mind and by her early thirties, she had the
apartment, the car, the husband, and a lover who could wangle her even
greater financial security. She'd felt safe, at last.

Until now, when it seemed her material well-being was in as much
danger of being taken away from her as it had been all those years
ago . . .

Once Ivy was back in her apartment, surrounded by familiar objects,
she began to feel better. It might not be homey, but she always felt at ease
in her spacious loft apartment.

Thank God, she thought. At least in here I can breathe.

Ivy had chosen the few pieces of furniture with painstaking care; no
one was more aware how others would judge her from her purchases.
Compromise made her shudder, and luckily her husband was happy to
fund her extravagance—or perhaps he realized it would be more trouble
than it was worth to argue. So from the retro refrigerator to the sleek
power shower, Ivy got her own way on everything.

There was irony too, for Ivy relished spiked humor. Take the neon-lit
sign on the wall, visible from the street when the blinds were up. Only
she knew it also advertised the whereabouts of her stash of cocaine in a
desk drawer beneath. She liked to have a tiny envelope put by for when
she was in the mood, and enjoyed mocking authority with the procla-
mation: COKE. THE REAL THING.

Ivy flicked on the kettle—a freebie from a lust-lorn photographer
who'd hoped if he let her keep it after a shoot it might help him get into
her knickers (it didn't).

Russell's right, she thought as she waited for the water to boil, I do
have a lot to lose, and it won't be easy get a similar salary elsewhere. I'll
get in touch with my headhunter, but I'm not hopeful. I suppose there's
freelancing, but all that having to be nicey-nicey to keep in favor and be
rehired—ugh. She shuddered. So there seems no getting around it, for
the time being I'd better stay put and make the best of a bad job. I'll have
to build bridges if I'm not to come completely unstuck. What a hideous
prospect.

Hmm, she calculated. Perhaps there is a way to salvage a sense of self-worth. I'm not going to fall apart like my mother . . . Oh no. I'll show Orianna I'm still a force to be reckoned with, bring her down a peg or three.

Yes. That's it, the way forward . . .

12. A capable and wide revenge

The shrill sound of Rob's alarm at 7 a.m. dragged him from a fulfilling dream about being the lead singer of a boy band, yet for once he was pleased to be interrupted. He knew it wasn't very nice of him, but the prospect of seeing Ivy was enough to propel him from bed at speed. He was dying to see if his client mentioned anything from the night before, and how she would paint it. Given Orianna's upset, perhaps his sympathies should have lain with her, but he so loved juicy gossip . . .

By the time he arrived at the gym, he'd had the journey to work himself into a frenzy of anticipation.

"Ivy!" He pounced on her before she was hardly through the door.

"Rob, hi."

She sounds tired, he thought, and there are circles under her eyes. She was already dressed in her workout clothes. "So what do you feel up to today?" He chose his words carefully, hoping she might reveal her state of mind.

"Something tough." She went over to the verti-climber, a challenging

test of endurance and coordination. "This? Show me how it works."
Given her apparent exhaustion, he was surprised.

Once she was up and running, he played his opening hand. "What
did you do last night?" He watched her reaction.

"Nothing much." Her face was expressionless.

"It's only I thought I saw you."

"Oh." If she wasn't so darned focused he'd be able to gauge more.
Still, he could swear she was taken aback. "Where?"

"Wardour Street." With luck she'd think he'd seen them in Cassio's
and offer her version of events.

But she was silent, scowling, then said, "Where, *exactly*?"

How infuriating! She wasn't making it easy. Rob hesitated. If I admit
I saw her hurrying down the street, she'll sidestep the issue, he calculated. And I can't confess I spent the evening with Orianna—that would
stir dreadful trouble. Best opt for middle ground. "I saw you and Orianna in the window of Cassio's. Looked like you were having . . . er . . . a
bit of a fight."

Ivy stopped pumping and turned to him, green eyes flashing. Lord,
he thought. She's terrifying! Though in a weird way, her scariness was
almost erotic.

"She fucked me over," said Ivy, straight out.

"Oh?" said Rob. Rob was a master of social extortion; at lightning
speed he decided he'd play Ivy's cohort, button up about his encounter with Orianna. He prayed Orianna wouldn't let slip that she'd seen
him.

"She went behind my back professionally. And it's not the first time."

At once Rob could see why she had been so livid, but feigned innocence. "She did?"

"The board offered her the post of creative director—"

"You don't say!"

"—without me—"

"Fuck!"

"—and she's chosen to accept it."

"*No!*"

"It's true. But far as I'm concerned, it's pretty much all down to her relationship with Dan."

Rob was confused. He couldn't see an obvious link between the two.

"In fact," Ivy slowed her stride a touch to talk, "I'm beginning to wonder whether she didn't start sleeping with Dan as a means to an end."

Before Rob had a chance to disguise his disbelief, out popped, "That doesn't sound like Orianna to me."

"You've witnessed how underhanded she can be, seeing Dan on the quiet for months on end."

Rob nodded.

"Nothing would surprise me these days." She paused for a moment, adjusting the machine to a less frenetic pace. "The thing is, Rob, this may sound ludicrous to you, not being in the business, doing something worthwhile like you do. You're in control of your own destiny; you dictate your own terms." She gave him a broad smile. "I admire you for that." He was flattered. "But our industry has a unique set of quirks and prejudices. The truth is creative directors tend to be art directors who've worked their way up."

"Really?"

"Yes. Certainly in more old-school agencies like Green."

"Why?"

"Because they tend to know more about production."

"Production—where Dan works?"

"Precisely. So Orianna being in with Dan the Man is bloody handy. She already understands about commissioning illustrators and photographers and he can help her gain more expertise. I can see them now, discussing printing techniques and Pantone references before they drift off to sleep." She snorted contemptuously. "It's probably their idea of foreplay—Orianna's such a workaholic I bet she finds it a turn-on. Nevertheless, that's something our board would hold in high regard."

"Right." Rob knew Ivy was being bitchy, but it did seem feasible.

"Don't get me wrong. I'm not saying she started their affair *just* to gain a promotion—I don't think even Orianna is that cunning—it probably helped, that's all." Suddenly she unhooked her feet and extricated herself from the machine. "I'm going to do some cycling now." She took several gulps of water from the fountain, then planted herself on an exercise bike. She knew what to do; he was more interested in encouraging her to continue.

"It doesn't sound fair to you," he observed.

"Oh, we writers, we're used to that . . . take it from me, the powers that be would never be happy promoting a *copywriter* to CD—we're just about the words, the *ideas*. The ignorant tossers on our board don't value them at all."

"Isn't that a bit shortsighted?"

"Of course. But take the Bellings Scott win a few weeks back. You might have seen the ads just out—'Get up and go with *That Sunshine Feeling*'?"

"With the traffic lights?"

"Well, I came up with that idea. I'm sure even Orianna wouldn't have the gall to deny that, if you asked her."

"Wow. They're great!"

"Thanks." Ivy purred. "Although maybe I'm wrong—I've gotten Orianna wrong before."

Rob was torn: last night he'd felt for Orianna, now he sympathized with Ivy. It must be tough to be treated so badly by any colleague, let alone one who was such a good friend.

"Yet despite the fact the account was worth a fortune to the agency, who do they choose to promote? The *art director*, of course. But then again, ad execs are rarely known for their long-term vision. Particularly at Green."

Gosh, thought Rob, with all the clients I've got from there, it's fascinating getting this inside perspective. "Why Green especially?"

"When the agency started out in the late nineties, they specialized in direct mail and promotions—'buy one get one free,' 'ten cents off your next purchase' kind of stuff, designed to give sales a quick fix. They were hardly about big ideas." Ivy adjusted the bike setting up a level. "So you can appreciate our bosses are the types who consider it more important that something makes a fast buck and looks OK than it has a great head-line or concept behind it. But their myopia is doing the agency no fa-vors." She leaned forward on the handlebars, close to his ear. "Despite that new account win, it isn't a secret that Green hasn't had a great run of luck recently. I've heard there might have to be layoffs."

Rob had a moment's panic. His clients! His income! He brushed his fears aside. "So, there's no way they'd have promoted both of you?"

"You've got it. I'm certain they can't afford more than one CD. If so, who would you choose? Orianna, the golden girl who sucks up to all the suits and is shagging the head of production? Or the ideas woman, who occasionally rocks the boat because she challenges the status quo?"

"I see," said Rob. Ivy sounded somewhat bitter, but given how un-fairly she had been treated, he was amazed she wasn't more so.

"You know the really sad thing?" Bizarrely, Ivy laughed. "In some ways I feel sorry for Orianna."

Rob couldn't see why, then realized, "Because she works so hard?"

Ivy stopped cycling and looked directly at him, dropping her voice even lower. "You mustn't breathe a word to a soul."

"No, no, of course." Pigs might fly, but still, she *had* asked.

"Because last night I heard something that really *would* upset her."

"Oh?"

"And it'll make your day."

Rob's heart started to race. And he wasn't even exercising!

"Your hunch was right, dear boy. There's clearly no smoke without fire, and Dan the Man bats for your team. Not that often, but occasion-ally, no question. I have it on authority from the agency's number one queen. He saw him at G-A-Y, one Saturday. Snogging some guy, then they went off together, one can assume they got laid. And," she winked at Rob, "I can't see our conventional little Catholic handling a partner who's AC/DC, can you?"

13. What is spoke comes from my love

The next morning, Dan woke before Orianna and lay watching her. She was facing him, unusually; they tended to sleep wrapped up like two Cs, her lowercase semicircle encompassed by his larger one. Yet that night she'd kept him awake, tossing and turning and rucking the sheets, grabbing the duvet and throwing it off, sighing and shifting and thumping her pillows. Eventually he'd retreated to the other side of the bed in an attempt to get some sleep himself.

Despite his disturbed night, he couldn't stay miffed with her for long. She looked so vulnerable and childlike. Her dark hair was spread across the pillow, tumbling in no particular direction, a contrast from the carefully styled tresses she presented during the day. Her mouth had fallen open, her lips relaxed and soft, and as her breath came and went, he was struck by how much he cared for her.

I see a different side of her, he thought, than the rest of the world sees; it's my Orianna, just mine, and I'm lucky to have her. She's fun to be with, generous, loving. Passionate, yes, a worrier, there's no doubt, even a little paranoid on occasion. Certainly Orianna had huge gaps in her self-esteem, which surprised him, given her talent. But that she wasn't driven by money was part of what attracted him to her. Instead he'd observed that perfectionism and the desire to be liked lay behind her ambition.

After all, he deliberated, it's only because Orianna's got a big heart that she's so churned up about Ivy; others would have been far more ruthless. Orianna is so trusting compared to the majority in our business. I hope she never loses that.

As Orianna exhaled heavily and began to stir, he put a hand out and softly stroked her cheek, wanting her emergence to consciousness to be a gradual journey out of her dreams.

Orianna caught the elevator to the top floor and edged through the doors of the creative department. She was clutching the cappuccino she'd bought en route in one hand, her bag and jacket in the other.

She was dreading seeing Ivy. How would she act after the night before? Moreover, how should Orianna act in return? Dan had been a sweetheart that morning, but she was still shaken. Nonetheless, she'd decided she was not going to apologize first; Ivy had behaved appallingly and made her look a fool.

By the time she reached their partitioned section of the office, her heart was racing and her palms clammy. Yet Ivy's chair was empty, her handbag nowhere to be seen.

Orianna opened all of her e-mails, replied to those that required it and some that didn't. Still no sign of Ivy. Her anxiety mounted. She examined her work schedule, filled in her time sheets, tidied her desk. Still no sign. Having finished her cappuccino, she fetched another coffee from the machine. She drank it, went to the loo (inevitably), returned to her desk, bit her nails. She wandered around to find out how Leon, one of the designers, was getting on with some artwork, but didn't really absorb his reply. She came back, *still* no Ivy. By now it was past ten and she was really unsettled. Was Ivy not going to show at all?

Then the phone rang.

Orianna jumped and picked up the receiver. "Hello?"

"Hi, Orianna, Neil here."

By this point she could do nothing but fret: her immediate reaction was to worry that he wanted to discuss her new position. Help, she thought, I'm not ready to talk about my plans.

But Neil said, "I see Ivy's not in yet."

"No."

"Perhaps you'd like to pop into my office," he said. "I've something to show you." Orianna, thankful to take her mind off Ivy, agreed.

Once she was standing opposite him, door closed behind her, Neil handed her a sheet of paper. The logo was familiar: *Trixie Fox.* Trixie was a woman for whom the word *headhunter* might have been invented. Her knowledge of hirings and firings was legendary, and although she must be seventy if she was a day, she considered herself unassailable professionally. Orianna had been rapped on the knuckles a while back for hiring a junior through someone else. The junior had turned out to be slow and stupid, and was let go after a month, while Orianna, humbled, had been forced to acknowledge that only résumés with Trixie's blessing warranted a closer look.

She examined this one now. *Cassie Goldworthy.*

"She's the art director I mentioned yesterday," Neil prompted. "You'll need someone after I'm gone, to work with Ivy. This girl's good."

Orianna noted her date of birth. Orianna had been born a decade earlier. You mean she's young, she thought, therefore cheap, though she didn't say so.

Although she felt uneasy about interviewing someone before she'd sorted things with Ivy, she hid her concern from Neil, determined to appear the confident soon-to-be boss. "I'll see if I can set up a meeting. If it's all right with you, I'll call Trixie from here, so I won't be overheard."

She picked up the phone and dialed.

Ivy got to the office at 10:05. She'd taken an extra half hour getting ready at the gym—she was damned if she was going to be early—and felt pleasingly well-groomed. She threw her stuff down on the sofa and cast her eye about.

Where the hell is Orianna? she wondered, venom fueled by her conversation with Rob. I've braced myself to see her. Oh well. Fuck it. If she's expecting me to hunt for her, she can think again.

Ivy wasn't ready to start work, but there was no time like the present for sorting pressing matters. She switched on her computer and located a folder, entitled, covertly, New Business. She clicked on the document she was after; she'd not updated it since she and Orianna had talked about leaving after Orianna's disastrous affair with Clive two years previously. Nonetheless, amending it wouldn't take long. She only needed to add a couple of new clients and change the dates.

There was still no sign of Orianna, and from where Ivy was sitting she'd see her coming. This was a good time to make that call. She picked up the phone and dialed.

"Trixie?"

"Speaking."

"It's Orianna here. Orianna Bianchi, from Green."

"Ah! Hi, hi. Long time no speak. How are you?"

"I'm well, very well."

"Good, good. So what can I do for you?" Trixie clearly knew to take her lead from her caller, not the other way around.

"I'm with Neil, in his office. He's got a resume here, and tells me the girl in question is worth a look." Orianna smiled at Neil.

"Ah, that would be Cassie?"

"Indeed."

"Yes, she's great. Just flown in from Sydney. Fantastic portfolio, ever so talented, charming too."

Neil tapped Orianna's shoulder and whispered. "It's OK, Trixie knows I'm leaving."

Orianna nodded. "I gather you've been informed about Neil. This is hush-hush so I'd rather you didn't make it public . . ."

"Of course, dear. Anything you say to me never travels further. Goes without saying."

"I'm going to be taking over."

"What, as CD?"

"Yes."

"Oh, my dear! But that's *great*! Fantastic news! I always knew you were so talented! I *am* so pleased! It's not often in this business we get to see a nice person do well. And so gifted too! Congratulations!"

"Thank you," said Orianna. Neil winked at her; doubtless he'd hitherto been on the receiving end of such gushing praise himself.

"And forgive me for taking a moment to say so, but I must also congratulate myself for being one of the first people to spot your potential." Orianna couldn't begrudge this. Trixie had found Orianna and Ivy their first job. "So, darling, next time I see you we must celebrate. Have a glass of bubbly, yes?"

"That'd be nice." Orianna was flattered, but keen to get back to Cassie. "Anyway, Neil and I thought I should see Cassie. Any chance of her coming in?"

"Sure. I'll see what I can do."

"Say around seven o'clock one night?" Ivy would have left by then. "Maybe tomorrow—though she won't want to do Friday . . . How about Monday?"

"Leave it to me," said Trixie.

"Trixie?"

"Speaking."

"It's Ivy Fraser. Copywriter. Remember me?"

"Ah! Hi, hi, the beautiful Ivy. Of *course* I remember you. How could I forget? How are you?"

"I'm well, very well."

"Good, good. It's been too long! So, what can I do for you?"

"I was wondering . . ." Ivy lowered her voice, "if it would be possible to come and see you."

"Yes, yes, dear, of course. I understand. Time to make a move?"

"Indeed," said Ivy.

"So I take it you'd like to show me your portfolio?"

"Please." Respect, thought Ivy. When it comes to the art of one-sided conversation, Trixie is a consummate professional.

"And forgive me for being direct . . ."

"Of course."

"But are you thinking of moving on your own? Without your art director? Oh, what *was* her name? Haven't spoken to her in ages . . ." There was a short pause. "Orianna! Orianna Bianchi, that's her."

"No, it'll just be me."

"Oh, really? Right dear. Well, funny you should say that, but that's great. Great. Because between you and me . . ."

"Yes?"

"It's always much easier to find something for a writer."

"Really?" Ivy felt heartened. Then she recalled Trixie didn't know the kind of salary she'd be demanding, and reminded herself not to get too hopeful. Still, it was worth a shot. She might even be able to find her something abroad, get her away from Soho altogether for a while. "That's good."

"Oh yes, dear. I've such a shortage of *good* writers. Whereas I've got dozens of art directors on my books. Dozens! Can't find some a job for love nor money, what with all the layoffs of late. Especially the juniors, dear oh dear, no one's willing to take them on. It can be quite a struggle. But copywriters, ah! You're worth your weight in gold. And with your experience, they'll be snapping you up, I'm sure. I hope you won't mind me saying so, but I always thought you were *so* talented. Thought perhaps Orianna was holding you back a bit, actually."

Ivy smiled. She could see through Trixie with ease, but she admired her skill. It was fun to be manipulated for once, rather than the other way around.

"So," continued Trixie, "how about coming to visit me here in my little pad in Belgravia? Early next week suit you?"

"That would be perfect." It would give Ivy the weekend to sort her portfolio.

"Tell you what. Why not come after work on Monday? I'll crack open a bottle of bubbly. Say around seven?"

"Hi," said Ivy, minutes later, when Orianna returned to her desk.

"Hi," said Orianna. "Sorry, I was just with Neil."

Ivy could tell she was nervous. Good, she thought. And so she should be. She'd decided how to play things already.

"I got you this." She handed over a small paper bag.

Orianna took it with trepidation. She peered inside. "Gosh, thank you." Wrapped in a napkin was a miniature panettone. "My favorite!"

Ivy understood that with Orianna, food equals comfort, which means everything's OK. "I stopped off at the deli," she said, "and there was a massive line—sorry I was late." She took a deep breath. Speaking to Trixie had given her the impetus she needed, reminding her of what a fine actress could achieve. "I'm also sorry I was such a cow last night. With hindsight I think I overreacted."

Orianna was clearly confounded. "Oh . . . er . . . Yeah, well, I do understand. I feel terrible about it, you know."

"I can imagine."

"I hardly slept a wink."

"Nor me."

"But I thought it was better to tell you sooner rather than later."

Not for nothing had Ivy been a leading light in her school drama group. She gave Orianna her most dazzling smile. "I appreciate that, having had some time to think about it. Honestly, O—I realize you meant well, telling me like that, and it *was* good of you to let me know that swiftly. It was just a shock, that's all."

"And for me, too." Orianna bit her lip.

"And, well, you know me, I have got a bit of a temper." Ivy could see the G&T flying through the air as she said it. And . . . *splat!* My, what a fine feeling that had been.

"Yes."

"Sometimes I can't help myself."

"No."

"But I lay awake in bed all night"—no mention of Russell obviously—"and thought things through carefully." This much was true. "And I decided the last thing I want is to jeopardize my friendship with you."

"Oh, I am so glad."

God, Orianna was such a sucker! "We've worked together for years without a single major hiccup. It would be a shame for something to come between us after all this time. And you're right when you say I've never been that interested in being creative director. I haven't."

"No?"

"No, no. I guess I'd always seen us working together as partners, that's all. But I'm sure we can still continue to do that."

"Yes, yes." Ivy could hear the relief in Orianna's voice. "That's exactly what I meant. I'm bound to need to work with a writer almost as much as I do now. It just means that I'll get tied up with lots of adminny stuff too, that's all. And, well, I know that's not really your kind of thing."

"No." Ivy couldn't resist a teeny jibe. "Bores me stupid, all that."

Orianna was plainly content to have her promotion belittled, if it meant making amends. "Not to mention getting entangled in politics."

Ivy snorted. "Yeah, rather you there than me."

"Oh, I am pleased!" Orianna smiled broadly. "Friends again?"

"Yes." Ivy beamed.

"Good!" Spontaneously, Orianna came over and gave Ivy a hug. Ivy struggled not to recoil, but Orianna failed to notice. She bounced back to her seat and took a huge bite of panettone.

Well, well, thought Ivy. That was easy. Peace bought with a piece of cake.

14. Perdition catch my soul but I do love thee!

The following Saturday, Orianna and Dan were shopping in Covent Garden. Orianna, in the mood for spending, had gone through an impressive amount of her forthcoming pay raise before it had even been agreed upon. Guiltily she compared her four shopping bags to Dan's one.

"If you see something you like, I could buy it for your birthday. Any thoughts?"

Dan hesitated, then ventured, "You know what I'd really like? A watch." He held out his wrist. "I've been making do with this, but it's not particularly me."

"I agree." Though she'd not said so, his lurid Swatch was not to her taste.

"I had a nice antique one that my uncle gave me, but I wore it in the sea last summer by mistake and salt ruined the workings."

"A watch is a great idea!" Orianna gave a little skip. The notion that Dan would carry a little piece of her wherever he went delighted her. A recent ad sprang to mind. "I think Paul Smith has some."

"Won't they be expensive?"

"Nah!" Orianna yanked him toward Floral Street. "I'm going to be creative director!"

Orianna took a moment to gain her bearings inside the dimly lit interior. Traditional oak cabinets, walls painted in muted colors, figurative oil paintings—the shop had been designed to seem as though it had been here forever. The atmosphere was hushed, almost reverential. She located the accessories, strode over with a purposeful clunk of heels on floorboard, and ran her fingers across the glass. Row upon row of pure wool socks. Roll upon roll of pure silk ties. Fold upon fold of pure cotton boxers. What a treat! Cuff links in every color and shape within the bounds of good taste. And, in the cabinet right at the back, the watches. It was all she could do not to choose one for him, but she held back, telling herself that despite his previous purchase (and the odd dodgy shirt she refrained from commenting on) Dan did have *some* idea of style.

Swiftly they narrowed it down to two.

"Which do you prefer?" said Dan.

She was pleased he seemed keen for her approval. One, in the corner, had a buff suede strap and a cream face with simple dashes indicating three, six, nine, and twelve. The other lay on a red spotted handkerchief. She wasn't enamored with its purple crocodile-skin strap, but the face, with plain Roman numerals on a white ground, was preferable. "That one."

"You don't mind that strap?"

"It can always be changed." She turned to an assistant hovering in hope of a sale. "Can't it?"

"I'm afraid we don't have any straps that would fit this particular design in stock at the moment."

"Oh," said Orianna.

The assistant coughed awkwardly. "We can order something for you?"

"We wanted to get something today though."

Dan interjected, "The face reminds me of the one I used to have." Then with a burst of confidence, confessed, "You know? I quite *like* purple."

Orianna bit her lip. In her opinion the strap should be black or brown leather, or, at a stretch, chrome so it would coordinate with anything. It's *his* present, she reminded herself and turned to the assistant. "We'll have it." Then to Dan, "But you must wait till your birthday."

"Oh I do love you!" Dan said, and kissed her with a resounding smack on the cheek.

Orianna's heart skipped a beat.

Then he looked at her sheepishly.

He obviously meant it! It was the first time he'd said the words, and if she had to compromise over a garish watch strap to get him to say it, she didn't mind a bit.

"She said *what*?" Chloë gasped so loudly her mother turned and glared.

Rob and Chloë were sitting in the church on Chiswick Green, await-ing the arrival of the bride. Chloë's brother was already standing at the altar looking nervous.

Rob leaned into Chloë and whispered as quietly as he could, "Ivy told me Dan is bisexual. Said she had it on good authority he'd been seen at G-A-Y. Before he was going out with Orianna, but still."

Chloë didn't answer at once. She reflected then whispered, "Yes, though he could have gone there to have a good time. I've been more often than I like to think, and I'm not gay."

Rob hooted, "But you're the biggest fag hag there is!" before he could stop himself.

"Shhhhhhh!" Chloë's mother scowled.

Rob and Chloë adopted penitent expressions and were silent. After a while Rob couldn't bear it. No matter that Ivy had said to keep quiet; telling Chloë didn't count—she was going back to New York in two days. He reached into his jacket pocket for a pen.

Dan was seen snogging a *GUY,* he wrote with relish on the program.

No need for her to write a response; her gaping jaw said it all.

Rob added, *And they were spotted leaving together!?*

To which Chloë mouthed, "Blimey."

At that moment there was a stirring and murmuring at the back of the church, and a unanimous turning of heads indicated the arrival of the bride. The organist thumped out the familiar tune, and Rob craned his neck around an array of hats that ranged from the fashionable and flamboyant (their generation) to the elegant and eccentric (Chloë's mother's) for a better view. In a cream, raw silk sheath that clung to her curves, the bride emerged, almost worthy of a spread in *Vogue*.

"Oh! She looks lovely!" Rob exclaimed. One thing he loved almost more than seducing a straight boy was a wedding, and by the end of the ceremony he was quite overcome. The bridegroom's angst had metamorphosed into proud happiness, and the bride's expression as they made their way back down the aisle hand-in-hand was a picture of womanly serenity, made all the more human by a touch of shyness. Rob clutched the defaced program to his chest. "They seem so happy!"

Chloë, dabbing her eyes with a hanky, seemed speechless for once.

I wonder if anyone will ever love me *that much?* wondered Rob. In spite of being amidst all these people, he suddenly felt very single and alone. He pushed away a wave of gloom, and turned his mind to Dan.

I want him sooo badly! he thought.

Don't go there, his alter ego argued. *If you're after even the teeniest degree of commitment, why bother?*

But he's gorgeous!

Are you sure you don't want him because you can't have him?

But now I know there might be a chance!

And what about Orianna? said the first voice. *She appears a very nice girl.*

According to Ivy, she's only with him to get a leg up professionally, countered the second. *She says Orianna's ambitious and money-grabbing and she betrayed her dearest friend. Why do you owe her any allegiance?*

Is a man who's at best a closet job, at worst in love with a woman, truly a good bet?

Chloë tugged his sleeve. "Come on. I've got to be in the photos."

Keen to appraise more outfits, Rob followed her rapid step down the aisle.

That evening, Rob told Chloë about Ivy's take on Orianna's promotion. He added only a few *very* minor embellishments of his own.

"So what do you reckon?"

Chloë frowned. "Isn't it possible Ivy has exaggerated Orianna's motives? I can't believe Orianna would date Dan purely to get promoted."

"Hmph."

"The girl I met didn't seem that conniving."

"Aside from Orianna though, d'you reckon it's true that Dan's gay?"

"He didn't give off that vibe to me."

"Well, he wouldn't, would he?"

"Eh?"

"You're a girl."

"That's my point—he seemed straight. And . . . well, sometimes you have a tendency to think all good-looking boys must be gay."

"I do not!" Rob bristled. "Like who?"

"Tom, Robbie, Kevin . . ." She cast her eyes upward. "Jason . . . According to you, every male star worth shagging is secretly gay."

"How do you know they're not?"

"I don't. But how do you know they are?"

"Come on you two," interrupted Chloë's mother. "You're like an old married couple. It's time to bid farewell to the bride and groom."

As Chloë led the way through the throng, Rob said, "Yes, though what you see isn't always what you get with people, is it?"

"One might say the same of Ivy."

"You've never even met her!"

"But I know what I hear. From what Orianna was saying, your Ivy sounds to be quite a woman." Chloë pushed past a distant relative with a polite but firm, "Excuse me," grabbed Rob's arm, and yanked him to the front.

Even though Rob was surrounded by attractive females, they were of the well-fed, well-turned-out, West London variety. Ivy's face flashed before him.

"She is." He sighed. For alongside Dan, Rob was also falling half in love with Ivy. Sex was the last thing on his mind, but his admiration had a suitor-like blind intensity. If Ivy were here she'd outshine everyone, he thought.

Chloë said, "It's possible Ivy made the whole thing up about Dan."

"No! She's clever and sharp, but Ivy's not like that. I swear."

"If you say so." Rob could tell she was unconvinced.

Pah! What does Chloë know? he reasoned. She's fallen for some rats in her time—she's not *that* clued-up about human nature. Whereas I've often seen through her boyfriends at once . . .

Rob was so preoccupied he didn't notice women congregating thickly around him until he turned to see he was hemmed in by shawls and sequins. It was too late to extricate himself, and before he knew it the newlyweds were poised at the top of the steps.

"*The bouquet! The bouquet!*" yelled Chloë's mum.

The bride threw her arm forward and up, propelling her pretty pink posy high . . . high . . . high into the air and down . . . down . . . down . . . The other girls pressed in but there was no stopping it; Rob could see it coming, but was too tightly wedged to move.

Thwack! The bouquet landed right in his arms.

"But you're a man!" protested one woman.

"You have it." He handed it to her.

"Don't be ridiculous." Chloë snatched it back. "Sorry." She turned to the woman. "He needs a boyfriend as much as you do. Come along, honey." She took his hand. "Time for more champagne!"

Perhaps this means I'm going to get lucky with Dan, thought Rob. Now that's a prospect worth toasting.

Orianna and Dan finally stumbled through the door to her apartment at 7 p.m.

"Phew." Dan dropped the shopping bags on the floor.

"Shall we get takeout?" said Orianna.

Dan agreed, and several glasses of wine and a DVD later, they tumbled into bed, prompted by some amorous fumblings on the sofa.

As they made love, Orianna experienced a tenderness that was new. Dan had been a caring lover from the outset, and she hoped she matched his thoughtfulness. When it came to slow caresses and gentle kisses they'd learned the geography of each other's bodies intimately, and both were open enough to communicate what turned them on. But nevertheless this particular evening there was something about the sensations of Dan's fingers on her skin, exploring her curves as if she were irresistible, that was not just erotically charged but sensitive and moving too. As he stroked her breasts she could sense his desire through his fingertips, and as he edged down lower, lower . . . then kissed and sucked where he knew she really liked it, she felt as if he was enjoying the experience even more than she was. At last he pulled her down the bed and entered her, and before too long she felt herself pause on the edge of such pure and intense bliss that she wished the moment would last forever. Then, as she felt him orgasm inside her, the pulses of pleasure tipped her over, and in a glorious, unstoppable rush, she came too.

I love him, she thought. Not in a shallow way that will burn itself out, but lastingly, deeply. And he loves me too. Maybe, just maybe, this is the one romance in my life that will have a happy ending.

15. And when I love thee not, chaos is come again

"What did you do this weekend?"

Ivy and Orianna were sitting at their desks opposite one another, sipping coffee in an attempt to rev up for the week ahead.

"I spent all Saturday shopping," said Orianna.

"Ooh, get anything nice?"

"A few little things for the apartment." Orianna downplayed her extravagance for fear Ivy might detect she'd been prompted by her pay raise. Yet she couldn't resist sharing, "And a Dolce and Gabbana skirt," knowing how much Ivy appreciated clothes too. Their tastes were different—Ivy preferred clean lines; Orianna was a sucker for frills and flounces—but they shared a passion for fashion.

"Describe."

"Deep plum color, some sort of satin, cut on the bias, with lace that crosses over at the front like this." Orianna stood up to demonstrate.

"Bet that really suits you."

Orianna smiled to herself, recalling the ardor with which Dan had undressed her after she'd worn it out the night before. No matter how much of a workaholic she was, it was rare to feel so content on a Monday morning. But a Sunday spent lounging in bed reading the papers, puttering in the garden, followed by taking Dan to meet some old school friends for supper was her idea of heaven, and she felt closer to him than ever. She was relieved to see Ivy was all smiles too, and the trauma of the previous week past history. She'd persuaded Dan to go easy on her workload to help smooth things over, convinced it was the best way forward for everyone.

I won't mention the watch, Orianna decided. No matter how amiable Ivy's being, she's sure to scoff if we seem too much the cozy couple.

It was as though Ivy could read her mind. "Did you see much of Dan?"

Orianna couldn't lie. "We spent quite a lot of the weekend together."

"I presume he didn't go shopping with you—I can't imagine any man keeping pace once you get going."

Orianna hesitated. She'd no desire to ram her happiness down Ivy's throat, and shopping was a pastime they'd enjoyed together. Nonetheless, she couldn't believe Ivy would see this as a threat, and she was sick of subterfuge. Recent experience had confused her; she was no longer sure where discretion ended and deception began. She admitted, "Actually, Dan came with me."

"A whole day of shopping?"

Orianna colored. "Yeah. He seemed to enjoy it, funnily enough."

"Well I never." Ivy leaned back in her chair. "That's a first. A straight man who likes shopping. Are you sure he's not gay?" She laughed lightly.

Orianna recollected their lovemaking. "Quite sure."

That afternoon, Orianna was primping in the ladies' room. She was due to interview Cassie Goldworthy—a fact she must remember to mention to Ivy, once they'd finished an urgent brief—and wanted to look the part. As she was fluffing her hair, her colleague, Ursula, emerged from one of the cubicles.

Ursula examined herself in the cruel florescent light. "God, I look like shit."

"No you don't," said Orianna. She'd always thought Ursula good-looking in an unconventional way, with her straight dark hair and pointy features. Orianna particularly envied her slender frame.

Ursula unzipped her makeup bag—"It's kill or cure"—and twisted up a dark red lipstick. "Hey, you know something?" Even though her mouth was contorted for the application, she never wasted a moment's talk time.

"What?" Orianna examined her makeup. Mm, it was fine. Any more would be overload. And she mustn't get too caught up with Ursula; she had to tell Ivy about Cassie . . .

Ursula checked behind her to ensure the stalls were empty. "I-heard-a-great-bit-of-gossip-the-other-day."

For all the trouble she'd been in lately, Orianna couldn't resist the bait. "Yeah? What?"

"About Dan."

Oh, thought Orianna. Ursula must have discovered we're going out. Word spread easily on the grapevine. Still, she'd worked with Ursula for years, and they'd forged a friendship built on mutual respect. Orianna would have told her personally soon enough.

"You'll never guess."

Odd way to broach the subject, thought Orianna. "What?"

Ursula was busy concentrating on her own appearance. "Apparently he was seen at G-A-Y."

Orianna frowned. "What's G-A-Y?"

"A club."

"So?"

"A *gay* club."

Orianna remained mystified. Dan had a couple of gay friends—Rob, for instance. So he could have gone with him, though why hadn't he mentioned it? "I don't understand what you're driving at. Lots of people go to gay clubs."

"Wouldn't mean anything," Ursula leaned closer, "except he was clocked *snogging* someone." She looked at Orianna, but read her shocked expression as mere surprise. "You don't get it, do you? Honey, sometimes you can be so naïve!" Ursula stopped, then delivered the punch line. "A *guy.*"

"Oh!" This couldn't be. It was almost laughable. "Who told you that?"

"Someone . . ." Ursula wrinkled her nose, trying to remember. But she rode her days at such full speed such details easily slipped her mind. "I can't recall who told me first. But everyone knows. I always thought Dan was a bit of a one, but *men*, I don't know." Orianna was speechless, but no matter. Ursula was talking again. "Apparently-it-was-a-while-ago-but-they-were-seen-leaving-together-so-they-probably . . . you know . . . *did it.*" At that moment her mobile rang. "Ursula speaking," she said, mouthed "Catch you later," at Orianna, and departed to take the call.

Orianna was left staring into the mirror, stunned.

At six thirty Dan popped his head around the partition.

"Hiya, girls."

"Hiya," in unison.

"Coming for a drink?"

Orianna spoke first. "You go ahead. I'll join you in a while."

"Typical." Dan raised his eyes to the heavens. He turned to Ivy. "Show this girl how to have a good time, will you?"

"I'm afraid I can't." Best be gracious, thought Ivy. "But thanks for asking."

"Aw, go on, just one. It's my birthday." Dan grinned, his face all boyish persuasion. At moments like this Ivy had to admit he *was* pretty attractive. The way his dark hair tumbled forward in defiance of grooming, the way his eyes creased up in the corners, the way he laughed, deep and loud. Not her type at all, but she could see what Orianna saw in him.

Still, she owed him no favors. "Birthdays are for mourning, not celebrating," she said. "I'm afraid I'm already meeting someone."

"Ask them along," suggested Dan.

"I couldn't do that. We're meeting at their place."

Dan shrugged, defeated. "Well, we're off now." He turned to Orianna. "Catch you down there—we'll be at the Pillars of Hercules."

Orianna grunted and went back to her Mac.

Ivy checked her watch. If she was going to make it in good time she'd better leave. She opened her handbag. A rapid reapplication of lipstick (she could apply it perfectly without a mirror), a swift brush of her hair (the electricity crackled and sparked), a swoosh of perfume (a gift from Ed), and she was set. Her portfolio was in the trunk of the car.

"You smell nice," said Orianna, glancing up.

"Thanks. Better dash. See you tomorrow."

"Have a lovely evening."

As Ivy rounded the corner to reception a girl pushed open the door. She was lugging a huge portfolio, so Ivy calculated she must be some sort of creative. What a coincidence, thought Ivy. She comes in for an interview as off I go for mine.

She gave her the swift once-over. Early to mid twenties, younger than Ivy was—bad. Bleached-blond hair that Ivy judged from her brows was naturally dark—tacky. A tan—passé. A round, pixie face—annoying. And petite—*unforgivable*.

She also looked lost. The receptionist appeared not to be around and Ivy was curious to find out more. "Can I help you?"

"Oh . . . er . . . yes please." Ivy detected a twang—Aussie?—she wasn't sure. "I'm afraid I'm ever so early. I'm not due till seven."

"Never mind," said Ivy. "I'll let whoever you're meeting know you've arrived. Take a seat."

"Oh thanks." She sounded relieved. "My name's Cassie. Cassie Goldworthy."

"And you're here to see . . . ?"

"Some funny name—oops, I shouldn't say that, should I?" She giggled. Ivy was reminded of that girl in accounts Russell had fancied and Dan had shagged—what was she called? Lara. Cassie rummaged in her bag. Pathetic, thought Ivy. She could have clarified the interviewer's name before getting here. "It began with an O . . ."

"Orianna?"

"Ah, yes, that's her."

So Orianna hasn't even got her feet under the creative director's desk and she's interviewing staff, noted Ivy. More to the point, she's doing it on the sly. And if my hunch is right, this Cassie is a junior creative. Orianna's entitled not to tell me, but this wouldn't have happened before her promotion. Then we'd have seen prospective candidates together . . . Further evidence of a rift between us. Ivy kept her tone innocent. "Are you a creative then?"

"Yes. An art director."

Bingo! thought Ivy. I wonder what her work is like. She was just about to connive a peek at her portfolio when the receptionist returned.

"Ah, Philly, there you are. So Cassie, I'll leave you here. I'd best be on my way."

Orianna liked Cassie at once. Trixie was right, her portfolio was very good. They chatted for about an hour, covering agencies where Cassie had worked, where she saw herself going, and what she felt were her strengths and weaknesses, but Orianna was convinced within the first five minutes she was worth hiring. She felt bad that she'd forgotten to mention the interview to Ivy, still, she'd been terribly preoccupied with that silly bit of gossip of Ursula's, and all the work they'd had that afternoon . . .

Not to worry, she decided as she cut across Soho Square to meet Dan, Ivy doesn't know I've interviewed Cassie, so no harm done. I'll discuss it with her in due course. As for Dan being gay, well that's just crazy.

She pushed open the door of the Pillars of Hercules. The atmosphere hit her at once—rowdy, crowded, jovial. The pub was small and low-ceilinged, with none of the pretensions of Cassio's or Lucifer's. Here people drank pints not cocktails, and you were lucky if the wine passed muster. Little surprise it was a favorite of Dan's.

Clustered tightly around a table on a platform at the back were her colleagues: Neil—now that his resignation was public he could work his final days in a relaxed state and he'd been enjoying more long lunches and early evening bevvies than ever; Dan's coworkers in production, Earl and Esme; Leon, who was in Orianna's opinion the most talented designer in the studio; and Gavin, who'd come along to prove he wasn't a step removed from the rest of the agency as a member of the board, though in fact he was, and everyone else would have felt more comfortable had he been absent.

Orianna fetched herself a drink, squeezed into a chair next to Dan, and joined in the discussion. They were in the midst of a debate about reality TV—"publicity-seeking idiots have got what's coming" (Dan, who'd already downed a couple of pints) versus "no one deserves to have their sexual incompetence splashed across the tabloids" (Orianna, swiftly taking up the baton as she was sober) when someone stumbled up the steps behind her and grabbed her chair for support. A helpless giggling interspersed with hiccups followed.

Oh no. Orianna winced. I'd know that giggle anywhere. She turned and took in the long, fair hair of Lara, from accounts.

Dan pulled up a stool. "Seat?"

"Yeth pleathe," said Lara.

Jesus, thought Orianna, she's at lisping stage already. Right then she missed her copywriter: she could rely on Ivy to have a good snipe. Instead hissing at Dan had to suffice. "Who asked her?"

"I did."

Worse and worse. Hadn't Dan been seeing Lara at one stage—how could he be so tactless?

Carried away by beer and birthday buoyancy, he failed to notice how miffed she was and held out his wrist. "Hey everyone, seen my new watch?"

There was a collective cooing and gasping.

"Who gave you that?" asked Lara. She took his hand and peered closely at the face. Orianna prickled. "Ooh, Paul Thmith. How flath."

Flash? seethed Orianna. It's not "flash" at all—it's *classy*. That Dan didn't pull away from physical contact made her fume more.

Dan glanced at her but his ability to pick up silent signals appeared to be malfunctioning, for despite Orianna's please-shut-up-it-will-embarrass-me vibe, he grinned proudly. "Orianna."

"Oh!" squealed Lara, and dropped his hand as if it would scald her. It landed on the table with a thud, as had, it seemed, Dan's confession.

"You *are* an item then?" said Earl, eventually.

"Yes," said Dan.

"I knew it," said Esme smugly.

"How long have you been together?" asked Earl. "No, let me guess."

"Since Easter," interrupted Gavin, keen to sound clued in.

"Since February," said Esme.

"Since Christmas," clarified Dan. Under the table he squeezed Orianna's knee.

"Stone me," said Leon. "I'm well out of date, mate. I thought *you* two were shagging." He nodded at Lara.

Orianna reeled.

Lara giggled.

"Us?" Dan sounded surprised, yet, thanks to several pints, unfazed. "Oh no. Not since last autumn."

"Ooh Dan," piped up Lara. "It wathn't that long ago." Another titter. "It was about thixth months."

Six months! For someone who works in accounts she's got a lousy head for figures, thought Orianna. Dan began to stroke Orianna's thigh more keenly. If he meant to indicate she was the one he was interested in, it merely irritated her further.

"Thweetheart, I'm thorry to have to correct you"—another titter—"but it was definitely latht winter. At the Image Focuth Chrithmath party."

Orianna started. Image Focus was a retouching house and invitations to their annual bash were limited to those in production, so Dan must have invited Lara. More importantly, it had only been the night before the Christmas party where *she'd* got together with him.

I remember it distinctly, she thought, because I was impressed Dan had the stamina for two parties in succession. Well, bloody hell, it

seemed like he had the stamina for more than that! Ugh! Lara of all
people!

Dan was still fondling Orianna's thigh, oblivious, and she pulled
away at once. Coping with his full public admission of their relationship
and Lara's revelation was a lot to take. But with Lara wedged in too,
shifting her chair would be impossible, so she lifted Dan's hand from her
leg and got to her feet. "Just going to the loo," she muttered.

Once inside the cubicle she locked the door and sat down. At least
here she could get some privacy, although her thoughts were racing too
fast for her to be able to pee.

Hmm . . . Insofar as I can remember, Dan didn't directly *lie* regarding Lara, she rationalized. I guess I never asked outright about timings,
because I was happy with his assurance their fling meant little and was
over. Nonetheless, he kept the truth from me. Surely it's important to
put a bit of space between different women? A healthy gap indicates a
new relationship is the result of clear decision-making, and makes it
more special. To go straight from Lara to me is at best impulsive, at worst
sordid.

She cast her mind back to the evening she and Dan had first tumbled
into bed, when they'd been playing that game, "Who would you shag/
marry/push off a cliff?" Hadn't Earl accused Dan of being more interested in shagging than anything? No wonder—as Dan's colleague in
production, Earl had probably been at the Image Focus party too.
Doubtless he knew Dan had spent the night before with Lara. She shuddered.

Plus, there was that gossip about G-A-Y, and Ivy's theory about
Dan's suspicious love of shopping . . . Orianna's mind whirled. Men,
women . . . who knew what, when? Certainly past experiences had shown
Orianna the opposite sex couldn't be trusted.

You're being silly, she scolded herself. Dan adores me. We have great
sex, and get along brilliantly. Hasn't he only just told me he loves me?
He's even suggested I might meet his parents.

Eventually a banging on the door brought Orianna to her feet.

"Sorry," she said to an impatient-looking woman waiting outside.

As she mounted the stairs, she forced herself to be sensible. The last thing she wanted was another public scene. She'd let it all wash over her, behave like a soon-to-be creative director should, and not pay any attention.

No one was going to spoil her happiness. Were they?

16. The thought doth like a poisonous mineral gnaw my innards

"Darling!" *Mwah, mwah.* "Lovely to see you. Let me look at you."

Trixie stepped back and Ivy paused on the threshold. Dressed in her favorite A-line skirt and a sharply tailored jacket, she was confident she appeared her best.

"Ooh, gorgeous, sweetie. Gorgeous. And I'm loving those shoes! Patrick . . . ? Hang on, let me guess . . ." Trixie peered down, examining the strappy suede stilettos, encrusted in tiny pearl beads. "No . . . a touch too practical maybe; seems you can actually walk in them . . ." Finally, "Oh go on, put me out of my misery."

"Topshop."

"Never!"

Ivy nodded. "Oxford Street special."

"You don't say."

Ivy, gratified she'd scored already, followed Trixie down the hall, heels clicking on the parquet flooring. She noticed a waft of lilies coming from an imposing display on the antique mahogany table.

"Thought we'd sit in here." Trixie led Ivy into the sitting room and lowered herself onto a chaise longue. Ivy took a seat opposite on a deep four-seat sofa upholstered in rose-colored silk. As she sank back into the cushions, she smiled inwardly: Trixie, perched above her, was able to maintain an elegant, formal pose with her legs crossed—she had magnificent calves, even at her age.

Whereas I'm forced to sit beneath her, noted Ivy. Still, it's interesting she's brought me into the lounge, not her office, where she saw me last time with Orianna. I guess these days she thinks me worthy of platinum treatment. Or maybe she's wanting me to see just how successful *she* is.

A bottle of champagne was cooling in a silver bucket on the smoked-glass coffee table, two crystal flutes by its side. Trixie removed the bottle using a linen tea towel, dried it, and deftly twisted the cork. It barely hissed, let alone emitted anything as uncouth as a pop. The champagne (for champagne it was, not some poor New World imitation) bubbled as she filled the glasses. Trixie waited for it to settle, and topped it up before handling Ivy hers.

"Well, my dear. Long time no see. Cheers."

"Cheers." They smiled at each other, and for a brief moment Ivy could see herself reflected in Trixie's eyes.

"Before we look at your portfolio, do update me, darling. Tell me *all* the gossip at Green. Am I right in gathering Neil's leaving?"

"Indeed." Ivy took a sip.

"And how do you feel about that?" A pained expression communicated sympathy.

Ivy shrugged. "I'm not bothered, really."

"Can't imagine he had much to teach you."

"No."

Trixie took a teeny sip of champagne. "Forgive my directness, my dear, but what I think you need is someone who can match your intelligence, your spark, your wit."

Three words of praise: Ivy knew she was being played, but nonetheless savored them all. "Oh?"

"I'm not sure Neil was the right creative director for you. Copy never was his strong point, was it?"

"No." Ivy often thought he lacked appreciation of her skills; it was good to have this verified by someone she respected.

"I'd like to see you working somewhere bigger, more high flying."

"Yes?"

"Where writing is viewed as an art form." Trixie uncrossed her legs and recrossed them the other way. She is *terribly* chic, thought Ivy, eyeing her dog-tooth tweed skirt enviously. "I'm thinking . . ." Trixie paused for effect. Ivy sat forward on the edge of the sofa. "Brothers and Sisters, perhaps, or even AMV . . ."

"Right." Ivy was delighted. She was talking about the crème, the very crème!

"With things so tight at the moment, lots of places aren't hiring, but for someone of your caliber, I'm confident we'll find something. If there's one area that's not been hit too hard by recession, it's direct mail, and with your experience, the DM division of these big agencies will be most keen, I'm sure."

Oh, thought Ivy, reassessing. She had assumed Trixie meant advertising proper. She was less thrilled about this suggestion—it wouldn't be very different from what she was doing now.

Trixie continued, "And if we don't pull that off, there are some other small agencies, real hotshots creatively, raking it in despite the economy."

You mean sweatshops, thought Ivy. Though all she said was, "Indeed." It's amazing, she observed, Trixie has talked me down from the highest-flying agency to the lowliest start-up in less time than it takes to air a commercial. And she hasn't even asked to see my portfolio or discussed salaries. She's quite brilliant.

Ivy decided to let her continue so she could see where the conversation went next. Sure enough, it proved even more interesting.

"After all"—a still more delicate sip—"it's probably time you broke away from Orianna, anyway."

"Oh?"

"I don't think staying there will do you any good." Trixie nodded in agreement with her own appraisal. "I mean, if you weren't learning much from Neil, you're hardly going to learn from Orianna, now are you?"

"No." With this at least, Ivy could wholeheartedly agree. "I'd been thinking I wouldn't mind breaking away entirely. Going abroad, perhaps."

"That's not such a bad idea. There's quite a demand for English-speaking writers in some places. The Netherlands, for instance."

Ivy nodded. Copious sex and drugs—Amsterdam could be fun . . .

"And it might be good to break from one another fully. One can be a mite too close sometimes. Claustrophobic." Trixie settled back, relaxing a tad. "Actually, I have a tiny theory I'd like to share with you."

"Oh?"

"About art directors and copywriters."

"Ah?"

"You see, I was an art director, once."

"Really?" This did surprise Ivy, not least because Trixie seemed far more chic than most art directors she'd known.

"It was many years ago." Trixie smiled. "I worked with a copywriter myself, Cherie, she was called." Cherie and Trixie, thought Ivy. They sound like matching dolls. She could see them now, for sale as a boxed duo, complete with miniature designer outfits.

"That must have been very unusual," said Ivy, admiringly. "Two women creatives, in those days."

"Oh, it *was*." Trixie almost beamed, recollecting. "We worked together in all the big agencies of the seventies and eighties. Bates, Saatchis, you name it. We had some fantastic creative directors in our time, I'm telling you. So when I say it's important to carry on learning from the best, believe me, I know." Suddenly, her face hardened. "But I guess all good things must come to an end."

"What happened?" Ivy was on tenterhooks.

Trixie's voice dropped to a hush. "She betrayed me."

"Gosh," said Ivy, genuinely surprised. "How?"

"She left the industry."

"She left?" Ivy was astonished. However ambivalent she felt about advertising, there was no better alternative, surely.

"Without telling me." Trixie was almost spitting by now.

"*Without telling you?*" My Lord, thought Ivy, what a coincidence. But she said nothing about her own experience with Orianna, just waited, keen to hear more.

"Yes. Out of the blue. One Monday morning, she announced it."

"What?"

"That she was going into *publishing*." Trixie spoke the word as if it were unclean.

"Publishing!"

"I know, extraordinary."

"But publishing—it—" Ivy could scarcely get the words out.

"Pays a pittance?" Trixie said helpfully.

"Yes."

"I know." Trixie sighed. "Cherie had a pang of conscience. Got involved in that feminism stuff, went off on some awful weekend workshop, women only, and discovered her inner being and with it her true vocation. When she came back she was never the same." Trixie seemed almost wistful, for a second. "Said she felt advertising compromised her. It was too competitive, rife with jealousy, driven by narcissism and greed. She decided to become a book editor. Wanted to work with real people, *genuine* writers, contribute something valuable to the world. Absurd! But that's how it was."

"Well I never," said Ivy.

"All true, I'm telling you."

Ivy took a sip of champagne. This was most illuminating, called for something special. She recalled Trixie indulged occasionally, too . . . So she leaned forward, opened her bag, and took out a packet of menthol cigarettes. "Do you mind dreadfully if I smoke?"

"No, do," said Trixie, pushing forward a crystal ashtray. "In fact, you've tempted me. May I join you?"

"Of course." Ivy handed her the pack.

Trixie took a cigarette, lit it, and inhaled. "I only allow myself one a week," she confided. "I appreciate it's dreadfully outmoded these days. But oh! How I love it!" As she exhaled, her lips formed a reverential kiss.

"I understand," said Ivy, who did.

"My point is this," continued Trixie. "Never get too entangled with anyone else professionally, my dear, however much you might like them or how well you work together. You never know what can happen— they might get married, be promoted, fall ill, or, like Cherie, have some peculiar, nutty freak-out. Whatever. Because if you tie yourself to someone, you're laying yourself open to being deserted."

Ivy nodded.

"And at the end of the day we all die alone." She sighed again, more heavily, then inhaled deeply on her cigarette. "I was terribly, terribly upset by what Cherie did to me. Never really got over it. But it taught me a lot. When I found out she was leaving, I went wild, reacted very strongly. I suppose . . ." She paused. "With hindsight I betrayed my own feelings somewhat."

"Oh?"

"It's nothing I want to go into." Trixie shifted in her seat, obviously uncomfortable with the confession. "But I got myself a bit of a reputation for being fiery, difficult. Which when you're a woman in advertising . . . It's bad enough already—or it was then, certainly—without having gossip and prejudice to contend with. And ultimately her leaving affected my career because I never really had my heart in being a creative after she'd gone."

"Oh dear." Ivy was strangely moved.

Yet Trixie brushed her concern aside. "There's no need to worry about me. I was fine, in the end. Without all that . . ." She gesticulated around with a sweep of her beautifully manicured hand. "None of this would have happened."

"Mm?"

"Shortly after I left agency life too," explained Trixie. "Or at least directly. I went into head-hunting. Set up on my own, working here. And

I assure you, I never affiliated myself to one person, or betrayed my real feelings, ever again."

"Ah," said Ivy. It was wonderfully clear. Never mind Neil or Orianna; the person she could learn from was Trixie. Though there was one thing further she wanted to clarify. "And Cherie?"

"Yes, Cherie." Trixie spoke the name with disdain. "She's in publishing to this day. Grand old dame of literature. Became an agent, in fact."

"Do you ever speak to her?"

Trixie tutted. "Sometimes, yes. When it's mutually beneficial for us to do so, professionally, whatever. We still have some friends in common. But we'll never be close, obviously."

"Obviously," agreed Ivy, and together they stubbed out their cigarettes.

By the time they left the pub, both Dan and Orianna were pretty inebriated; Dan more so, having started earlier, and because no matter how much wine Orianna knocked back, she couldn't shake her sober mood.

"Taxi!" shouted Dan, waving his arm at a passing black van and lurching rather alarmingly onto Tottenham Court Road.

The busy thoroughfare worried Orianna. She ran after him and led him to safety. "Let's walk," she urged, taking his arm. Dan's place was just over a mile away.

"Walk!" Dan stomped back to the pavement edge. "Walk?! I don't walk on my birthday!"

Orianna had to laugh. "It might be wise. Clear our heads a bit."

"Oh, OK," said Dan, drunkenly obedient.

"Good for your weight, too."

"Am I fat?" He looked at her, worried, and patted his tummy. "You think I'm a Dough Boy!"

"No, silly. I'm teasing."

He linked his arm in hers, walked a few paces, and promptly tripped over a paving stone. He looked at her, mouth turned down in cartoon contrition. "Sorry!"

They stumbled on a while, Orianna steering Dan in as straight a line as possible. They were past Sainsbury's and Muji; alongside a row of tired-looking electrical shops; crossed Stephen Street, checking for vehicles taking a sudden left; ignored some beggars sitting beneath the HSBC ATM with their dog—getting home, not homelessness, had to be her priority right now. Dan entertained himself by kicking a Coke can along with them, but after a while it bounced out of reach.

"Halfway there," she said, when they reached the Warren Street subway station.

He swung her arm gleefully. "Not far now!" He gazed down at her, then observed, voice slurred, "I do love you, you know."

"Do you?" She glanced up at him. "*Really?*"

"Of course! You're my best girlfriend, ever!"

She smiled. She could hardly be cross with him like this. But patience was not one of her virtues; she didn't want to sit with her doubts longer than she had to. Plus several pints of Stella might mean he hadn't the wherewithal to lie.

"So you do consider me your girlfriend, then?"

"Yes! Of course!"

They crossed with the light and headed up Hampstead Road.

Orianna let go of his hand. "Dan, can I ask you something?"

"Whatever you like."

"Did you spend the night with Lara after the Image Focus Christmas party?"

"Oh, um . . ." He frowned. "I think I did." He looked at her again, his expression guilty. "Is that *very* bad of me?"

She sighed. "I s'pose not."

"I wasn't going out with you then, was I?" He nodded, sure of this. "I didn't start seeing you till after that."

"No . . ."

"And I've never had anything to do with her since, I promise." He leaned in and kissed Orianna's cheek. She could feel a touch of saliva; damp, warm, reassuring. "You're *much* lovelier than Lara!"

This went some way to consoling her. "But Dan, it was only the *night* before!"

"The night before what?"

"The Green party, when you first went out with me!"

"Really?" He stopped by the curbside, brow furrowed, struggling to recollect. "Was it that soon?" He glanced at her sideways, biting his lip. "I think you might be right."

"That's only twenty-four hours!"

"Mm." Sheepish.

Tears pricked behind Orianna's eyes. "I thought I was more special to you than that."

"You *are* special."

"It makes me feel like some sort of tart!" Orianna knew if anyone was a tart Dan was, but she felt it nonetheless. "As if I'm one of hundreds of women"—then she remembered Ursula's remark—"people, *men*, I don't know, you're just shagging."

But this seemed too much for Dan to process. He stood swaying, appearing to try and sober himself up, fast.

Orianna struggled not to cry. "I hate feeling I'm one of a string of conquests—that you leaped straight from her bed into mine." She voiced a particularly distressing fear. "You did have a bath between, didn't you?" Then the tears started to fall.

Dan stomped his foot. "Of *course* I had a bath!"

Orianna gulped back her upset. "You did?"

"Well, a shower, at any rate. I always have a shower. Every morning. You know that. Look . . ." He stopped, turned to her, held her gaze, and said firmly, "You must appreciate the situation. I did have a fling with Lara and I'm not going to hide that from you—you've always known that was the case."

"Yes." Orianna's voice was small.

"But that was all it was: a fling. I never was that into her. She's too young for me. And let's face it, she's nowhere near as bright as you."

"She's thick!"

"Well, I'm not sure about that."

"She *is!*"

"OK, OK, if you say, she's stupid. Dumb—"

"—blond," quipped Orianna, and laughed through her weeping.

He took her face in his hands and wiped her damp cheeks. "Listen. I'm a bit of an idiot, sometimes, but you have to believe I really can't remember much about that night with Lara; it was months ago, it wasn't particularly important to me. It only happened that evening because it had once before."

"But you must have invited her," Orianna pointed out. "If you went with her to the Image Focus party."

"I seem to recall she saw the invitation on my desk and asked me if she could come. I could hardly say no, could I?"

"I guess not . . ."

"So we went and one thing led to another. But after that first night with you, I never had anything to do with Lara again. I promise."

"Honestly?"

"Honestly." They resumed walking; Dan took her hand, seemingly sobered by the conversation.

Orianna remained uncomfortable about one detail. "Did you ever finish it, though? I mean, tell her it was over?"

He paused. "I thought it would be unnecessarily cruel—not to mention presumptuous—to sit her down and say I didn't want it to happen again. After all, it wasn't as if Lara and I were going out or anything—we only slept together a couple of times." He examined Orianna's face to check she understood him. "Honey, I'm sorry; maybe that was a bit cowardly, perhaps I should have told you both. But you wanted us to keep things about the two of us quiet; I didn't want to hurt Lara, or you, come to that. I thought you didn't have to know every tiny detail of the run-up to our going out; and she didn't have to know I'd rather have a proper relationship with you than have something casual with her."

"Oh. I see." That did make sense; in a way it was flattering.

By now they were at the front door of Dan's building on Mornington Terrace. He reached into his jacket pocket for his key as the porch light came on automatically. Slowly they climbed the stairs in leaden rhythm. Once inside his large studio, Orianna kicked off her shoes and threw down her bag on the sofa.

"I'm exhausted!" Dan made a beeline for the bed. He fell immediately onto the duvet flat on his back, clothes and all. Orianna followed him and he pulled her down on top of him, their bodies entwined.

One final concern, then Orianna could undress and go to sleep. She lifted her face up from his and said, "So you're not gay, then?"

"Gay?" Dan hooted. "Now you're being daft. What on earth gave you that idea?"

"Something someone said at work." Orianna was too exhausted for a second confrontation.

"I've never heard of anything so ridiculous."

"Really?"

"Sweetheart." Dan reached for her hand and put it on his crotch. "What do you think?"

There, indeed, was proof of his desire for her, and she wanted to believe him with all her heart. But when she woke the next day, a small cloud of worry still remained.

17. Make all the money thou canst

As Neil worked his final days, Orianna decided to ignore her worries about Dan's promiscuity, in order to focus on gleaning as much as possible from her boss. Despite his waning interest, it was unusual to have one's predecessor on hand, and she was determined to turn this to her advantage. She spent days with him in his glass-walled office, the door closed so they could oversee the department while chatting in private.

She encouraged him to offload information about their clients, debrief her on unfamiliar projects, steer her on new business, give her guidance on handling colleagues she'd not hitherto worked with closely, and impart as much as he could about the sequestered machinations of the board. Discreetly, she lured him into revealing more about the agency's finances. These in particular were an eye-opener: the balance sheets were in a worse state than Orianna had realized.

"It's an expensive business, running an agency," said Neil. "Best ask Russell if you want a thorough explanation."

There were other shocks too. "I didn't realize Ivy earned so much!"

"Oh yes." Neil nodded.

"Has she been at this salary for long?"

"I can't recall." Orianna felt he could remember all too well.

But I work harder than Ivy, she thought. *I'm* the one they chose to promote. I might be at a higher salary now, but why on earth was she paid more than me before?

"That's why we can't afford to hire someone senior to work with her," Neil pointed out. "We haven't got the money. Did you speak to Cassie, by the way?"

"Yes. She's starting next Monday."

"She'll be good, I'm sure."

"A real asset," agreed Orianna. In her years as group head at Green, she'd interviewed several art directors, but rarely one as gifted or charming as Cassie. In fact, Orianna had been so convinced of her talent and that others would take to her as swiftly as she had, that she'd offered Cassie the job the very next day.

"It's one of my regrets I won't see her in action," said Neil.

"I'm looking forward to teaming her up with Ivy, seeing what they come up with as a duo." Orianna recollected the early days when the two of them had first been put together—Ivy had taught her so much. "Ivy's so good at bringing new people on. Though you've reminded me, I *must* have a chat with her about Cassie."

"You've not told her yet?"

"Er . . . no." Orianna felt guilty she'd not done this before, but she'd been awfully busy, and by the time she'd thought of it again, Cassie had accepted the job. "I'm sure Ivy will like Cassie too."

"How could she not? Nonetheless, you're planning on them working together?"

Orianna nodded. "Although I'll still team up with Ivy as well."

"I see."

She reassured herself. "Ivy and I have always got along with the same people in the past."

"Mm," said Neil, but Orianna detected concern.

She thought for a moment. It was Thursday already, no time like the present. She rose to her feet. "I'll have a word with her now. I can shift things from my old desk while I'm at it." Neil had acquired a stack of empty boxes, ready to pack his personal possessions. She picked up a couple. "Can I borrow these to put my books in while I move them around here?"

"Sure. Take the trolley, too."

"Good thinking." Orianna grabbed it and wheeled it through the door. "Back soon."

But when she reached her desk, Ivy wasn't around. She decided to start packing regardless. These days she was much in demand and couldn't hang about.

Ivy hurried to the office, panting. It was a lot to accomplish, to and from Knightsbridge in a lunch hour—she'd actually been gone far longer. As she walked into the creative department and slowed to a more measured pace, she could see Orianna's head bobbing over their partition wall.

Bugger, thought Ivy, sneaking her Harvey Nichols shopping bag deep into the jackets on the communal coat stand. I hope she hasn't noticed I've been out for ages. She tiptoed around to the other side of the department and headed to her desk from a different direction so it wouldn't appear she'd just come in the main door. With luck Orianna would assume she'd been in a meeting.

Several boxes were piled on Orianna's desk, filled with books, files, and magazines, and Orianna was on all fours under the table. Judging from the mesh of cables nearby, she was struggling to unplug her computer.

Ah, so she's moving to her new office, Ivy observed.

"Hi," she said breezily, slipping past to take her seat by the window.

She felt a lurch of sadness at the thought that she and Orianna would no longer be sitting together. They'd not been more than four feet from each other in over a decade. But then a rush of envy sent sensitivity flying.

It's not fair, she fumed, Orianna having all that room, when I'm still stuck here. *And* she's taking our reference materials. Typography manuals, Pantone guides, creative handbooks—I use them too! And I'm not even sure those magazines are hers.

Presently Orianna peered out from beneath the desk, her face dusty and sweaty. "Do me a favor? Save whatever it is you're writing, and turn off your machine so I can unplug everything?"

Ivy tried to think why she couldn't accommodate this request, but failed. "OK." She shut down her PC but didn't offer to get down and help. "I'll have all this space to myself," she said, biting back irritation.

At that moment Orianna surfaced. She stood and faced Ivy. "Actually, I did want to talk to you about that. There's someone starting soon and I was thinking you might like to have her sit here."

"Oh?"

"An art director."

Ivy started. I hope to God she's not referring to that nauseating blonde I met in reception, she thought.

"She's called Cassie," Orianna went on. "She's . . . er . . . a bit younger than us, but she's ever so good."

If Orianna sounded unsure, Ivy certainly wasn't going to make it any easier. She was silent, checking her nails as she assessed the evidence.

I'm not stupid, she thought. Orianna won't just be planning on Cassie *sitting* opposite. I bet she's intending that the two of us *work* together.

"In fact . . ." Orianna said tentatively, "I was going to suggest that you teamed up with her from time to time."

Ha!

"I was hoping you might teach her a thing or two—you're so good, so experienced."

Stop trying to butter me up, thought Ivy. What on earth will I get out of it? What can some tart who's just got off the plane from Oz show *me*?

The harder she considered it all, the more incensed she grew. This is just typical of the new, power-crazed Orianna that she's hired Cassie without consulting me, she ruminated. Teaming me with someone half my age! She bit back her anger, but couldn't resist saying, "You didn't think of introducing her to me, then?" as she continued examining her cuticles. She glanced up to check: Orianna was blushing. Good.

"You can meet her, if you'd like."

"But unless I misunderstand, you've hired her anyway?"

"Um. I, er . . . yes, I have. She's very nice."

"Not much point in my meeting her now though, is there?"

"I'm sure if you had a problem with her—"

"You'd renege on the job offer?" Ivy snorted. "Orianna, sweetie, that's hardly your style." Orianna looked even more uncomfortable, but Ivy was keen to make her squirm. "When does she start?"

"Monday."

"Monday!"

"Yes."

"Hardly much time to hook up beforehand, is there?"

By now Orianna was scarlet.

"Don't worry," said Ivy, knowing Orianna would, a lot. "I'm sure if you like her . . ."

"That's what I thought."

"I guess we often chose the same candidates at interviews before."

"Precisely." Orianna sounded relieved.

"And I trust your judgement."

"Thank you." Orianna clarified, "And you do know that I'll still be teaming up with you too?"

"Indeed." I won't hold my breath, thought Ivy. How much work did Neil ever do with a writer? But she merely smiled. "I'm looking forward to it."

Orianna beamed back. "Me too," she said, and resumed her packing.

Ivy sat watching her lift the boxes onto the trolley.

Eventually . . . "Phew." Orianna sighed, exhausted. "I better get one of the guys to help me wheel this through."

"Don't want to hurt yourself." Ivy pictured Orianna tumbling, headlong.

"No." Orianna puffed and lifted the last box with a grimace. "So you'll see Cassie's taken care of?"

"Nothing would please me more."

"I knew I could rely on you. Well, best get on." And with a squeak of straining wheels, Orianna was off to her new room.

Ivy sat glowering at the empty desk in front of her. Its laminated surface bore traces of Orianna's presence—years of marker stains, scalpel-knife scratches, coffee-cup rings. Beneath where her computer had been, an unsavory collection of dust, crumbs, and used staples now lay exposed.

So, she'd been left again, deserted. Just like Cherie deserted Trixie . . . And from where she was sitting, Ivy could already see Orianna unpacking, happily lining books along the shelves Neil had cleared for her, playfully color coordinating the spines.

While I'm being made to work with some *junior*, crammed in the same cubby hole I've put up with for years, she seethed. Just look! Orianna's got *four* shelves, where I've got one—a shelf I'm to share with some bimbo. Orianna's got a big, wooden desk with a return; I've barely room for a sheet of A4 alongside my keyboard. Orianna's got a large, comfy, leather chair with armrests and a high back; I've got this old swivel thing more suited to a typist. And Orianna's got a shiny new speakerphone with a direct line and lots of buttons; I've got this grimy extension with mangled wires.

Wherever Ivy turned, echoes of the past reverberated around her. It was the story of her adolescence, all over again.

18. The green-eyed monster which doth mock the meat it feeds on

To: Everyone
From: Orianna Bianchi
Date: Monday, July 1, 8:41
Subj: New recruits

As most of you already know, today is my first official day as creative director. You will now find me permanently based in Neil's old office at extension 450.

Although in the long run I may well make changes to the department, I don't intend to implement any dramatic alterations yet. I plan to get settled before looking at the way we operate.

I would like to say, however, that from the start I wish to foster an atmosphere of openness and trust. I want anyone—and I do mean anyone—to feel they can come and talk to me about work. If my door is open and you want a quick chat, please pop in and share. If you've something lengthier to discuss, I still want to hear about it, so e-mail me and we'll sort a time out.

Finally, I'd also like to take this opportunity to announce that a new member of staff is joining us today. Cassie Goldworthy is an art director and she'll be sitting opposite Ivy, at my old extension, 457. I'll be bringing her around to introduce her to all of you, so please make her feel welcome.

Orianna

She'd just pressed *Send* when Philly called to announce Cassie was in reception.

She's early, a good sign, Orianna noted, and she headed down to meet her. She bounded out of the elevator, into reception, and held out her hands in welcome.

"Hi, Cassie!"

As Cassie got to her feet and warmly took Orianna's hands in hers, Orianna was struck by how incredibly pretty she was.

Later that day, Ivy was sitting at her desk, once again focused on the space in front of her, glowering. The only difference was Cassie was opposite, and Ivy had shifted her computer screen so she could send negative vibes without being seen.

I loathe her, she thought.

Of course she'd been sweet as pie when Orianna had introduced Cassie, purring that she remembered her. But underneath the sugary smile Ivy had been glowering then, and she was glowering now.

It wasn't merely that Ivy had disliked Cassie's youth, appearance, and manner from the start; it was that she promised to be an ever-present reminder of the widening gulf between herself and Orianna.

Worse, Cassie seemed to attract men like bees to a honeypot. Although Orianna had hauled Cassie around the agency on the customary round of introductions that morning, it seemed this had only whetted the appetites of the male population of Green, and that afternoon one by one they came to pop their heads around the partition wall and ogle.

Gavin was first, then Earl, then Leon. Leon stayed laughing and teasing Cassie for several minutes about her Aussie roots, and if Ivy wasn't mistaken there was a little sexual frisson there. This increased her rancor, as she'd long appreciated Leon's Jamaican good looks, and previously enjoyed a mild flirtation with him herself. Moreover she was struggling to write a leaflet about mortgage interest rates, and could have done without the distraction. But then came not one, but five account handlers.

The supercilious little creeps, thought Ivy, treating Cassie like she's a piece of new business to be wooed and won.

Yet Cassie was equally sweet to them all, and rather than basking in their attention, handled it with natural ease.

To add insult to injury, at four o'clock Russell sauntered by on the pretext of heading for the coffee machine. He leaned against the partition, bantering lightheartedly with the two of them, but Ivy knew him well enough to appreciate his nonchalance was feigned. She observed that he primarily directed his conversation to Cassie, and his eyes seemed to linger on her petite, bronzed form.

I always suspected he had a thing for small blondes, she bristled, recollecting his lust for Lara. She sent imaginary daggers flying through the screen of her PC at both of them.

Lastly, who should come bounding in, with a chuckle and an amiable slap on the back for Cassie, but Mr. Long-Limbed Handsomeness himself.

Dan folded his legs onto the small two-seater sofa and grinned. "Seems you've been quite a hit."

"Oh?"

But loyalty to the boys' network meant he wouldn't elaborate. "So, tell us a bit about yourself, Cassie."

"What do you want to know?"

"I gather you're from Sydney."

Cassie shook her head. "In the immediate sense, yes, I suppose I am, but actually I'm from close to Alice Springs—I grew up on a sheep farm. My parents emigrated there after the war."

Good grief! Brought up in the outback? Daughter of a farmer? No wonder she's so lacking in guile, thought Ivy.

Cassie continued: "I went to college in Sydney then got my first job in an agency there. After a couple of years, I decided to come to London."

Strange choice, advertising, pondered Ivy, for a girl like her. Still, she was heartened. With a background like that, it would be like shooting fish in a barrel. One parochial agency in Sydney was hardly going to give Cassie the edge that working in Soho required. So if Ivy was going to get one over her—which as the day wore on she was increasingly keen to—the advantage was all hers.

"I see. And what brought you to the Big Smoke?"

"I came on the off chance—I've always wanted to work here. After all, the standard of creative work is reputed to be the best in the world."

"So they say."

"It's a great opportunity for me, this. A sort of dream come true."

"Hard to imagine working here being anyone's dream." Dan laughed.

Ivy couldn't agree more, but Cassie didn't seem to mind. "And how 'bout you, Dan, where are you from?"

Well, thought Ivy. I've never asked him that. Could be telling.

But the answer was dull: "Me, I'm a North London lad. Born and bred in Hampstead."

"That's nice," said Cassie. There was an almost undetectable pause while they both searched for where to take the conversation next.

At this point Ivy, finished with her leaflet copy, decided to interrupt. "You ought to be especially nice to Dan. He's not just any old head of production, you know."

"He isn't?"

"No." Ivy chose her words carefully. "He's our creative director's partner."

"Oh?" Cassie turned to Dan. "You and Orianna are married?"

Dan didn't even blink before answering. "Not yet."

It was all Ivy could do to contain her surprise. "Is there something I don't know?"

"Oh no." Dan's tone was congenial.

"You're not engaged or anything?"

"No, no. I'd have to put in some groundwork with my family before considering that."

"But it is pretty serious then?"

"Mm." Dan nodded, looking embarrassed to be discussing this in front of Cassie. "Er . . . I guess you could say so."

"Oh," said Ivy. She had deliberately avoided asking Orianna about the relationship—hearing it was going well would only increase her sense of isolation, and Orianna hadn't spoken much about Dan either. This revelation pained her; she knew that if Dan was prepared to admit publicly it was serious it must be; men like him tended to keep such personal revelations to themselves until they were sure.

"Well, best get going." Dan got to his feet, clearly keen to avoid further questioning. "Catch you later."

"See you." Ivy nodded.

"Nice to meet you," said Cassie.

"And you."

Ivy sat there, thinking. At once she buried her discomfort, concentrating instead on how she might make herself feel better. So he was *that* serious about Orianna, was he? Very interesting . . . Yet he'd jumped at the chance of meeting Cassie, albeit in probable innocence. Unlike the other boys who'd made a beeline for Cassie that afternoon, Ivy was pretty convinced he was curious and being genuinely friendly. Still, here might be a great way to wipe the smile off not just Orianna's face, but Cassie's too.

Two birds knocked from their perch with one stone.

Hmm.

Now *that* was a truly creative idea.

19. Dangerous conceits are in their natures poison

"Well, hey."

"Hey." Cassie swiveled around in her chair.

It was Leon, who'd come to show Cassie some artwork. He loped over to her desk, dreadlocks swinging, and spread a large color run-out before her.

In a tie-dyed T-shirt and floppy black trousers, he's by far the coolest-looking guy in the agency, thought Ivy. And he's sexy to boot.

She felt a stirring of desire, but pushed it away, and focused instead on her two colleagues. She'd been sharing space with Cassie for several weeks, during which time Cassie and Leon had been working together on some ads. Yet while Ivy acknowledged it was common practice for art directors and designers to collaborate, she recalled that in the past his behavior had been rather different. Leon was talented but frequently got so caught up in details that he'd run late on jobs, and when Orianna had worked with him, she used to have to check up on him regularly and chivy him along. Often she'd have to sit by his Mac and oversee his work.

Whereas with Cassie, he seemed one step ahead of her requirements all the time.

That Ivy had been attracted to Leon for years on the quiet herself increased her curiosity. Her computer screen still blocked her vision of Cassie, but she could see Leon and hear Cassie's responses. And although they merely talked of tints, logos, and images, she saw Leon's hand brush Cassie's more than once, and there was something about Leon's lowered voice and Cassie's giggling that led her to conclude they fancied one another, big-time.

Ivy was determined not to have anything put past her again, so when he'd gone, she said, "I think he rather likes you."

"Oh?"

Ivy gently slid the wheels of her chair sideways and sneaked a peek at Cassie's face. Hmm . . . Her head was down, concentrating, but she was blushing. Ivy pushed further. "In fact, I'd say he's got the serious hots."

Cassie flushed pinker still. How pitiful they are, thought Ivy, these women who can't disguise their feelings. Yet maybe there's more than a simple flirtation going on here—a few weeks is a long time where lust is concerned. I wonder if they've gone further than mutual appreciation already? What the hell, I'll ask.

Ivy could tell Cassie was intimidated by her—like most young creatives—so to gain Cassie's confidence, she turned on the charm. She wheeled her chair along farther, leaned around, and eyed Cassie so pointedly that she was forced to look at her. Then she edged in close, over her desk. "Is there something going on?"

Cassie almost dropped her pen. "Er . . ."

"You can tell me," Ivy cajoled. "I won't breathe a word."

Cassie, who normally had an answer for most things, was speechless.

"He's very attractive—I wouldn't blame you." With luck her approval might encourage a confession.

"D'you think?" Cassie's tone was nervous.

"Ooh, *yes!*"

"Actually . . ." Now Cassie leaned in close too, arms resting on Orianna's old desk. She lowered her voice so she wouldn't be heard over the partition. "He asked me out last Friday."

Today was Monday. "And?"

Cassie's face took on a glazed expression. "We had *such* a lovely time."

Bugger lovely times, I want to know if you've done the dirty deed, thought Ivy. "I'm not surprised. He's a nice guy, Leon. Where did you go?"

"The movies." Cassie smiled at the memory.

"And?" Ivy raised an eyebrow.

"Then we went back to his."

"And?"

"I stayed over," blurted Cassie.

Ha! "Well . . . ?"

"Well, what?"

"Did you . . . ?"

More blushing. She's as bad as Orianna, thought Ivy. No wonder those two have taken to one another. She prompted, "Was he good?"

"Fantastic!"

Damn. She'd always suspected he would be. Jealousy seared through her, but it was important to establish the extent of the attachment. "Do you think it might happen again?"

"It already has," admitted Cassie.

Ivy blanched.

"We ended up spending Saturday together too."

Echoes of Orianna and Dan; a sexual attraction swiftly and joyfully consummated, with potential for serious romance. Yet again Ivy was pierced by loneliness; except for a trip to the gym on Saturday, she'd spent the weekend alone. Russell was up in Hertfordshire with his family, as usual, but even Ed hadn't called her. Not that she'd really wanted him to—these days she and her husband never had much to say to one another—nonetheless, it brought home their lack of intimacy.

Orianna, Dan, Cassie, Leon—they're all so smug and self-satisfied, she thought. Oh for the days before Cassie's arrival, when Orianna was bumbling and romantically incompetent, Dan was just an affable colleague, and Leon was more interested in flirting with *me*!

She crept in even closer and whispered, "Actually . . . if I were you I wouldn't tell anyone you've been seeing Leon."

"Why?"

"I know it seems silly, but they can be funny here about casual agency relationships, trust me."

"Really?"

"Yes."

"I wasn't planning on telling everyone anyway. Not now. It's early days."

"No, no, of course you weren't. It's just, well, it's easy to share, isn't it?" Ivy reached out, her fingers almost touching Cassie's.

"Yes, I suppose."

"Honestly, Cass, I'm not kidding you; they believe relationships interfere with our work."

"They?"

"The board. I think it stems from Russell originally; he can be funny about things like that. Likes to keep the professional and the personal separate, you know, and it's sort of an unspoken part of the company philosophy."

"But what about Orianna and Dan?"

"What about them?"

"Well, they're quite open about their relationship, aren't they?"

"Yes, they are now. But rest assured, Orianna and Dan kept quiet for months before going public. Ask anyone."

Cassie looked perturbed. Ivy guessed in the normal run of events she would have blurted to all and sundry once her relationship with Leon was a few weeks old.

"I know what it's like, so if you have to tell someone, perhaps tell me?"

"OK."

"Good. It can make people look a bit unprofessional when things go wrong."

"I guess."

"Just imagine, Orianna would feel dreadfully humiliated if her relationship with Dan unwound itself, now that everyone in the agency is aware they're dating, wouldn't she?"

"I don't think that seems very likely—they seem so happy."

Ivy's mind worked fast. "I wouldn't count on it."

"Really?"

"Oh, it's probably nothing." She looked away.

"What?"

"Well . . ." She hesitated as if to appear reticent, then continued, "If you remember, when you started, and Dan came to have a chat, he seemed to avoid going into much detail about how serious it was."

"Er . . ." Cassie frowned.

"I certainly don't think he'd consider marrying her, for instance."

"Why not?"

"Because he's Jewish, for a start."

"Me too."

"Really? That's a coincidence!" Ivy affected surprise. Cassie *Goldworthy*? I mean *please*.

"Yeah, my father's Polish, my mother's American, but Jewish too."

Ah, that's where *Cassie* comes from then, noted Ivy. The U.S. of A. No wonder it sounds like something from *Little House on the Prairie*. She continued, "I don't know about your parents, but I gather Dan's family is quite religious—you might remember him mentioning it."

"Yes."

"That's not the only thing."

"Oh?"

"I heard something extremely interesting . . . just the other day. At the gym."

"Yeah?"

By this point Ivy was wedged in, resting her elbows on Orianna's old desk too. Their faces were only inches apart. "But you mustn't breathe a word, Cass, to a soul."

"No, I won't."

Ivy suspected however much she liked Leon, Cassie wouldn't be able to resist a compliment, so revealed, "Because someone else fancies you—not just Leon."

"Wow. Really?"

"Though I gather he is very keen, so he's holding off."

"Oh?"

"He knows it might cause a few ructions."

"Why?"

"He's seriously entangled with someone else."

"Oh? Who?" Ivy could almost hear Cassie's heart racing with excitement.

"Because it's *Dan,* Cassie, that's why."

"No!" A gasp. "How do you know?"

"Why do you think he was in such a hurry to come and say hello? And so embarrassed to talk about Orianna? Think about it . . . He's been around here a lot." Of course he has, you silly cow, thought Ivy. It's his job.

"Er . . . I suppose."

"It's not me he's coming to see, let me assure you."

"Oh." A pause while Cassie assimilated it all. Then, "But who told you?"

"Rob," said Ivy. "He's my personal trainer. Dan's a client of his, too."

20. Weigh'st thy words before thou giv'st them breath

Dear Mr. A. B. Sample,

As a valued customer, it is my great pleasure to be writing to offer you a new way to go about paying for your home. And indeed, all of your monthly standing orders and direct debits. It's called an Offset Mortgage.

Jesus, with copy this clichéd, no wonder the last agency lost the business, Ivy observed. And now I've been given the unenviable task of rewriting this letter in line with an idea developed by Orianna, without my input at all.

Orianna had left her scribbled concepts and a note asking Ivy to "tidy up the headlines and write the body copy." How insulting. Ivy checked the brief. *Target Audience: B2C2 Adults.* Cheers, she thought, that helps a lot.

The letter was needed for the end of play, so she had to get a move on. In her mind's eye she envisaged Mr. and Mrs. Middle England, living in their Barratt home on the outskirts of Birmingham, with two children, a Labrador, and a Ford Mondeo. She began to type.

> Dear A. B. Sample,
>
> You've been banking with us for many years, but that's no reason to stick with the same old way of managing your money. Your life's moved on—you've probably got children to think of, a home to manage, a car to run. With so many demands on your energies, you simply haven't the time to bank in the way you used to. Yet you still want to be in control of your finances, enjoy the best service, and, above everything, earn the best rates of interest.
>
> If that's the case, then an Offset Mortgage is right for you . . .

Ivy paused and reread her version. Yes, that was better.

She was good at this, making a convincing argument, altering the tone to appeal to certain sectors of the population. She'd written to mums about supermarket prices, teenagers about spot remedies, beer aficionados about widgets in cans, pensioners about investment opportunities. Like an actress taking on different roles, Ivy didn't have to believe in what she was doing in order to play each part. In advertising the line between fact and fiction was always blurred, and she'd discovered telling some of the truth—"brand so-and-so tastes better than other butters" for instance, and ignoring the full picture—"it contains more salt, will make you fat, and costs more than its competitors"—was how to sell more products and thus make a success of herself.

These lessons had reinforced those she'd learned as a child: just as her father had falsified evidence of his income to avoid paying child support so, in fact, everyone the world over lies, or avoids the truth. Over her years in marketing, Ivy had seen how easily people can be duped, and it was a small leap to altering her tone of voice on paper to doing it

in person. Ivy had discovered that friends and colleagues, just like cus-
tomers, could be persuaded to believe what she wanted them to.

Less than an hour later, Ivy was ready to show the letter to her boss.
Orianna's door was open and she was sitting at her desk, eyes fixed on
her computer screen. Ivy coughed, and Orianna looked up.

"I've done it. Here." She handed over the sheet of A4.

Orianna skimmed it. "That's great." She smiled appreciatively. "As
always, I knew I could rely on you." She hesitated. "Er . . . would you
mind awfully taking this down with the scribbles I gave you earlier and
showing everything to Ursula? I trust you to talk her through it and I'm
trying to get my head around some figures."

"Oh right," said Ivy. Gone are the days Orianna and I presented ideas
as a team, she noted. *Quelle surprise.* She was poised to leave when Orianna
stopped her.

"Ivy?"

"Yeah?"

"I just wanted to check—are you OK sitting with Cassie, working
together and so on?"

Ivy gleaned from Orianna's expression she was keen to hear it was.
Tempted as she was to say Cassie irritated the hell out of her, Ivy saw
more potential by responding otherwise. "It's fine. She's very talented. I
don't mind working with her . . ."

"Good—that's what I hoped."

". . . so long as I'm not bothered being interrupted by a constant
stream of boys." She laughed lightly.

"Oh?"

"Her admirers."

"Really?" Orianna fell straight for it. "Such as who?"

"The guys in the studio, you know what they're like. They've all got
the hots for her."

"Doesn't surprise me."

"And God knows how many of the suits."

"Well, I never!"

"Even your Dan, he can't seem to resist popping in from time to time."

Orianna paled.

"Though I'm sure there's nothing in it, of course."

"No."

"He's only being friendly."

"Yes." Orianna gulped.

"That's just what Dan's like."

"True . . ."

"And I have to respect a girl who can wrap so many men round her little finger. Don't you?"

"Er, yes." A hesitation. "Dan was only being friendly?"

"Orianna, sweetie, of course he was! It's simply his way—he's like that with almost everyone, isn't he? Just having a laugh."

"I guess . . ."

"He's a normal red-blooded male, that's all." Ivy paused, twisted her hair. "He's only got eyes for you. When I see the way he looks at you—it's *completely* different."

Orianna appeared relieved.

So, the knife. "She's ever so pretty, isn't she?"

"Mm."

"Anyway." Ivy altered her tone. "It's fun working with her. Reminds me of what we used to be like. Full of enthusiasm and impractical ideas. We have such a giggle."

Orianna smiled wanly. "I'm glad."

No, Orianna convinced herself, if Ivy says there's nothing in it, there isn't. Dan's like that with everyone. She shifted her focus onto the positive—at least Ivy and Cassie seemed to be getting along well.

See, she thought, we do have similar taste in people, and whatever others say, Ivy's much more generous spirited than she's given credit for.

Orianna recalled the copy she'd read minutes ago. There was no doubt Ivy was a first-class writer; fast, shrewd, and to the point. So what if she occasionally takes a long lunch? Ivy would never miss a deadline. And if she's a bit abrasive every so often, does it matter that much? She's been perfectly OK with me recently, and now she's going out of her way to befriend Cassie too, which is really sweet of her. And to think I was worried I should have let Ivy meet her sooner.

As for Dan, Orianna couldn't process that right now. She turned back to her computer, focusing on the figures she'd been e-mailed, and bit her lip, perplexed.

Call me stupid, she thought, but shouldn't our biggest overheads be salaries, office rental, print, and production? Even taking these outgoings into consideration, it seemed running an agency was bewilderingly costly. Orianna was anxious that if things didn't look up soon, there would have to be layoffs, and she was eager to impress those members of the board who'd been cynical about her appointment—namely Russell—so she had been working harder than ever to bring in new business. Lately she'd assigned several teams to work on each project simultaneously—something Neil had never done. This had inspired some of the lazier creatives to make more effort and encouraged others who were set in their ways to look at briefs afresh. The sense of competition had increased the tempo of the department and raised standards. It also allowed her to choose the best work to present at pitches, and as a result Green had recently won two major new accounts, and several existing clients had put extra business their way.

Yet in spite of the additional income coming into the agency, there seemed an awful lot being paid out. Math had never been Orianna's strong point; perhaps she'd gotten something wrong. She sighed. Office politics, sorting figures, whipping people into shape who'd previously been her peers—none of these did she enjoy.

No, what Orianna liked about advertising was it gave her the chance to produce exquisite creative work and benefit from having decent budgets to play with. She genuinely believed in the goodness of her fellow human beings and was convinced that advertising was about communicating choice. When she and Ivy had been together as a team, they'd chatted about their different perspectives, even argued, but the result was they'd often taken the middle ground. Certainly Orianna had tempered Ivy's misanthropy, while Ivy had helped Orianna sharpen her act. Yet now that they were separated the gulf between them was widening, and Orianna the optimist was flying high.

21. Can anything be made of this?

That lunchtime Dan had an appointment with Rob. He got changed, and, as was customary, met Rob on the stretch mats.

"Can we start with some sit-ups?" he asked, convinced a succession of boozy nights that had started with his birthday meant his paunch was returning. Moreover, he was hoping to lure Orianna on vacation—he was concerned she was working too hard—and he might soon have to display his torso in public.

"Of course," nodded Rob. They lay down alongside one another. Rob hoisted his legs in the air and folded his arms above his head. Dan followed suit. "And one . . . and up . . . and back . . . and down . . ." This was one of the toughest abdominal exercises, and after a hundred crunches, even Rob appeared short of breath. "Enough?"

"No. Let's do the same again."

"OK."

Next they lifted weights (Dan upped the level), rowed (Dan increased the resistance), and ran (well, sprinted) four miles. By the end of his session, Dan felt absolved by the most rigorous workout he'd done in weeks.

He'd made the effort to get into work early today so he could spend extra time at the gym over lunch.

Now's a good moment to see if I am out of shape, he thought, so asked, "Will you do me a favor and take my measurements quickly? I'll have to get back to the office shortly, but it's been a few months since we last did them."

"Sure. Come into the staff room."

Dan's weight was his Achilles' heel, and though he knew it was OTT, he was so concerned he'd piled on the pounds that he took off his sweatshirt, trainers, and watch, hoping the scales would be kinder.

"Hop on," said Rob. Dan obeyed. "One hundred ninety pounds. Not bad—you've only put on a bit."

"How much?"

"Two pounds."

Dan was relieved—he'd anticipated worse.

"So how are things between Orianna and Ivy these days?" asked Rob. "Ivy's appeared in pretty good spirits when I've seen her."

"They seem much better, actually," said Dan. Rob's remark only verified what Orianna had told him: that lately Ivy had been extraordinarily genial.

"Right, now your flexibility. Sit down here." While Dan was sitting on the floor trying hard to reach his toes, Rob continued, his voice casual, "And how about between the two of you?"

Dan exhaled. "Me and Ivy?"

Rob noted how far Dan could stretch. "No, no. You and *Orianna*. Is it going well?"

Dan paused for a second. From what I gather, Rob hasn't had a partner in a while, he thought. It would be tactless to bang on about how happy we are.

Something in Rob's tone suggested this question wasn't as disinterested as it appeared. Dan wasn't presumptuous—far from it—but he noticed that Rob still seemed nervous around him. So he said, "Um, it's going fine, thanks," hoping Rob would gather this was all he was willing to impart. There was a silence while Rob measured around his upper arm, his chest, his waist and wrote down all the figures. It was all going swimmingly—Rob said Dan hadn't altered shape that much—until Rob bent down to measure his inner thigh.

"Hee hee." Dan jumped. "Stop! I'm ticklish!"

"Sorry." Rob sprang back and whisked away the tape. There was no mistaking it; he was blushing. "Er . . . do you want to do this bit your-self?"

"Please," said Dan. That seemed a wise idea. Yet as he reached to take the tape measure, something couldn't help but catch his eye. Good grief, he thought. Rob's got an erection!

To: Chloë Appleton
From: Rob Rowland
Date: Monday, September 2, 8:52 p.m.
Subj: How embarrassing is this?!

OMG! Remember I told you that Dan may be bisexual? Well, you know me, and of course it's only got my imagination working overtime. I will confess I had the *hottest* dream about him last night so when he came for his appointment today I found it a bit hard to concentrate, particularly as now I know he might actually be "up" for something (as the actress . . . 'n all that).

So then, this lunchtime, in the gym, Dan is just looking soo gorgeous—in a white T-shirt and these satiny shorts, he's got a body to die for—and as we were doing sit-ups, I happened to notice that he has the most enormous package. I swear, Chloë, it had to be seen to be believed.

Anyway, I carry on, like the true professional I am—we lift weights, do some rowing, go running—and then, at the end of the session, when he would normally have to *rush* back to the office in a frightful hurry (we'd already been working out for a good hour) he says, "Will you take my measurements?" Can you imagine? It was all I could do to stop myself from saying, "Looks like eight inches to me!" And so we go into the staff room for me to weigh him—which is private as you know—and my God, he takes off first his trainers—I appreciate lots of people do that, though mainly women I must say, so it's strange for a guy to do it—then his socks and finally his T-shirt!!!! And he's standing there in front of me, virtually stark naked, with that incredible chest, and that gorgeous face, and, I mean, what is a boy to do? It was all I could do to keep from fainting.

And I'm thinking, this is most unusual, a guy stripping off, perhaps it means he truly is gay, maybe he wants me as much as I do him. He *insists* I take all his measurements, his upper arms (ooh), his chest (aah), his waist (yum), and finally . . . his inner thigh.

As I'm doing this I think to myself, hey Rob, maybe the best way to get him to open up to you is to ask him a few leading questions, so I inquire about Orianna, and he's sooo evasive, he just says it's fine, which I think is odd, considering, and changes the subject.

At his point I get the tape measure and wrap it around his thigh—it's all taut and a little sweaty from exercise—and I tell you, my face is almost pressed against his shorts and I swear his package is just *unbelievable* that close up, and I can't stop myself feeling turned on, and all of a sudden, it's as if he feels this huge sexual vibe too, and he jumps about fifty feet in the air and he says he can't cope because he's ticklish!

Meanwhile I've got a big hard-on by now, and I'm positive
he sees, and clearly he doesn't know what to do, so he just
grabs his T-shirt and trainers and says he'll see me next
week and runs out of the staff room.

I AM MORTIFIED!

But I do reckon he *could* be a closet job, really. Consider all
this evidence. Feedback please—pronto!!

Rob
xxx

22. Is't lost? Is't gone?

Orianna and Dan were snuggled up under a blanket on the sofa. Orianna had her legs slung over Dan's; Dan was enjoying a sci-fi film full of laser missiles and planetary battles. It was one of the things he liked about his girlfriend—she didn't pester him to watch profound movies. Meanwhile Orianna was reading a romantic novel; from the corseted bosom on the cover, Dan guessed she was deep in the nineteenth century. She had her book in one hand, in the other she held Dan's and was stroking his fingers absentmindedly when a particularly loud intergalactic explosion forced her to lift her eyes from the page.

"Where's your watch?" she asked suddenly.

Dan removed his hand, and checked his wrist. He pushed up his shirtsleeve just to be sure. Oh Lord, she was right. Had the buckle come undone? When? Where?

He cast his mind back. Taking a long lunch meant he'd been more frantic than usual that afternoon. He'd been so busy typing up purchase orders he'd barely looked up from his PC. When at his computer he used the onscreen clock—this was the first time he'd noticed the watch was gone. It could have been missing for hours.

"Shit."

"You've lost it!"

"No, no, I haven't," said Dan hurriedly.

"Where is it then?" Her voice rose. She put down her book, pulled her feet from his lap, and sat up.

Dan racked his brain. It could be at work, on the train, anywhere. Surely he'd have noticed if it had slipped from his wrist? Heard it fall? The buckle seemed secure. Though compared to his old Swatch, it was slim enough to slide under his shirt cuff.

"Er . . ." He glanced at her.

"Oh, *Dan*!" Her eyes filled with tears.

You idiot, he said to himself. You stupid, clumsy oaf. She'll never forgive you.

"I've only just bought it for you!"

He bit his nails, distress mounting.

"Think," she ordered. "What have you done today?"

Desperately he retraced his movements again. Perhaps he hadn't even put it on? Maybe he'd left it on the bedside table.

He got up, hurried into Orianna's bedroom—but the table was bare. He sat on the edge of the bed, thoughts hurtling. He'd had it that morning, surely. An illustrator had come in with her portfolio—hadn't he checked his watch when she'd gone? He'd been worried he'd be late for Rob . . . Ah! That was it. He returned to the living room.

"I must have left it at the gym."

"The gym?! *Where* in the gym?"

"I'm not certain . . . In the changing room, probably."

"But someone could have nicked it! Oh, *Dan*!" Tears began to fall.

"I'm sure they wouldn't," said Dan, though he wasn't sure at all. The gym had hundreds of members. No doubt most were honest, but it only took one . . .

"Call them."

Dan consulted his wrist. Doh! He checked the LCD on the DVD player. It was 10:05 p.m.

"They'll be closed." He winced.

"Oh no!"

"I'm sorry."

"It's OK." Orianna sniffed. "Are you *sure* you left it in the changing room? Would you have put it down on one of the benches? Wouldn't you have put it in your locker?" Her voice was hopeful, her eyes wide, expectant.

Dan thought long and hard. "Mm . . . I tend to keep it on when I'm exercising, because it's waterproof." He scratched his head ferociously, maybe it would help clarify. Then all at once he remembered. "Maybe . . ."

"Yes?" Orianna sat forward.

In an instant, Dan envisaged Rob's erection, his own hurried exit. He could feel himself flush at the memory, but was too embarrassed to tell Orianna. How on earth could he confess he was so conscious of his weight he'd taken his *watch* off? How ridiculously vain was that? If he explained about Rob and the erection, she might just think he'd provoked Rob in some way. She'd muttered stuff about him fancying men before. Though he found this a bit odd, Dan didn't wish to stir trouble—he got along with Rob very well; he was almost a friend. So . . .

"Oh nothing," he muttered, cheeks burning.

"What do you mean, *nothing*?"

"I think I remember where I left it."

"Where?"

"Um, er . . . In the staff room."

"In the *staff* room?"

"Yeah."

"Why?"

"I took it off. I'll call in the morning, first thing."

"Well, at least that means no one will nick it." She sat back, relieved, then peered at him more closely. "Why have you gone all red?"

———

The next morning Rob was heading to the changing room when Jane, the receptionist, waylaid him.

"Hey, Rob! Hang on a minute."

He stopped in his tracks.

"This was found in the staff room last night. Is it yours?" She held out what appeared to be an item of jewelry.

He went over. In her palm was a rather elegant man's watch, with a white face and a purple leather strap.

He frowned. He was sure he recognized it. He took the watch from her, examining the logo. *Paul Smith.* He'd seen someone wearing it but couldn't recall who.

"Apparently it was by the weighing scales."

That was it. *Dan.* He'd been in the staff room and had removed some of his clothes to be weighed. Rob remembered noticing he'd taken off his watch, thought it odd at the time. And—Rob's toes curled at the memory—Dan had left in an awful hurry.

"Yeah, it belongs to a client of mine," he said. "He's not due in till next week so I'll give him a call." Then he had a better idea—his next client could pass it on. He plucked the watch from Jane's palm. "Not to worry, I'll take it to give to him."

At 7:58 a.m., Ivy arrived. No time for niceties with the receptionist—she flew into the changing room, slung the bag containing her work clothes and toiletries into a locker, and turned the key. She attached the safety pin to her sports top, pulled her hair up into a high ponytail, checked herself in the mirror—yes, she looked better than most of the other girls scrambling into or out of their clothes around her—and bounded out of the room.

"Ah, Rob!" He was by the stretch mats waiting, dressed in his uniform of trainers, navy tracksuit bottoms, and a white vest.

"Ivy, hi."

Mwah. Mwah. "So, what today?"

"Actually, before I forget, I wonder if you could do me a favor?"

Ivy never agreed to favors before finding out what they were. "What?"

"Are you going to see Dan today?"

"I expect so. Why?"

Rob reached into his trouser pocket. "He left this." Ivy recognized it at once as the watch Orianna had given him for his birthday. "Oh?"

"I'm not seeing him till next week, so I wondered if you'd return it."

"Sure." Ivy didn't hesitate. "I'll wear it, that's simplest." She pulled it around her slender wrist.

"Great."

Careless of Dan, thought Ivy. He should take more care of his possessions. "He left it in the changing room I suppose?"

"In the staff room."

How odd, Ivy reflected. "What was he doing taking it off there?"

"I gave him a fitness assessment. So I weighed him and stuff."

Ivy looked at him sideways, the same persuasive gesture she'd used on Cassie. "Yeeess . . . ?" To her delight, Rob blushed. God, it was so easy to make some people color up! She had a true gift for it. "What on earth would make Dan take off his watch to have a *fitness* assessment?"

"Don't ask me." Rob shrugged.

"Are you sure that was the only reason?" Ivy gave him a nudge. Goodness, she thought. Did I really hit on something with my suggestions of Dan's bisexuality after all? What fun!

"Quite sure." Then he gushed, "Though it was weird. He took all his clothes off for me to weigh him!"

"*All* his clothes?"

"Well, he kept on his shorts, but otherwise, yeah."

"*No!*" Ivy clapped her hands. "How scandalous!"

"Do you think?"

"Of course. He must have been coming on to you, I reckon."

"Honestly?"

She could detect hope in his voice. "Take it from me."

"I'm not so sure . . ."

Nor was Ivy, in truth. She liked to weigh herself when she came out of the shower—it gave a more accurate reading—but this wasn't about honesty. "It seems a mite suspicious."

"Mm."

"Who asked for the assessment?"

"He did."

"He must have known that would mean you two got to be alone."

"I suppose . . ."

"I'll give it to him later." She coaxed one last time, "But, really, nothing happened?"

Rob blushed some more. How quaint, thought Ivy, he has a major crush. "No."

"Promise?"

"Promise."

"I believe you," said Ivy. "But thousands wouldn't."

Dan phoned the gym the moment he got out of Tottenham Court Road station. Orianna had gone ahead to pick up a coffee.

It seemed to take ages for anyone to answer and his heart was thumping by the time a girl picked up the phone.

"Who am I speaking to?" he asked.

"Jane."

"Ah, Jane." He always said hi to her. She seemed efficient, good. "It's Dan Cohen. I wondered, has a watch been handed in at all?"

"What's it like?"

"It's a Paul Smith one."

"With a purple strap?"

"Yes."

"One of the instructors found it in the staff room last night."

"Oh, thank God!" Dan could feel his heart slow in relief. "Can I come and collect it?"

"Actually, I've already given it to Rob."

Dan stopped outside Green's offices. "Ah."

"He said he'd give it to you."

"But I'm not seeing him till next week." Oh help, he thought, heart-beat quickening again. Maybe Rob's going to use it as a ruse to meet up.

"I'm sure he'll call you. Hang on a sec, I'll check his appointments . . ." There was a pause. "He's booked up all morning, but if I catch him, I'll tell him you called."

"Thanks."

"Do you want his mobile number? I doubt he'll answer when he's training but you could leave him a message."

"I've got it," said Dan, and called Rob straight away. As he stood waiting for Rob to pick up, several colleagues passed him on the steps to the office. I'd better hurry, he thought. Rob's voice mail clicked on—that was a blessing—he could avoid a conversation. He was about to begin speaking, when Earl nudged him to say hello. Thrown, he blurted his message, "Er, Rob, hi mate, it's Dan here. Give me a call, please?" Then he leaped up the stairs into work, happy that his watch was in safe hands.

23. I have a thing for you

When Ivy arrived at Green, Cassie was not around, but evidently she was already in the agency; her stuff lay strewn on the sofa by their desks.

Perhaps she's nipped to the ladies' room, thought Ivy. She was poised to get on with her copy, when she did a double take.

A zip-up rectangle of shiny red leather, with a pert little handle, like a schoolgirl's lunch box lay open on the cushions, its jaws wide, hungry: a patent invitation.

Ivy stood on tiptoe and checked left, right, over the partition walls.

Then she pushed up the sleeve of her jumper, unbuckled Dan's watch from her wrist, and swiftly dropped it into Cassie's handbag, between her mobile and purse. She stood back and examined her handiwork. No; not obvious enough. She glanced about again and pulled the strap out a little, so it protruded from the top of the bag. The bright red leather offset the purple strap brilliantly.

Now what?

Few thought faster than Ivy when opportunity called.

First, she located Cassie. Sure enough, she found her in the loo, combing her hair. Little surprise; Cassie spent a lot of time grooming since she'd started seeing Leon—she couldn't go half an hour without checking her appearance.

"Ah, Cassie, there you are." Ivy stepped alongside her in front of the mirror.

"Ivy, hi. How are you?"

"I'm OK, thanks, I suppose . . ." She halted, adopted a pained expression, and sighed. "Though, I wonder if you could do me a favor?"

"Sure," said Cassie.

How amenable she is, Ivy observed, agreeing to a request without knowing its nature. "Only I've got *terrible* period pains."

"You poor thing."

Ivy clutched her abdomen. "I'll live." She leaned against the sink, as if she could scarcely keep herself upright. "It's one of those things," she said bravely. "Some months are worse than others. If I didn't have to get those damn headlines done, I'd have come in later . . ." Menstruation was such a handy excuse. Even in this day and age, most people were too embarrassed to question symptoms.

Cassie peered at her. "You don't look great."

Cheeky cow! "I don't feel great."

"You're *ever* so pale."

"I was wondering . . ."

"Did you want me to get you something?"

"Ooh, yes, if you don't mind."

"Hang on—I might have some aspirin in my bag."

Blast—that wouldn't do at all. "Oh no," Ivy said rapidly. "Not painkillers. I avoid drugs whenever possible—they're not good for you." She calculated at the speed of light. "I was hoping you might get me some Rescue Remedy. It's much more natural—made from flowers—I swear by it." Did she hell. She wasn't even sure what it was for, though she seemed to remember Ursula saying it helped her calm down.

"Right." But Cassie appeared worried. "Where can I buy that?"

"I think they have it at the pharmacy on Broadwick Street," said Ivy.

"Not at Boots?"

Boots was nearer. "No, I'm pretty sure they don't."

"Oh."

"The shop's called Zest." Ivy flinched in pain. "It's on the corner, with a bright front. You'll find the herbal remedies at the back."

"I haven't got any money . . ."

"I do." Ivy let go of her stomach to hand Cassie the fiver she'd been clutching. "That should be plenty."

"OK." Cassie took the bill and put away her comb. "I'll just get my jacket."

"No!" Ivy snapped, and hastily added, "I wouldn't bother—it makes it obvious you're going out of the office."

"I suppose." Cassie didn't think to argue that getting medicine for a colleague might qualify as a good reason. "All right then, I'll see you in a minute."

More like ten, thought Ivy, and returned to her desk.

Orianna was about to tuck into a breakfast muffin when she had a call on her internal line. Her swish new phone declared who was calling.

"Ivy, hi."

"Am I interrupting? It won't take a sec."

"What is it?"

Ivy sighed. "It's just I'm having some problems with the headlines for those travel offers, Orianna, and I wondered if you could spare me a moment of your wonderful brain—it's the kind of thing you're so fantastic at."

Orianna was surprised, yet flattered—it wasn't often Ivy asked for help. "Sure, do you want to come by?"

"Can you come to me? Cassie's nipped out, but they're all up on my screen and the printer's jammed."

Funny, thought Orianna, the printer looks to be working from here—she could see Leon waiting for his run-outs to emerge as they spoke.

Ivy added, "It's some problem with my machine. The guys from tech support are coming to fix it but I need to e-mail these off as soon as possible."

"Ah, right." Orianna got to her feet and headed over.

Ivy was sitting at her desk. "Hi." She smiled.

"Hi."

Orianna was about to plop herself down on her old chair at Cassie's desk when Ivy said, "Oh, Cassie will be back in a tick, but feel free to clear a space on the sofa."

Orianna duly turned to take a seat. But just as she was lifting Cassie's jacket to make room, something caught her eye.

She looked at it more closely, heart thumping.

There was a watch, very like Dan's, protruding from a handbag. The bag wasn't Ivy's—Orianna recognized the large Louis Vuitton purse on the floor as the one Ivy always took to the gym—so it must belong to Cassie.

She picked up the watch, examined it. She scrutinized the face. *Paul Smith*, jeered the logo. She started to tremble. She had her back to Ivy, but she could feel her cheeks burning up, her hands going clammy. She could tell Ivy was watching her, eyes boring into her.

Sure enough: "Something the matter?"

"Nothing," said Orianna quickly. She slipped the watch into Cassie's bag again—and sat down on the sofa, struggling to remain calm.

"Are you sure?"

"Yes."

"Oh, well." Ivy was chirpy. "These are the lines I was thinking of. What d'you reckon? They're for holiday discounts. There's this one: 'One hundred percent Ireland for ten percent less.' And this one: 'Going Dutch—Holland at half price.' Or how about, 'A top-dollar US trip for next to nothing'?" She read out several more, but Orianna couldn't think straight, let alone listen.

It's not as if Paul Smith is a common make of watch, she thought. There can't possibly be two of the same in such a small agency. But what on earth is Dan's watch doing in Cassie's handbag? Cassie doesn't go to the gym.

Orianna could make no sense of it at all.

With a lurch, she remembered that the night before, when she'd asked Dan about the watch, he'd gone scarlet. Why had he blushed like that? Was he guilty? What was he hiding? Had he recollected where he must have left it, and concocted some cock-and-bull story, knowing it was with Cassie? It seemed ludicrous, but why else would it be here, in her bag?

She recalled Ivy saying Dan had been hanging around Cassie's desk a lot; and thought how similar Cassie was to Lara, physically. Dan had failed to tell her the exact truth about the Image Focus Christmas party, which meant he was quite capable of deception when it was called for . . . Then there was his reputation before he met her, the gossip about G-A-Y and his friendship with Rob . . .

That Orianna had pushed these anxieties aside for weeks meant they all came rushing in at once. What other explanation would there possibly be for Dan taking his watch off? He must have undressed because he'd been *having sex* with Cassie.

Suddenly, Orianna was overcome by violent nausea. She felt giddy and hot; her vision clouded by wavering bright orange lights, and the world seemed weirdly disconnected, as if she were in a bubble. She struggled to get up, but as she did so, the blood rushed from her head; she felt even more peculiar, her feet slipped from under her, her knees buckled . . .

Ivy leaped to break Orianna's fall. She laid her on the floor, and while she was out cold, extracted the watch from Cassie's bag and slipped it in her own desk drawer. Then, still moving fast, she pulled a copy of *Grazia* from the bookshelf and knelt down. She was fanning Orianna when Cassie returned moments later.

"What's happened?"

"Orianna's fainted."

"Fainted!"

"Yes."

"Why?"

"I'm not sure what brought it on."

"Should I get someone?" Cassie was most concerned, even panicked.

"No, no." Tenderly Ivy lifted Orianna's head onto her knee. "She'll be fine, honestly. I've seen this happen to her before."

"Gosh, really?"

Ivy knew it was hard to imagine someone as robustly built as Orianna frequently fainting, but if anyone could convince Cassie, she could. "I bet she hasn't eaten any breakfast." Orianna skip a meal? A likely story.

"You should rub her temples."

"Don't tell me what to do!" barked Ivy.

Cassie looked mortified. "I was only trying to help. Are you feeling better now yourself?"

"Sorry," said Ivy, more gently, stroking Orianna's hair. "I'm fine. I worry, that's all. Orianna has probably been overdoing it again." She sensed her patient beginning to stir. Orianna's eyelids fluttered, one of her hands twitched. Ivy glanced up at Cassie. "I reckon it would be a good idea if you just left us a moment, would you? She'll be OK in a minute, I'm sure, but she might not want you to see her like this."

As Cassie turned to leave, Ivy noticed the paper bag from the pharmacy clenched in her palm.

"Oh! Cass? Before you go—give me that please?"

"Er, of course, yeah." Cassie handed it to her.

"I think Orianna could do with some Rescue Remedy, don't you?"

24. Work on, my medicine, work!

Orianna felt something cool and glassy being slipped between her lips and an alcohol-flavored liquid on her tongue.

"Eh?" Gradually her eyes focused: she appeared to be staring straight into Ivy's face, and, very strangely, above Ivy were the white polystyrene tiles of the ceiling. Orianna struggled to get her bearings. Ivy seemed to be holding a tiny pipette.

"Don't worry. This is Rescue Remedy."

Orianna sensed Ivy's fingers running softly through her hair. Her touch was comforting, but what was the ceiling doing up there? She checked to her left—green partition wall. And right—mint-colored sofa. So, she was on the floor by her old desk . . . Why? She was dreadfully nauseous . . .

All at once she remembered. The sofa—the watch—Dan—Cassie . . . The blood rushed to her head. She tried to prop herself on her elbows to see the evidence again.

As she jerked up, Ivy gently restrained her. "Hey, hey!"

She managed to establish—yes, there was the bag, the vile red handbag, but—Orianna sat up—where was the watch? It had vanished! She shook her head to clear her vision. She was on a level with the sofa, the bag was inches away, yet the watch had completely disappeared. Another wave of sickness washed over her. Surely it had been there seconds before? She must be going mad. Or hallucinating.

"Sweetheart, take it easy," said Ivy. "You fainted."

"Did I?"

"Yes, so don't rush. Here." Ivy swept aside Cassie's jacket to clear space on the sofa and patted the cushion. "Head between your knees."

I've never fainted in my life, thought Orianna. It was Dan's watch that did it. She checked the handbag again. From here she could see right inside. There was Cassie's mobile, change purse . . . The watch was gone, no doubt about it. Unless it had slipped into the depths, and she could hardly start rummaging inside it in front of Ivy.

"What do you think brought that on?" Ivy sounded anxious.

"I don't know." Orianna was too shocked and bewildered to admit what she'd seen. If the watch had been there, the implications were so awful she needed to think them through. And if she'd imagined it, she was clearly going crazy, which was hardly consoling.

Presently, Dan came hurrying to her side. He lifted up Cassie's bag, dumped it on the floor, and sat down beside her. "What's up?" He seemed even more anxious than Ivy.

"She fainted."

"Yes, Cassie told me."

Cassie told Dan? She must have rushed straight to him. Orianna felt sick again.

"Yeah, she's very worried."

I bet she is! thought Orianna.

Dan brushed aside Orianna's fringe, looked into her eyes. "Honey, I'm worried too. This isn't like you at all."

She searched his face for a clue his concern was genuine. It seemed to be, but who could tell when she couldn't trust her own eyes?

"You've been overdoing it," said Dan. "I've been trying to say this for weeks."

"Me? Overdoing it?" The gall—turning his indiscretions into her fault!

"Yes. I want you to stop working so hard."

"No!"

"Maybe take some time off—have a vacation."

And give him the chance to spend time with Cassie? "*No!*"

"I just care about you——"

Yeah, me and a million others. Orianna winced. She'd had enough of being made to seem a fool; the way Ivy and Dan were treating her only exacerbated her anger. She would look after herself. "I'm fine. Honestly. See?" She struggled to her feet.

"Well, I think you should eat," advised Ivy. "Have you had anything yet today?"

"Er . . . I'd been going to——"

"I'll run out." Ivy picked up her purse. "Do you fancy a panettone? That should raise your blood sugar." And before Orianna could explain she had a muffin back at her desk, Ivy was gone.

"Honey——" As Orianna also made to leave, Dan reached to catch her hand.

She snatched it away. "What?!"

"We need to talk——"

"Too right we do. Though I don't think now's the moment, do you?" And, still shaky, she ran back to her office and slammed the door.

Tap tap. Ivy poked her head around Orianna's door. Orianna was sitting at her desk but not working; instead her eyes were focused on the space in front of her, features distorted into a painful frown.

"Here." Ivy went over and handed her the paper bag. "This should help."

"Thanks." Orianna opened it and pulled out the panettone. Ivy was surprised she didn't dig in to it at once, as was her normal custom. Instead she put the bag down, placed the panettone on top, and stared at it.

"You OK?"

"Mm. Leave me a bit, will you?" She seemed lost in thought.

"Yeah, sure." Ivy hesitated, and was about to leave, then added, "I don't want to pry or anything, O, but—"

"What?"

"It's not about Dan, is it?"

"Why?"

"Oh, I'm not sure." Ivy shrugged. "I got a vibe things weren't that great between you. And now you seem kind of upset with him. So I wondered—"

"I don't want to talk about it!" Orianna kicked the hard drive of her computer under the desk.

She must be very distressed to risk damaging it and losing her work, thought Ivy, feeling a mixture of guilt and satisfaction. "No, OK."

"I just need to work out what I think, first."

"Sure." Ivy nodded. "You know where I am when you want me."

Orianna smiled wanly. "Cheers. And thanks for looking after me just now." She paused. "You're a good friend, Ivy."

Ivy nodded. "It's no trouble. Isn't that what friends are for?" Tactfully, she retreated from the room.

Bugger guilt, she thought, back at her own desk. She opened up her drawer with an efficient *swoosh,* picked up the watch, and headed to production.

Dan was leaning over Esme's screen. Ivy swiftly detected they were sorting a schedule of the departmental workload. "Dan, hi."

He looked up. "Ivy, hello. Did you get Orianna something to eat?"

"Yes."

"Good. I'm ever so worried about her."

"Me too."

"But she doesn't seem to want to talk to me about it."

"No. I wouldn't take it personally, Dan—you know Orianna—she's such a workaholic. I bet she thinks you'll tell her to go easy on herself, but she doesn't want to hear that."

Dan scratched his head, clearly agitated. This was going better than

Ivy would have dreamed possible. "I don't know what to do with her sometimes," he said. "I wish she'd slow down. She might make herself seriously ill."

Ivy bit her lip to mirror his concern and exhaled. "Take it from me, we've been friends for years. Sometimes Orianna won't listen to reason."

"Esme and I were seeing if we might cut her workload a bit, though I'd prefer her to go home."

"She won't do that."

"No, I realize. I thought we might shift stuff around, so she's not doing as much."

"Good idea." Ivy switched tack. "Anyway, with all the hooha, I forgot to say earlier, Rob gave me this." She held up the watch.

"Oh! Great!" Dan reached for it eagerly.

"I had a session with him this morning."

"Of course." He buckled the strap around his wrist.

"He said you'd left it in the staff room."

"Yeah."

"I won't ask why you took it off."

"I had a fitness assessment."

"I see." Ivy was conscious that Esme, who'd not said a word, was all ears.

"And, er, he weighed me."

Esme interrupted. "You took your watch off to be *weighed*?"

Dan blushed.

Fantastic, thought Ivy.

"Um . . . yeah."

"Right." Ivy laughed. "Apparently that's not the only thing he took off." She raised an eyebrow.

"Really?" Esme was on the edge of her chair. "Dan, what else?"

"My trainers," admitted Dan.

"And?" prompted Ivy.

"My T-shirt."

"Your *T-shirt*?" squealed Esme, incredulous.

Dan stammered, "I wanted to get an accurate measure of my weight." He was evidently mortified.

"Fair enough," said Ivy, all understanding. "I usually weigh myself with nothing on too. You ought to be careful though, my boy."

"Why?"

"It's hard for Rob, when you undress like that."

"Who's Rob?" asked Esme.

"Our fitness instructor," explained Ivy. "And when I say hard, I mean *hard* . . ."

Dan went crimson.

"You've made him blush!" shrieked Esme, delighted to see her boss embarrassed.

Ivy continued innocently, "Rob really fancies you, Dan."

"Do you think?" asked Dan.

"Do I *think*? Sweetheart, I *know*."

Not much later Dan tapped on Orianna's door.

"Yes?"

He went in. Orianna was at her desk; it seemed she'd had a bite of the panettone, but only a small one. She was scowling, glaring into space.

"Honey—"

"Don't 'honey' me!"

He knew she didn't like to be seen as professionally lacking in any way; still, he couldn't grasp why being encouraged to let up should enrage her so. "I appreciate you don't want to talk now. It'll keep till later."

"Too right it will."

"But please take a look at this. I've shifted work around to give you a bit of a breather."

He leaned across the desk to hand her the revised schedule, and as Orianna reached out to take it, she cast her eyes downward to avoid his gaze. Then she said, "I see you got it back." Her voice was odd, icy.

"What?"

"Your watch."

"Oh, er, yeah. Ivy gave it to me."

"*Ivy?*"

"Yes. Just now."

She shook her head. "Don't lie to me, Dan."

He was baffled. "I'm not lying! She brought it to me. Rob gave it to her earlier."

"I don't think so." She glared at him, her expression cold and hard.

"What are you talking about?"

"Cassie sneaked it to you, didn't she? I'm impressed—quick-thinking little cow."

"Eh?"

"When I collapsed she must have come and given it to you."

"I don't know what you mean. She's worried about you."

"Charming. Bloody charming. She's worried about me, eh? A likely story."

"Orianna—" He moved to touch her.

She recoiled sharply. "Don't come near me!"

"This fainting has affected you more—"

"Oh, for fuck's sake! Do you think I'm stupid?"

"I'm trying to help. Cassie—"

"Shut up about Cassie, will you?"

Dan gulped, at a loss. *I know she's sensitive,* he thought, *but she's talking in riddles—this conversation is absurd. She's being paranoid.*

"Leave that here." Orianna slammed the desk to indicate he should put down the schedule. He did as he was told. "Now, go."

"Go?" He was aware he sounded dumb and somehow was making things worse, but he couldn't make her out. Normally he knew how to handle her—he prided himself on his diplomacy—yet everything he said seemed to be wrong.

Surely suggesting someone take it easy after collapsing isn't a crime, he thought. *And what does she mean,* Cassie *gave me the watch?*

He hovered for a second, desperate to smooth things over. But Orianna just glared at him, her expression glacial, until finally she snapped, "Christ, Dan, *piss* off, will you?"

25. Farewell the tranquil mind! Farewell content!

Left alone, Orianna took another bite of panettone; she could only lose her appetite for so long — her instinct was to comfort eat if miserable. She picked up the revised schedule.

When Neil had been in charge he'd chosen not to have his workload included in the listing, reasoning it was his role to oversee the other art directors and copywriters and be "involved in everything." But Ivy often griped that this hid the fact he frequently did very little creatively at all, and Orianna acknowledged this was the common perception of Neil within the department. Thus upon her promotion she'd asked Dan, whose responsibility it was to sort work flow, to allocate specific briefs to her and include them in the schedule. "I still need to be involved in coming up with ideas," she'd said. "Getting sucked into a purely administrative role would be dreadfully dull. And I want my colleagues to see I'm pulling my weight."

This week Green was particularly busy—the agency was pitching for two new pieces of business. Orianna had been due to work on one— for another Bellings Scott brand—and had requested she be teamed with Ivy. They were due to start the moment the brief was ready. She was also due at a shoot, and later in the week had been marked with a day out of the office for a presentation. So as always she had a lot going on, but at least the work would be challenging. Pitches were always fun, and the shoot involved working with a talented photographer Orianna had been hankering to commission for ages.

So when she first examined the revised schedule and noticed the pitch and the shoot had both been struck from beneath her name, she was a little disappointed. Nevertheless, her predominant reaction was relief. She desperately needed some headspace to think through what to do about Dan.

Orianna was preparing to concede it wasn't *that* bad of an idea to take on a bit less after all, when she decided to check who'd been allocated her work instead. She ran her finger down the schedule, found both projects, then traced across to see whose name they were under.

Cassie.

She went hot and cold; again had to steady herself.

If it's not bad enough they're having an affair, she thought, now Dan's giving Cassie my prized jobs! I can't believe he's that brazen. If the evidence wasn't right in front of me, I wouldn't have thought it possible. No; it's more than brazen—it's *callous.* If he can be so callous about that, who knows where he'll stop?

Try as she might to focus elsewhere, as she sat mulling over the schedule, she couldn't shake images of Dan and Cassie in bed together. He'd undress Cassie with the same relish he had her . . . With a shiver, Orianna recalled how he'd admired her Dolce & Gabbana skirt, but said he liked her naked best of all. She thought of Cassie—her neat, petite figure, naked; her bleached-blond hair disheveled by lovemaking, and recoiled. There was no doubt that Cassie was every inch the male fantasy—even more so than Lara—and it made Orianna feel horribly, hugely insecure.

I'm really fat in comparison—"cuddly" Dan calls me, and he's not the first. I bet Cassie's so confident that she merrily removes Dan's clothes herself . . .

She pictured Cassie playfully unbuttoning his shirt, trying to take it off, then realizing that the cuffs were still done up around the wrist and having to undo his watch to remove it . . .

Was that what happened—he'd left his watch at her place because they'd been so keen to get naked? Orianna had made love to Dan often enough, not to mention read a good many steamy novels, to know this was all too possible, and here was the revised schedule, compounding the evidence.

She had to escape from the office a moment, clear her thoughts. She checked the time—not yet her lunch hour.

To hell with it, she decided. I'm the boss, I've just fainted.

So she picked up her bag and headed for the elevator.

Once outside, she crossed the road and went into the public gardens in the center of Soho Square. Although it was only early September, the day was chilly, so the small park, normally a favorite with sightseers and shoppers, was relatively empty. Orianna found a free bench and sat down.

How could everything change so fast? Until that morning she'd believed Dan might well be The One.

She struggled to assimilate. I've had concerns, she thought. I was worried he's been flirting with Cassie, and that he'd fibbed about Lara, and there were those weird rumors of his bisexuality. But Dan's been so good to me; he's so kind and supportive, and we get along extremely well, I couldn't see how they were true. I believed he fancied me rotten—he always said he did—and I fancy him too, or I did . . . She shuddered again, picturing Cassie. Christ, she thought, I'd even been thinking we might settle down together, have children . . . How could I have been so naïve?

Now it seemed that Dan—indeed the whole world—was not as Orianna imagined it at all.

That she'd been hurt by men before and was sensitive to betrayal meant it didn't take much to undermine her trust. That she was such a romantic only made the gap between reality and her idealism greater. From such heights it was easy to fall, and when she fell, Orianna fell heavily. She could feel herself falling, slipping, losing control now; her happy ending destroyed long before she'd gotten there.

She looked up at the trees. The leaves were just beginning to turn, edged with brown, orange, and tawny gold. The flowers were past their best, the grass was tired and worn after months of tourists' trampling. Everything seemed to be declaring summer was over. Even the sky was gray, clouds poised on the verge of rain.

Softly, quietly, unnoticed, Orianna began to cry.

26. Lie with her? Lie on her?

Somehow Orianna got through the day at work. She was in too much of a state to think clearly about anything, let alone that it might be a good idea to go home. When she returned from Soho Square, she phoned Esme—not Dan—to say she'd like to retain the work she'd been origi- nally allocated, thank you, and asked her to revert to the original sched- ule. Then she checked the concepts of a couple of junior teams, went through illustrations with Earl, and chivvied Clare for the brief on the pitch, reminding her that every hour she ran late reduced the time available for development of creative ideas. All the while she endeavored to be as diligent and chirpy as ever, but thoughts of Dan and Cassie were there beneath the surface, gnawing away at her like a slow-release poi- son. By the end of the afternoon she had nothing to do other than wait for Clare, and without anything to occupy her mind, the toxicity could permeate. At last Clare called.

"Shall I come up to you?" she suggested.

Orianna jolted herself back to professional mode. "If you wouldn't mind. I'll call Ivy."

"I think we'll need Dan, too," said Clare. Orianna's stomach lurched. "It's a complicated one, and I'd like him to be up to speed."

"All right," agreed Orianna reluctantly. What could she do? The last thing she wanted was to have Clare think she couldn't separate business and pleasure—Clare was on the board and Orianna had promised she'd be able to handle an agency relationship when her promotion had first been mooted. "I'll call him."

Dan picked up his phone almost before it had rang. "Orianna?"

"Yes."

"Are you OK?"

She wasn't going to lie. "No, I'm not. Though it'll have to keep till later—I don't want to talk about it now. I spoke to Esme. I'd like my work schedule left as it was. Clare's coming up to brief us on this Bellings Scott launch, and she wants you here."

"In the meeting?"

"Yeah."

"I'll be right there."

Orianna suspected he was going to use the opportunity to snatch a second with her in private, but she couldn't face seeing him alone yet. Not only did she wish to avoid a confrontation in the agency, she feared she would force him to reveal truths so hurtful that she needed to prepare herself first. She asked, "Give it five minutes, will you?" Then she could ensure Ivy was present too, and be protected.

She replaced the receiver, hands shaking alarmingly. Still, she ought to phone Ivy.

"Fine—I've been ready for Clare since two," said Ivy. Within an instant she was in Orianna's office.

Thank God for Ivy, thought Orianna, as her friend took a seat at the round table in the center of the room. At least I can trust *her*. She's known me for ages, seen me through other romantic disasters; she's exactly who I want by my side right now.

Sure enough, they seemed on the same wavelength, for Ivy said, "Are you alright, sweetie?" before Orianna could draw breath.

Orianna exhaled. "No, not really."

"I thought not. You still look ever so pale."

"Mm."

"Anything I can do?"

Orianna shook her head as she pulled her chair up next to Ivy.

"Not at the moment—the others will be here any minute." She smiled to show she was grateful.

Ivy only had time to squeeze her hand supportively before they were interrupted by Clare and Dan. Clare took a chair next to Orianna, Dan opposite.

"Sorry about the delay. I was waiting for some facts to come over from Bellings Scott," said Clare.

She handed out copies of the brief, and launched straight into an explanation. But as she talked through the product background, Orianna found it increasingly hard to concentrate on the skin-softening properties of a new washing-up liquid. And as she saw Dan flick over to the second page of the document, all Clare's talk of palms and cuticles led her attention elsewhere. She'd noted months ago Dan's hands were especially attractive—they were so male; big and powerful, with neat, square-cut nails and strong, long fingers . . .

Those hands have stroked me, she thought. They've massaged my back and rubbed my feet when I've been tired, and touched me gently when we've made love. Those fingers have even made me come, for God's sake, only last night . . .

Yet now there was something hideous about them, cruel. Had those very same hands also touched Cassie? Had they massaged, rubbed, and stroked *her*? Helped her relax, then aroused her, brought her to the peak of ecstasy too? Orianna was completely repulsed by the thought, nonetheless she couldn't stop staring at Dan with macabre fascination. She watched him run his hands through his hair.

I always believed it indicated that he was apprehensive about something when he did that, she thought. But if Dan can sleep with someone else while coolly proclaiming his love for me, can I really read him? Do I understand him, truly know him at all?

"It's this hand conditioner," Clare reached the last page, "that makes

Sparkle such an amazing innovation. So, guys"—she turned first to Orianna and then Ivy—"it would be great if we could match this with some equally innovative creative work, just like you did for *That Sunshine Feeling*."

"Sure," said Ivy.

Help, thought Orianna. For several minutes she'd not listened to a word.

"I guess that wraps it up," said Clare. "When would you like to show me something? How about Thursday?"

"It'd be good to have a work-in-progress before that," said Dan.

Ivy decided for them. "Close of play Wednesday?"

The four of them got to their feet, and as Clare headed out of the door, Ivy said to Orianna, "I appreciate it's late—still, did you want us to start on this straight away?"

Dan broke in. "Er, before you two sit down, I'd like a word with Orianna in private."

Ivy raised her eyebrows at Orianna as if to say, Shall I hang around?, but try as she might, Orianna failed to communicate that she did, and before she knew it the two of them were alone in her office.

"What's this all about?" Dan said directly.

"You tell me."

"You seem ever so pissed off with me."

"Is it surprising?"

"What?"

"That I'm pissed off with you? Frankly, I'd call that an understatement."

"Well, er, yeah, I mean"—Dan scratched his scalp—"I know I might have stepped out of line a bit, what with it being work and all, but if you don't mind me saying, it seems you're getting things a little out of proportion."

"Out of proportion!" That was downright insulting.

"Yeah. It's not a big deal, surely—my wanting you to slow down a bit?"

"Gee, thanks." Orianna felt as if he'd punched her. Her instinct was to hit him back. Yet she was also acutely conscious they were surrounded by the glass panels of her office—walls that had eyes as well as ears. She took a deep breath. "Dan, we obviously feel completely different about this. But it's too complicated to go over right now. Can we talk about it tonight? Please?"

"I can't tonight."

She gripped the table, patience stretched to the limit. "Why?"

"That's why I've been trying to talk to you all day."

"What on earth are you doing tonight?"

"I've got a press pass."

"When was that organized?"

"Yesterday."

"Can't you cancel it?"

"You know I can't cancel a print run."

She did know—the agency would miss a deadline and lose lots of money. "Do you have to go?"

"Well, um, yes, I do. The client's insisted."

"Where is it?"

"Leicester."

"Can't you come to me after?"

"The first running sheets aren't due till nearly midnight."

"Oh."

"So I won't be home till after two."

"I see."

"Can't we at least talk about this swiftly now?"

"Get it over with in five minutes?" Orianna shook her head, disbelieving.

"I just don't want it hanging over me all night."

"So you'll give it five minutes? Is that what you think I'm worth? Jesus, thanks, Dan."

"No, of course I don't think that's what you're worth. But, if this is about the watch, you know I didn't mean to lose it; I reckon you've got it all rather out of proportion—"

It was all Orianna could do to restrain herself from socking him. But out of the corner of her eye she could see the rest of the department; a flying fist would never go unnoticed. She took another deep breath. "You know what I've said about bringing our business into the agency and we're obviously getting nowhere now."

"So when *are* we going to talk?"

Orianna was loath for it to keep, but for all her disillusion and upset, her job was very important to her; the more so in the face of losing the other main priority in her life. She simply couldn't afford to muck it up professionally too. "Tomorrow night." No sooner had she said it than the thought of waiting a whole twenty-four hours seemed unbearable, so she added, "What time are you leaving?"

"Leicester's a good two and a half hours away. I need to leave by seven."

Orianna checked her watch. It was approaching six. "I thought you said the run-outs weren't due till midnight?"

"They are. But I'm picking up Cassie on the way."

"You *what?*"

"Yeah—she has to go home first. She has a doctor's appointment or something."

Orianna was so shocked it took several seconds to gather herself. "Sorry, let me get this straight. You're taking *Cassie?*"

"Yes."

"Fucking hell. You're incredible."

"God, Orianna! Why do you have to make such a big deal of every-thing? Cassie wanted to be at the press pass—you know she's dead proud of that pack, the envelopes involve some tricky die-cutting. She thought it would be a good idea to see a printer on the job too—she's never been to one in this country. So she asked me if she could come and check it out, and I said yes. You've always encouraged her to take pride in her work. I think she thought you might be pleased. It's not during office hours, after all."

"*Pleased?!*" By now Orianna was too incensed to know what to argue. She picked the first of a million protestations that sprang to mind. "But neither of you told me!"

"I didn't think we had to."

If Orianna had wanted to punch him before, now she had a mind to slaughter the pair of them. "Let. Me. Get. This. Straight. You and Cassie are pissing off together for the night and you *didn't think you had to ask me*?"

"Yes!" It seemed Dan was cross too. How ludicrous—what right did *he* have to be angry?

"Well, it'll have to keep till tomorrow then, won't it?" she reiterated.

"If you won't talk now, I guess it will."

"Yes." She laid on sarcasm with a ladle. "Me and my 'five minute chat' . . ."

At that instant there was a tap on the door. Orianna still wasn't thinking straight, so without asking who it was, she said, "Come in."

And in walked Cassie.

"Orianna—" Then Cassie saw Dan. "Oh . . . er . . . sorry, I didn't mean to interrupt."

"Sure," snarled Orianna. "You've *interrupted* us before; why not interrupt this too?"

Yet her biting tone seemed to pass Cassie by. "I just wanted to check with you that it's OK if I go to the printers with Dan tonight?"

Christ, thought Orianna. Now she wants my blessing that she's spending the night with my boyfriend! She was so appalled she couldn't respond.

Cassie continued, "I'd really like to—"

"I bet!"

Cassie seemed to cotton on that this was not a good moment. She flushed and looked nervously from Orianna to Dan. "I guess I'll, er . . . catch you later," she said and made a rapid exit.

"What on earth did you do that for?" asked Dan.

"What for?"

"Bite her head off?"

"Why do you think, Dan?"

"Orianna," Dan said. "I really don't understand what's got into you. Perhaps you should go and see a doctor. Come to that, a shrink might be a better idea. Whatever, I think you need a day or two to calm down." He picked up his papers. "I'll speak to you tomorrow." And he turned and left with another bang of the door.

27. I had rather be a toad . . . than keep a corner in the thing I love for other's uses

Orianna arrived home, poured herself a huge glass of wine, and sat down heavily on the sofa. The longer she sat there, the more she thought about Dan and Cassie. Where were they now? She checked her watch. It was 7:35. He'd be at her apartment. Were they having sex before leaving for Leicester? Maybe they hadn't gone to Leicester at all.

And to think I liked her, thought Orianna. I gave her a job—I even believed she was pretty! She imagined Cassie opening the door to her home, dressed in a baby-doll nightie, blond bob painstakingly coiffed like someone from the cover of a Jacqueline Susann novel. God—of *course*—Cassie had been doing a lot of that recently, hadn't she? She was always in the ladies' room at work. Primping and pouting. No bloody wonder.

Orianna took a large gulp of wine, reached into her bag, and pulled out her mobile. Perhaps Dan had tried to get in touch. Come to his senses, realized he was being a jerk and wanted to see her later.

She looked to see if there were any messages—she even called her voice mail in case the icon had failed to show up on the screen. She got up, checked the landline. The answering machine wasn't flashing—but she dialed 1471 to see if Dan had called. No one had called that day at all.

She returned to the sofa, took another gulp of wine, checked her watch again. Where were they now? Doubtless on the M1. If not . . .

She shivered.

I can't stand this, she thought. I have to call him.

She tapped his number on speed dial, then, just before the line connected, decided better of it. To hell with him. If Dan could toss her out of his life like that after so many months together, pretend all she was worth was a *five-minute conversation,* then she wasn't going to flatter him by phoning. The last thing he deserved was an ego massage. She was a creative director for Christ's sake! She was older than him, more powerful. She earned more, anyway. Who did he think he was?

Another swig of wine.

Orianna was not normally one for drinking alone, or so fast, and at first it seemed to be helping, calming her. But after another ten minutes her fury had subsided, allowing pain and sorrow to take over. Shortly she started to cry; tears gave way to sobs, sobs to howls. She didn't know she had it in her to make such a noise, but at least no one would hear her.

Then the phone rang.

She jumped and stopped weeping. Dan? She picked up the receiver. "Hello?"

"Orianna? It's Ivy."

"Oh, hi." Her heart sank. Then her spirits lifted slightly; perhaps Ivy was the next best thing.

"I was just calling to check if you were feeling better."

"Er . . ." Given a sympathetic ear, Orianna's tears started to fall again.

"You're not, I can tell. Are you crying?"

Orianna sniffed loudly.

"What's up, honey?"

"It's Dan!"

"Oh, sweetie, I'm sorry. What's happened?"

"He's seeing someone else!"

"My God—*no!* Who?"

"Cassie!" Then out it poured in one long rush: the watch, the revised schedule, the trip to Leicester. "And he seems to think I'm an idiot for being upset about any of it!" she finished.

"He's a piece of shit," said Ivy.

Orianna winced. It was one thing if she thought this; another to have it articulated by another person, even her best friend. It underlined the dreadfulness of Dan's behavior.

"Do you want me to come over?"

Orianna considered for a moment.

"I can bring some wine. Pick up a pizza on the way or something. I could even . . ." she paused, obviously not wanting to impose, "stay over if you like."

The image of Ivy and herself curled up on the sofa with a pizza was therapeutic. She sniffed again. "Actually, that would be good."

"I'll drive," said Ivy. "Give me a sec to get my stuff together."

"Great. Thanks."

"See you in a bit," said Ivy, and hung up.

Orianna got to her feet and went to the bathroom to check her face in the mirror.

I look dreadful, she thought. Blotchy red cheeks, mascara smudged everywhere. She blew her nose. Ivy could cope with her au naturel, but she should clean her face. As she removed her eye makeup she reflected on Ivy.

How much easier it is to be friends with a woman, she sighed. It's far safer emotionally. I've never been hurt by a girlfriend like I have by men, or betrayed, or even particularly confused or upset. I understand women; we speak the same language. And of all the women in my life there's no one I value as much as Ivy; right now I appreciate her more than ever. With Ivy I know where I stand, how our relationship operates. Goodness—Ivy coped with my seeing Dan in secret and then forgave me the promotion. She's even been gracious about working with Cassie. What man would deal so well with all that?

Orianna checked her watch again. Ivy didn't live that far away, and knowing the speed she liked to drive her BMW, she should be here in a few minutes.

"I'm going out," said Ivy, slinging her mobile into her bag.

Ed stopped pouring himself a Scotch midflow. Slowly he put down the bottle and glass. "But I said I wanted to talk."

"And I said I didn't."

"You never want to talk."

"Not about certain things I don't, no."

"But it's our marriage, Ivy. We've got to sort this out sometime."

She glanced at him. In a dreadful lumberjack shirt and with the hideous beard he'd grown since she last saw him, he looked like an off-duty Canadian Mountie. How could she *ever* have found him attractive? She got to her feet. "It'll keep."

"God, Ivy, this is the first time I've seen you in weeks."

"I know. Sad, isn't it?" She headed to the bathroom.

Ed followed her. There wasn't space for both of them so he stood at the door. "What on earth's that much more important than our relationship?"

"Quite a lot, actually." She reached up to pull her sponge bag down from on top of the cabinet.

He grabbed her wrist. "Where are you going?"

"To see a friend." Ivy snatched her wrist away.

"What kind of friend?"

"Mind your business."

"A boyfriend?"

"If it was, do you think I'd tell you?" Ivy started to load her toiletries.

"Are you coming back?"

"Tonight? No."

"*Fucking hell, Ivy!*" He kicked the door. It rocked on its hinges.

"Careful," said Ivy, sweeping past him. "You might hurt yourself."

Five minutes later she was in her Z4. Before she turned on the ignition, she phoned Orianna's favorite pizza parlor in Islington and placed an order. Then she set off, stopping in Shoreditch en route to pick up a bottle of red—no point in spending too much as Orianna would never notice in the state she was in, though she couldn't stand utter rubbish herself so begrudgingly parted with nearly £10—and presently she was drumming her nails on the countertop at the pizza place, waiting for their pies. By nine o'clock she was pulling up outside Orianna's apartment.

It's months since I've been here, she thought, mounting the steps to the front door. How weird it feels, being back.

But it didn't seem to have changed much. A nearby streetlamp revealed the same geraniums in the window box as ever, valiantly attempting a last burst of scarlet before the autumn frosts set in. There were the familiar curtains, covered in a design based on Leonardo's botanical sketches, drawn as it was dark. And there, by the doorbell, the label that Orianna had proudly designed on her Mac when she'd moved in all those years ago. It said O. BIANCHI, GARDEN APARTMENT in swirly lettering.

We used to hang out here such a lot, before Dan, recalled Ivy. Since Orianna started seeing him she hadn't been invited that often, and when she had she'd suspected that Dan would be there too. The idea of hanging out with such a cozy couple was the last thing Ivy wanted to do, so even when she had been asked, she'd made her excuses.

Well, she thought, putting down her bag and tucking the pizzas under her chin so she could press the buzzer, with any luck that could change. Soon I might not be the one feeling excluded. Because the way things are panning out, it doesn't look as if Dan will be visiting this apartment quite so often in the future.

28. Tonight, I do entreat that we may sup together

"Shall we stop to eat?" said Dan. They'd just passed a sign for Leicester Forest East Services. "I'm starving and we're making good time."

"That would be great," said Cassie. "I could do with going to the restroom."

As they pulled into the parking lot, Dan wondered if he should try phoning Orianna again. He'd tried before they'd hit the M1, but her phone had been engaged.

Almost before he'd come to a stop, Cassie had undone her seat belt and opened the door. "Sorry, you'll have to excuse me. I'm desperate!" Dan had to run to catch up with her, and it wasn't until he was inside the building that he realized he'd left his mobile in the glove compartment of his Fiesta.

Blast, he thought. I'll lose Cassie if I go back for it.

Eventually Cassie emerged from the loo.

She looks tired, he observed, yet she's replenished her lipstick. Does she never let her image slide?

"Right then," she took his arm. "Food, here we come."

So the moment to call Orianna passed.

In the cafe, Cassie selected a small salad and mineral water. "I don't fancy eating much."

As he helped himself to fish and chips, Dan thought fondly of Orianna. With such a spread before her, she'd never be able to resist something fattening either. Her passion for food is one of the things I love about her, he thought. I'd rather that any day than someone like Cassie who seems to count every calorie.

But over the meal he decided he'd better make an effort. He was aware he was normally far chummier with Cassie than he'd been thus far. Perhaps it would be friendly to ask about her love life. He ventured, "Now that we're out of the agency, tell me . . . Are you seeing anyone at the moment?"

To his surprise Cassie almost choked on her lettuce. "Er . . . Why do you ask?"

He shrugged. "Just wondered." It's not that strange a question, he thought. After all, half the men at Green seem to have the hots for her.

Eventually, she admitted, "I have been seeing—um—someone, yeah."

"Oh." Dan nodded. "Is it serious?"

"Kind of," said Cassie.

"Anyone I know?"

"Maybe." Cassie toyed with a piece of tomato. Dan wished she'd hurry up and eat—it was well past suppertime, for goodness' sake, and she barely seemed able to get through a bowl of leaves without any dressing. The contrast made him feel greedy. At last she blurted, "Actually, yeah."

Well, well, thought Dan. This is a more interesting topic than it first appeared. He didn't share Orianna's insatiable appetite for gossip, but he did enjoy the odd bit of intrigue if it involved his colleagues. And perhaps he'd find out something he could impart to Orianna—she'd relish that. He leaned forward. "Who is it?"

"I'm not sure I should tell you. I've been advised to keep my private life to myself."

"You can tell *me,*" he urged.

"Why are you so curious all of a sudden?" Cassie looked at him suspiciously.

"I was just interested in you, that's all."

Cassie flushed. "I wouldn't dream of going out with you, if that's why you're asking. Not when you've been seeing my boss."

Now Dan nearly choked on his dinner. "What on earth should give you that idea?"

"Oh, nothing," said Cassie. "I guess I made a mistake." But she didn't appear convinced. She hesitated, as if considering whether to explain herself more fully, then decided to play it safe. "Nonetheless, I'm not sure it's a good idea to be discussing this. I understand you and Orianna kept things quiet for a while, and if you don't mind, I'd prefer to do the same."

"OK. Whatever." Strange girl, he thought. Assuming I fancy her! If there's one thing I can't stand, it's a presumptuous woman. In any case, she's not my type.

"Thanks for coming over."

"No worries." Ivy put down the pizzas on the coffee table and wandered into the kitchen. "Corkscrew?"

"I've already got one open," said Orianna.

It's not like Orianna to drink alone, thought Ivy, but sure enough, there was less than half a bottle of Chianti on the side table. She located the corkscrew and returned to the living room with both bottles and a glass for herself. "I expect we'll get onto this one too," she said. She unzipped her boots and took them off so she could sit cross-legged, and lifted the two pizzas onto her lap. She pulled the lid off the top one to check the contents and handed the box to Orianna. "I got you this."

"What is it?"

"Quattro formaggio."

"Ooh yum!" Orianna examined the gooey, creamy topping. "What's yours?"

"Arugula and parmesan." Ivy picked up her glass. "Cheers, anyway. Sorry you've had such a shit day." Clink. "Men, who needs 'em, eh?"

"Exactly."

"Wankers." They were silent a while, focused on eating.

Perhaps a small admission will prompt Orianna to reveal more about Dan, thought Ivy. She said, "In fact, I was glad to get away."

"Oh?"

"I left Ed. Back at the apartment."

"Right." Orianna swallowed. "How are things with him?"

"Not that great."

"Oh, I'm sorry." Orianna looked genuinely sad for her.

Her pity made Ivy feel uncomfortable. She laughed. "No change there. But God, O, you should see him—he's grown a beard!"

"A beard!"

"Not even a goatee. It's a *proper* beard!"

"A bear beard?"

Ivy grimaced. "Even his neck's hairy. One thing's for certain. He's not kissing me like that—let alone anything else." She winked suggestively.

"No way." Orianna nodded. She looked downcast for a moment. Ivy guessed she was thinking about Dan.

"Enough about Ed—it's all the same old, same old. What's going on with you two?"

"We three, more like." Orianna sighed. "As I said, seems Dan's shagging Cassie."

"Really?" said Ivy. She made her surprise sound fake.

Orianna picked this up at once. "Did you know about it?"

"Er . . ." Ivy hesitated. She bit her lip as if she was struggling to protect her friend from the truth.

Orianna's eyes welled up. "You might as well tell me."

"I didn't know anything for definite."

"No?" Orianna sounded relieved.

"Or I'd have told you."

Orianna nodded.

"Though I did notice he was hanging around her a lot. I mentioned that, if you recall."

"Yeah, yeah, I know you did. It's only I never really saw it myself."

"I guess he tended to do it when you weren't there. He probably knew you'd cotton to it otherwise. But sharing work space with her, obviously I couldn't miss it."

"No." Tears began to fall properly now.

Ivy felt a pang of guilt. "Here." She handed Orianna a tissue.

"Thanks." Orianna wiped her eyes and laughed at herself. "Good thing I took off my mascara."

"Just make sure you don't go out like that," teased Ivy.

Orianna pulled off another slice of pizza. The cheese stretched into thin strings which she scooped into a huge, consoling mouthful. "D'you think it's been going on a long time then?"

"Truthfully, I don't know. I'll tell you something though."

"What?"

"She's always in the loo, Cassie, isn't she, primping?"

"Too bloody right!" Orianna stopped crying.

"So if that's any measure, I guess it's been a while."

Orianna appeared mortified.

"Yet she looks god-awful for it," scoffed Ivy. Privately, she had a faint suspicion Cassie was doing more than preening and primping, though she kept the thought to herself.

"D'you reckon?"

Ivy gave a shudder. "Ooh yes! I've never known anyone to spend so much time on their appearance." Her own trips to the gym didn't count, of course.

"Nor me."

Ivy noted Orianna was dubious. "You don't think Cassie's pretty, do you?"

"Er, well . . . I'm not sure. Lots of men seem to think so."

"Men with no taste," said Ivy, before she could stop herself. Oops— Orianna appeared hurt. Better criticize Cassie, not Dan. "I don't think she's attractive at all."

"You don't?"

"Her skin's *orange,* Orianna!"

"Is it?" Was it possible Orianna hadn't noticed?

"Oh yes. Definitely tanning bed. I mean, whoever has a tan all year round? In this country? It's so dated, darling." She patted Orianna's knee.

"I suppose."

"And her hair!" Never mind Orianna's upset, Ivy was enjoying herself.

"It is a bit split," Orianna conceded.

" 'A bit split!' " Ivy flicked her long hair away from her face. She had bonding like this down to a fine art, confident both she and Orianna had flawless complexions and thick, glossy tresses. "It's *yellow*." She was on a roll. It was such a relief to vent her own misgivings.

"I mean if you're going to dye your hair"—she checked her own streaks in the mirror behind the sofa—"at least make sure it's done *properly*." She noticed Orianna surreptitiously check her appearance too. Ivy knew what she was doing—Orianna's brunette waves were natural. "I have to say though . . ."

"What?"

"It's not the only thing that's false about her, I reckon."

"Oh?"

Ivy lifted her chin, displaying her fine profile to full effect. "Well . . . put it this way . . . I might be wrong . . ."

"But?"

She could tell Orianna was on tenterhooks. "I don't want to stereotype, of course, but still, it's quite rare to see a Jewish girl with a nose like that."

"Pert, you mean?"

Ivy nodded. "Snub."

"Gosh." Orianna sat back, stopped chewing. "You think she's had it done?"

"Obviously I can't prove it."

"Mm."

"Still, it's like a ski jump."

"True." At last the implications took full effect. "God, Ivy, I hadn't thought of that."

"What?"

"That Cassie's Jewish."

"Hadn't you?"

"I mean obviously I realized she was, but I didn't think that was why . . . well, you know. Dan is too."

"Really?"

"His parents would love that. Well, *her*." She scooped another consoling mouthful.

"Surely he wouldn't be so swayed by what they thought, would he? He's not that much of a mummy's boy?"

"Actually, he's very close to his family." Trust Orianna to see this as an asset. "Or so he says. He's never introduced me to them."

"I see."

"Not yet."

"Because you're not Jewish?"

"I don't know. Maybe." Orianna's voice was forlorn. She glanced up at her friend, eyes full of tears. "Do you think he really likes her, Ivy?"

"Lord knows. Can't see it lasting, myself." Ivy allowed herself a sip of wine. "It'll probably blow over. My guess is he'll tire of her eventually, Jewish or not. But you can't hang around waiting forever. So"—the million-dollar question—"what are you going to do about it? I presume the last thing you want is to be made to look a fool."

"Is that what people think?"

Hell, Ivy thought, if I'm to be single again—or, more specifically, devoid of a husband, if not a lover—at least I'll have Orianna to hang out with. "No one's said exactly that as far as I know."

"Not yet. It's probably only a matter of time. I know how they behave at work—it's *just* what happened with Clive!" She began to cry again. "I'd better talk to him, I suppose."

Ivy sighed. "I guess you had."

"Maybe I should finish it." An extra loud wail. "But I really care about him, Ivy!"

If Ivy felt a twinge of remorse, but the moment soon passed. I can't change my tune now, she thought. "I know you do, honey. I thought he seemed like a nice guy, too."

"Did you?"

"Yeah. I suppose he had us all fooled."

"But he told me he loved me!"

"Of course he did."

Orianna looked mystified.

"That's what men do."

"Even when they don't?"

"Yes. That way they can get you to do more for them. Cooking, cleaning, mothering"—not that Ivy did any of these, but still—"sexual favors . . . No better guarantee of a good blow job than the old 'I love you' trick."

"Oh." Orianna was silent.

Poor Orianna, thought Ivy. She's such a sap! "Frankly, I don't believe in love, myself."

Orianna seemed shocked. "You don't?"

"Not really."

"At all?"

"Not the kind of love you're talking about, no."

"Oh."

"The important thing is to love yourself."

"Right."

"I don't know many people who know how to do that."

Orianna took a huge bite of pizza.

As she was chewing, Ivy continued, "This is what you should remember now: to look after yourself."

"Does it mean dumping Dan, then?"

Clap, clap! "Well, it's up to you."

"Though would you, if you were me?"

Ivy could barely restrain from squawking, *"There's no way I'd go out with Dan!"* but bit her tongue. "Oh yes. Also, I wouldn't give his excuses the time of day."

"You mean you wouldn't even *talk* to him?"

"And give him the chance to explain himself?" Ivy shook her head.

"But I want to confront him."

"What's the point? He'll only deny everything."

"I'm not sure..." Orianna frowned. "He's not that dishonest, surely?"

"He's a man, isn't he?" Ivy waited for Orianna to nod. "I don't trust any of them as far as I can throw them."

"Oh. None of them?"

"No. Not the ones with any intelligence, anyway. The only men you can trust are the dumb ones." Like Ed, she thought. "Talk to Dan and you give him the chance to come up with something; persuade you that Cassie means nothing to him. Or worse, he'll turn it back on you, convince you you're imagining it." She stabbed at the crust of her pizza.

"I'm sure he wouldn't do that."

"Don't you bet on it. That's what my father did to my mother."

"Mm?"

"She suspected he was having an affair, he made out *she* was the bonkers one. I'm positive it didn't help her already fragile mental state." Ivy had shared this story before and once she saw Orianna was nodding again, continued, "When they're caught on the hop, there's no telling what some men will do. Dan could suggest somebody is stirring it, I don't know." She laughed. "He might even try and blame me, you never know."

"You? Why would he do that?"

"Well, I don't think he's ever terribly liked me, put it that way."

"He hasn't ever said that to me."

"Honey, he's hardly going to do that, now is he? He knows how close we are."

Orianna sighed.

Some pep talk this is proving to be, thought Ivy. With luck Orianna won't know what to make of Dan anymore. "Whatever, don't let his excuses wash."

"Right."

"Though if it was me? I'd cut him out. Schwum!" She sliced through the air with her pizza knife.

Orianna jumped and—for a split second—looked a little scared. "I see. You really wouldn't speak to him?"

Ivy could tell Orianna was hanging on her every word. She held her gaze. "No."

"What would you do then?"

"I don't know *precisely*. E-mail him, write to him—tell him it's over. Maybe I'd simply not speak to him again. It would piss him off, I know, but nowhere near as much as he'd have fucked me over. Talking will only give him the chance to lie to you again. Still, that's me. You must do what's best for you."

Orianna swallowed the last mouthful of pizza.

"However you handle it," Ivy smiled sympathetically, "after that it's onwards and upwards, my friend. Men—we're better off without them."

29. I understand a fury in your words, but not the words

Hell, was it seven thirty already?

It was half past three before Dan had got to bed. A nighttime trip to the printers was always a chore, let alone one in Leicester. Left to his own devices, he'd have sped home to the accompaniment of his Ibiza mix on full volume, instead he'd had Cassie chatting incessantly all the way back. If he could have gotten away with it, he'd have dropped her at the taxi stand in Camden to get herself home. But that would be unkind, he'd told himself, so had driven miles out of his way to see her safely to her door.

To add insult to injury, his morning journey to work was fraught. The number 24 was packed, and he was wedged between a workman with bad BO and a woman of considerable bulk who kept treading on his toes. As the bus stop-started down Gower Street, he turned his mind to Orianna.

One of the things I like is her straightforwardness, he thought. She's so much easier to understand than most women—I felt I "got" her, and she "got" me. I mean I was even on the verge of suggesting we move in together. But yesterday—what was all that about? I couldn't get the measure of her remotely.

It was all very confusing and upsetting, and Dan was just hoping that today would be different when the bus took a 90 degree turn, swung onto New Oxford Street, and the large lady lost her balance and trod on his foot again. Dan grimaced in pain and was forced to acknowledge the signs did not bode well.

Arriving at his desk he saw his computer screen was already covered in Post-it notes from Ursula. Typical—she must have gotten into the agency at the crack of dawn and worked herself up into a state about what might—or might not—have happened at the printers. Totally uncalled for, of course.

It was at that moment Orianna phoned and said she wanted to see him. Whereas the previous afternoon he'd been feeling sympathetic, worried, and fond, but right then a confrontation with his girlfriend was the last thing he felt able to deal with. His heart sank at the prospect, nevertheless he headed over to her office, and shut the door.

"Orianna."

"Dan." She was sitting at her desk, a steaming cappuccino before her.

He pulled up a chair. "You wanted to see me."

"Yes."

"How are you? Feeling any better?"

"Not really, no."

Great, he thought, heart sinking further. "Oh dear," he said, but whether he meant "oh dear" for her or "oh dear" for himself, he wasn't sure.

"I think we should stop seeing each other."

While Dan knew she was angry with him, he was utterly unprepared for this. It was as if he'd been kicked, hard; and he'd felt emotionally knocked around already. However dire things had been the day before, they hadn't been that bad, had they?

"Oh," he said. It took a few seconds before he was able to ask, subdued, "Why?"

"You know why."

He frowned. Did he? He didn't pretend to be perfect, and his immediate reaction was to feel guilty. Though I haven't *done* anything, he thought, I don't understand what she's angry about. Damn it, I've tried my hardest to be good and kind and generous and yet it seems that isn't enough. I do my best, and all at once there's no pleasing her.

"Think," she said bluntly.

He scratched his scalp. In the past, if he'd upset a girlfriend, he'd have been able to see a conversation like this coming, but this was a shock. How could she perform such an enormous turnaround in such a short space of time? Usually Dan tried not to succumb to clichéd views of female behavior, but her conduct seemed to bear the hallmarks of a totally irrational, possibly hormonally induced mood swing. Though it's no mere mood swing, he thought, she's had a complete change of heart. And, because he genuinely loved her, this shook him to the core. Overwhelmed, he was unable to articulate any of his feelings. So, instead of protesting, asking for an explanation, or saying he cared, he simply shrugged, stumped.

This seemed to increase her fury: "Perhaps the name 'Cassie' might guide you?"

"Huh?"

"Oh, come *on*, Dan."

"No, *you* come on," he said, patience wearing thin. "I honestly don't know what you're talking about."

"Do me a favor, Dan."

He hated this: *Dan.* She never used his name formally, like this. It made him feel like a naughty little boy. And she was staring at him, her eyes cold and hard, just as she had been yesterday.

"You're shagging her, aren't you?"

If what she'd been saying before was unfathomable, this was farcical. Cassie? Tedious, talkative, lettuce-loving Cassie? She was so irritating— the very idea! He laughed. Then he recalled Orianna had made a similar accusation the previous day. "What on earth makes you think that?"

"I'm not stupid, Dan."

"I never said you were."

"Admit it, will you? It would save us a lot of time."

"There's nothing to admit!"

Orianna sighed. "I knew you'd try to deny it."

"Deny *what*, for God's sake?"

"Look, Dan, do one thing for me. Don't let me be the last to know. OK? I've been through that before."

"Orianna, sweetheart—"

"Don't 'sweetheart' me!"

"OK. OK." He held up his hand, a request for pause, peace. "I don't have a clue where you got this crazy idea from, but—"

"Don't tell me I'm crazy!"

Dan shook his head. "I wasn't."

"That's so typical! Men! You always try and make out it's our fault. Please don't bother."

He bristled. He resented it when women swept all men into the same pile. Nevertheless, he detected Orianna was fighting back tears. He had an impulse to extend a hand, touch her, hug her, but restrained himself, scared he'd make matters worse.

"It's exactly what happened with Clive—he ran off with that stupid little receptionist, and I thought she was a friend of mine and everyone knew before me. I told you that and I imagined you understood." She gulped.

He looked down, trying to stop himself from reaching out and grasping her, shaking some sense into her.

"I really cared for you, Dan, I really did." Her voice rose to a crescendo, then down with a bump that conveyed her disappointment and pain. "I thought more of you, of us, I suppose. And I believed you felt the same."

"I do!" Dan took a deep breath. He was desperate to explain she was wrong, yet she seemed averse to logic, to listening. "I don't know what you've heard, or who told you," he said, struggling to be rational and calm. "But it's not true. There's nothing going on between me and Cassie. Nada. Zero." He held up three fingers, a pathetic gesture from his childhood all he could think of. "Scout's honor."

She glanced up at him. For the first time he thought he could detect a touch of hope in her expression. Then her lips set in a firm line. "You gave her all my work."

"Eh?"

"You allocated the Bellings Scott stuff to her instead of me You planned to send her on the shoot."

"I was trying to help you!"

"Oh come on, Dan you took her to the printers. What kind of fool do you think I am?"

"It was business, for fuck's sake! Where on earth did you get the idea I'm having some sort of thing with Cassie?"

"I saw the evidence with my own eyes."

"What did you see, exactly?"

"Oh, Dan." Orianna shook her head, her dark locks swaying sadly. "Do I have to go into it all? I can't face it. I'm tired. I hardly slept a wink last night."

"Nor me," he whispered, equally miserable.

"Just take it that I've seen things—your watch in her bag—"

"What?"

"You heard me. I saw your watch. Your Paul Smith watch. In Cassie's handbag."

"How could you have? When?"

"Yesterday. Yesterday morning."

"But my watch wasn't in Cassie's handbag!"

She was vehement. "Yes it was; I saw it there."

"No." Dan shook his head emphatically. This was extremely alarming. Was Orianna deluding herself? "You're wrong," he said firmly. "Rob had my watch. He gave it to Ivy. Ivy gave it to me."

"Nice one, Dan. But it's too late. I said: don't bother denying it."

"*ARRRRRRRGHHHHHHHH!*" Dan roared, frustration getting the better of him. He banged the table with his fist. "You're fucking bonkers!"

"I am *not* fucking bonkers!" Now Orianna was shrieking too. Dan glanced nervously behind him through the partition wall. He could see their colleagues coming and going, oblivious. Thank heavens the door was closed. "Do me the courtesy of not lying. And *don't tell me I'm imagining everything*! I've seen things, heard things—other stuff too—that means I won't believe you, whatever you say." Her voice fell again, she finished, in a hush, "I don't trust you."

Dan exhaled heavily and sat back in his chair.

"Anyway, I don't know why you bother trying to explain. It's pathetic. She said you'd make all these excuses."

"*Who* said?"

"Never mind."

"Did someone *tell* you about me and Cassie?"

"No. There was no need for anyone to tell me."

"Who have you been talking to?"

"Ivy," admitted Orianna, after a pause.

"Ivy? When?"

"She came over last night."

"Did she?"

"Yes."

"Ah." Perhaps here, finally, a potential explanation. He wasn't sure why, but he didn't trust Ivy at all.

"What d'you mean—'*ah*'?"

"Has she put you up to this?"

"*No, she damn well hasn't!* And don't you *dare* blame Ivy. She said you would. But I won't have it. I simply won't have it. You hear?"

Dan felt like he'd been punched again. However hard he tried, Orianna seemed determined to smother every word.

"She's been sweet to me, alright? She saw me through last night, and I'm not sure I'd have gotten through it without her. In fact, you could learn a thing or two about loyalty from Ivy. Just keep your observations about her—or anyone else, come to that—to yourself."

So the final avenue was blocked. The portcullis was down; he was shut out of Orianna's world.

30. O! O! O!

Orianna's hands were trembling so much she could scarcely pick up her coffee. Slowly, she raised it to her lips. The liquid tasted the same as ever—warm, comforting, milky—yet everything, *everything* was different.

She looked at her watch. Nine fifteen. Was it possible such a lot had happened in so little time?

Through the glass wall it was business as usual. There was Ursula, striding across the department clutching some artwork, long hair flying behind her, purposeful as always, doubtless headed for the studio. There were Esme and Earl, chatting as they waited at the photocopier. Here came Ivy, carefully carrying a cup from the soda machine back to her desk—a black coffee, Orianna presumed. And then, right past her door, bounced Cassie—ghastly, bleached-blond Cassie—without a care in the world. And, by her side, Russell, of all people: they were laughing, or rather he was laughing; she was giggling.

Now Cassie's sucking up to *Russell,* thought Orianna. Before I know it, she'll be after my job. Well, she can steal my man—though Dan's a lying, conniving worm so she's welcome to him—such betrayal, they deserve each other. But she sure as hell can't have my career. It's all I've got left, and no one is taking *that* away.

No sooner had she avowed this than she was flooded by a wave of longing for things to be back the way they were; memories of her and Dan together, at their best.

How could he? she wondered. I don't understand. He told me he loved me; he acted like he did. What on earth have I done to deserve this? I was good to him, wasn't I? And he seemed to fancy me . . .

Oh no, she thought. Perhaps that's it. He doesn't find me attractive. I'm chubby, after all, especially compared to Cassie. And I feel horribly fat after that pizza . . . But I always thought Dan liked my curves. He said he did, although maybe he was only saying that to make me feel better. But why should he be bothered about making me feel better, if he doesn't care about me? He must have cared about me, surely, a bit. Though if he'd cared about me, how could he have slept with someone else?

Round and round her thoughts went, yet the harder she tried to puzzle them out, the more chaotic they became. She couldn't figure him out. She'd believed she'd known him, when she hadn't at all.

If I've got Dan so wrong, what else—who else—have I misunderstood, misinterpreted? Have I gotten everything—everyone—wrong, all these years?

Orianna cast her mind back to the morning, earlier that summer. She'd been gazing out of her bedroom window, contemplating the geraniums. That moment of complete happiness, when her future had stretched before her, filled with possibility.

How alive I felt! How blessed! she thought. It seems eons ago now. The world's not the way I thought it was; people aren't kind, loving, generous. It's the only explanation that makes sense.

Orianna held this observation, absorbed it, and braced herself. She could see Leon headed toward her, about to knock on her door. She had to face the day ahead.

This is how to play it in the future, she vowed. I'll never be so naïve again.

From her desk facing Orianna's office, Ivy saw Dan leaving, shutting the door behind him. He was whiter than she'd ever seen him.

Orianna must have finished it then.

To make sure, she went to fetch a coffee and sneaked a sideways glance as she passed. Through the smoked glass she could see Orianna at her computer, ashen-faced.

Good.

There's no time like the present for verifying what's happened, thought Ivy. She and Orianna were due to work together that morning.

"Sometimes I can't believe Ed," she said once she was seated opposite her old partner and they were both poised to come up with ideas. She knew Orianna would be flattered by the admission. "He comes all the way down to see me, claims he wants to talk. Says he thinks we've been growing apart, we don't communicate the way we used to. Is it any surprise if I've a *bear* to contend with? Would *you* want to talk to a bear, let alone kiss one? And when I ask if he'll please shave his beard off—of course he won't! I make the effort to look good, every single day. Yet no, he's the innocent party—expects me to alter my behavior. And it's typical. Abdicating responsibility, making it our fault. That's guys for you all over."

It was satisfying to offload her ill feelings about men—their ineptitude, their inability to commit, their lack of worth—and it seemed that Orianna was more willing than ever to take her opinions on board. Moreover, for once Orianna didn't seem remotely with it professionally, and today Ivy was glad to take the lead, knowing that finally they were back on an even keel.

Come lunchtime and her weekly appointment with Rob, Ivy felt the best she had for ages. Lord, she was almost happy. And though she usually disguised her feelings, her personal trainer was able to pick up on her mood the moment he set eyes on her.

"Good God!" Rob exclaimed. "What's happened to you?"

"What do you mean?" She could barely restrain from grinning.

"You look fantastic."

"Do I?"

"You're glowing, and there's a sparkle in your eyes." He paused, peered more closely. "You've got a new man, have you?"

"Oh, *no,*" said Ivy. Though come to think of it, she was in the mood for sex. Perhaps she and Russell could get together later. Mm . . . All this talk of keeping men in their place was quite a turn-on. With any luck she might persuade Russell to be tied up.

"Whatever your secret, it's doing you good."

"Thanks."

"You changed your diet, or something?"

Ivy shook her head. Let's change the subject, she thought, this is beginning to feel like an interrogation.

"I'll tell you something though," she said. "I've got some interesting gossip for you."

"What?" He was eager already.

"I'll tell you in a minute," she taunted, and disappeared into the changing room.

Rob sat perched on the arm of the sofa, endeavoring to be patient.

I could do with some light relief, he thought. I miss Chloë. Living with John isn't the same. We just don't click as well.

Rob and John had socialized together for a long while, so apartment-sharing should have been OK, but Rob was discovering the kind of friendship that made for a great Saturday night on the town did not necessarily satisfy come Sunday, when all he wanted to do was snuggle up on the sofa with Potato and feel cozy.

It didn't help that Chloë was having a great time in New York. According to her e-mails, she was dating countless different men, whereas in London her love life had often been as spartan as his was—if not more so. Previously Rob had been inclined to settle for one-night stands, but recently his heart hadn't been in it.

I must be growing old, he ruminated.

At that moment Ivy bounded out of the changing room, ponytail swinging.

"So?" he inquired, getting to his feet.

"Let me stretch first." Ivy always preferred to expend her energy working out rather than warming up so it wasn't long before they were side by side aboard rowing machines. "Well," she volunteered. "They've split up."

Rob's heart leaped. Could she be referring to the "they" he hoped she was? "Who?"

"Dan and Orianna."

"No!"

"Yes, indeedy." Ivy was soon rowing so fast that he had to push himself to match her. "Heard it from the horse's mouth. This very morning."

"Oh?"

"Orianna," Ivy illuminated. "I've been working with her on a pitch."

"Ah." Rob nodded. He had a fleeting suspicion perhaps this was why Ivy seemed so content all of a sudden, yet pushed the thought away. No, not Ivy; she'd got over her resentment of those two months ago. Hadn't Dan said as much? "Do you know why?" He struggled to keep his voice light.

"Your guess is as good as mine." *Schwoom, schwoom,* went the rowing machine. But then Ivy turned to Rob and winked.

"You don't mean . . ."

"Honey, it's truly not in my power to say."

Ivy hesitated, and continued rowing for a second in silence, her face turned away. Eventually she turned back to Rob. "Orianna's my friend. You know I would tell you if I could."

"Mm," said Rob, disappointed.

"It's only, what with Dan being your client too, and all . . ." She scrunched up her nose and shook her head. "I'm not sure it's terribly fair."

"No," agreed Rob. He wondered if he would be so discreet in similar circumstances, and worried he wouldn't. Frustrating though it was, he quite admired Ivy for this and in a way was reassured. It meant that if he was ever to confide in her, he knew she could be trusted.

"Anyway." Ivy smiled. "You've got a vivid imagination, I'm sure. Let me say that whatever it is you're thinking, it's probably true. There were other people involved."

"What? You mean Dan—"

"I'm sorry," Ivy interrupted. "That really *is* all I'm going to say. I've already said more than I should have, frankly. Orianna's my dearest friend. She'd be most pissed off if she knew I'd told you this much. I only thought you should know so you don't put your foot in it next time you see Dan. Whatever he's done, however much he's brought it on himself, he's still human. He's going through a lot. He probably needs time alone, to think and sort himself out so I'd probably tread carefully with him for a while. When he's ready, I'm sure you'll be one of the first people he'll turn to. After all, he knows you—more than anyone—will understand."

31. Guiltiness will speak, though tongues were out of use

Autumn was Ivy's favorite season. Spring wasn't her thing—all those bursting buds and frolicking animals—such brazen exuberance made her skin crawl. Summer she could take or leave; the fact people *expected* you to be happy because the sun was shining only made her feel churlish. Christmas, pah! All that gift-giving and altruism was such a trial. The compulsory celebrations—the work party with its inevitable scandals, the dinners out with old friends, and worst, the painful gathering of her dysfunctional family at her mother's increasingly worn home—Ivy always counted down until the month was over.

But, aah, autumn. Ivy loved it, especially when it had truly taken hold. The shortening days and lengthening nights—if she felt like going out she could; but she wasn't *obligated*. No longer was she forced to compete with bronzed summer beauties; this was when her coloring came into its own. The cool light perfectly offset her pale complexion, the turning leaves complemented her flaming hair, the shops were filled with clothes in dark hues that enhanced her air of mystery.

Then there was Halloween—the one tradition she did enjoy.

Moreover, the day before was her birthday. According to her birth certificate, it was her thirty-ninth; according to her CV, her thirty-fifth. Not that either would be a cause for rejoicing, save it allowed her to wangle expensive presents out of Russell and Ed, without an obligation to give in return. But this particular birthday appeared to have brought an extra gift her way. A gift that, with any luck, might end the indignity of having to work with a junior colleague.

Ivy had long suspected something was up with Cassie; something in addition to her affair with Leon, which Ivy surmised was carrying on apace. Her suspicions had been aroused several weeks previously, when she'd noted Cassie making an increasingly absurd number of trips to the toilet every morning, after which she'd emerge looking off-color, even through the bronzed glow. This in itself might not have been sufficient proof, but it also seemed that Cassie was being even more finicky about her diet than when she'd first arrived at Green. She'd been eating fewer salads, and she'd developed an unlikely appetite for frozen strawberry mousses.

By her birthday, Ivy was virtually 100 percent certain. By now there was another sign: Cassie was wearing looser, more layered clothes and, though it had been getting colder, Ivy was unconvinced Cassie would have kissed good-bye to her man-magnet wardrobe without good reason.

Then, finally, on the very afternoon when Ivy needed perking up (for she was privately discomforted at only being a year from forty), she received the confirmation she'd been waiting for.

Approaching the end of the working day, Ivy was at her PC, Cassie was sitting opposite, when the lights overhead went out, plunging the office into semidarkness, lit only by computer screens. Ivy braced herself. She knew what was coming; sure enough, within seconds, Orianna had appeared at her side, brandishing a cake replete with candles (thirty-five, Ivy quickly counted, relieved). Ivy had been waiting for this magnanimous gesture all day, so she smiled sweetly at her colleagues as they clustered around her desk congratulating her, wishing her well, gasping in amazement that she was a day over thirty.

A minute after Orianna came Russell, carrying three bottles of champagne on a tray and a dozen glasses. He popped the corks, poured several flutes, and handed them around. Ivy first, naturally, then the other creatives.

"Er . . . no, thank you," said Cassie quietly.

"No?" Russell held out the glass. "I thought you antipodeans liked bubbly?"

"Um . . ." Among the fawning and gabbling and back-slapping of her colleagues, Ivy sneaked a glance at Cassie. She looked fazed. "I do, but er . . ."

"Go on, just one."

"I'm afraid I couldn't." Cassie was firm. "I'm not drinking."

"Not drinking?" Russell was astonished. Everyone, but *everyone*, liked—*needed*—to drink in advertising. He, like Ivy, knew that if someone didn't drink, it was only because he or she had once fancied it rather too much or too frequently. "Dear me. Why?"

"Because . . . er . . ."

Ivy watched, fascinated, curious to see what excuse Cassie would come up with.

Eventually Cassie brought it forth. "I'm on medication."

"Oh," said Russell.

Mm, thought Ivy, not bad. He won't push her on that. As expected, he moved on, handing out glasses.

But it was enough. Jubilant, Ivy knocked back her champagne.

I wonder if Leon knows about this, she thought. She checked to see if he was keeping a protective eye on his girlfriend, yet he was joking with the other guys from the studio, so seemed blissfully ignorant.

Regardless, *she* had no doubt. Moreover, she was the only person in the agency who knew who the father was. Happy birthday indeed.

Merrymaking was the last thing on Dan's mind. Not because he didn't enjoy champagne, but because he didn't feel like celebrating Ivy's birthday. Over recent weeks he'd an increasingly nasty taste in his mouth about Ivy.

I couldn't say why, he thought, but I get the impression she's not remotely concerned that Orianna and I have split up. Quite the opposite: she seems to be doing her damnedest to conceal the fact she's pleased. I don't like to believe ill of people, but I'm not stupid, and having Orianna single suits her—she's free to hang out with her socially once more.

Dan had also observed they seemed to have got close again professionally, and Orianna was keen to work with Ivy whenever possible.

And Ivy being a constant presence in Orianna's life makes it nigh on impossible for anyone—let alone me—to get a word in, he decided. And I can't point this out as Orianna will see any criticism of Ivy as a personal attack and rush to her defense. The chances of her listening to me are nonexistent.

Dan couldn't avoid seeing Orianna, but he found being in such proximity difficult. Even though it was a couple of months since they'd split, the fact that the woman he still loved ignored him except when forced not to by professional circumstance upset him a great deal. So much so that earlier that day he'd vowed to look for another job, to get away from Green and the pain of working together forever.

Anyway, he'd an appointment with Rob at the gym that evening, and alcohol was incompatible with exercise. Just then he overheard Cassie say to Russell that she wasn't drinking. Well, if she could refuse and not be scoffed at, with luck he could too.

"For the latecomer?" Russell proffered him a glass.

"I won't, thanks."

"Not you as well."

"Going to the gym."

"Ah, right." Russell snorted and moved away.

Charming, thought Dan. Russell is so rude at times, and he doesn't think fit to offer any alternative. He turned to Cassie. "Can I get you something?"

"Oh . . . er . . ." She looked uncertain.

"There's some orange juice in the kitchen. I'd rather have that. Want a glass?"

Cassie smiled. "Yes, please."

So Dan went to fetch it.

———

"Did you see that?" said Ivy.

Of course she had. Orianna didn't miss the merest hint of contact between Dan and Cassie, let alone something so marked.

Ivy dropped her voice. "I hate it when he rubs your nose in it."

Orianna winced. "Me too." On the whole she had to concede Dan had been pretty discreet about his affair with Cassie, and for this, at least, Orianna was grateful. Whether it was out of humility, diplomacy, or embarrassment, Orianna didn't know or care—she just appreciated it made working together slightly more bearable. But seeing Dan bring Cassie a tumbler of fruit juice reminded her that *she* had been the one he'd attended to until recently, and it cut her to the quick.

Orianna had kept busy since they'd parted in an attempt to anesthetize the hurt. She'd thrown herself into work with a maniacal vengeance, aided by Ivy, who had been keen to do all she could professionally to help. "I've missed you," she'd said, and Orianna had been touched. Orianna had avoided much contact with Cassie; instead getting Ivy to oversee her work—Ivy, bless her, had been most amenable. What was more, to Orianna's relief, Ivy had also volunteered to fend off their colleagues' inevitable questions about her split with Dan. "I tell them not to pry or else," she'd said, and laughed. "And you know how frightening I can be." This had given Orianna the strength to go out in the evening occasionally too—often with Ivy. Once or twice they'd even had something approaching fun. But deep inside, Orianna's heart was bleeding; an unremitting ache was with her every hour of every day, and most nights she sobbed into her pillow.

For all his despicable behavior, I'm not over Dan, she admitted to herself. Sometimes I wonder if I ever will be.

Her thoughts were broken by Ivy nudging her in the ribs. "Wonder why Cassie's not drinking?" she whispered. "Always thought she liked a tipple, myself."

But Orianna was watching Dan—those familiar hands curled around the glass—and only half listening.

———

"Some sit-ups to finish?" suggested Rob.

"I suppose," said Dan. He'd hoped a trip to the gym might lift his spirits, get his endorphins going, but even after fifty minutes of intense aerobic exercise followed by weight training, he still felt a heaviness of spirit.

What's the point in toning up my abs when there's no one to notice the benefit? he thought, lowering himself onto the mat. He was reminded of Orianna and her affection for his little tummy, which only made him more morose.

"Ready?" said Rob, taking his place alongside.

But as Dan looked up at the ceiling, he decided: the only six-pack he was interested in right now was the kind to help him numb the pain.

Screw it, he thought. A tiny glass of champagne is one thing: a pint of beer another. It's time to drown my sorrows. With any luck, Rob might be happy to have his ear bent.

Dan had found the last few weeks tough—and he didn't have many male friends he could confide in; not that way. He always felt more comfortable exposing his vulnerability to a woman, usually whoever he was going out with at the time. And there was no one of the opposite sex he'd ever been able to talk to as intimately or frankly as Orianna. Yet he didn't have her to share his most heartfelt emotions with any longer . . .

However Rob might be more open than Dan's straight friends, more inclined to listen. After all, Rob probably had had his fair share of trauma, coming out, and he seemed to enjoy talking about people and intimate subjects.

Without bothering to complete the exercise, Dan sat back up. "What are you doing this evening?"

Rob turned to face him. Their eyes met, and Dan thought he detected a flash of understanding. "Nothing. You're my last client. Why?"

"Great." Dan sprang to his feet. "Fancy going for a bevvy?"

32. This is the night that either makes me, or fordoes me quite

It's looking good, thought Rob, as Dan headed off to buy a third round.

He watched Dan make his way to the bar—my, what a great rear view he had! Nicely rounded, yet firm. He's got me to thank for that, Rob congratulated himself. Though I did have fine raw materials from the start.

Rob could tell Dan had been far from happy of late, but had held back from pressing Dan too closely about the state of his love life during their sessions at the gym. He'd decided to follow Ivy's advice and wait for Dan to take the initiative. Now they were in a social environment, he was hoping Dan would open up.

From this it's only a small step to an admission we're mutually attracted, he thought, and from there it's but a skip and a hop to a snog.

Rob was confident he was pretty hot stuff, and had every faith they might reach the point of no return in the taxi ride that would whisk them both back to his place . . .

Going out together was even suggested by Dan—he was *lying next to me* on the mat when he mooted it. I mean, speculated Rob, how revealing of Dan's unconscious motives was that? *Purlease!* They'd locked eyes, for heaven's sake!

To compound things, Dan had suggested they come to Freedom on Wardour Street, a bar known for its mixed crowd of gays and straights. It had a late closing, so time was on Rob's side and a dance floor downstairs with dark alcoves virtually purpose-built for seduction. Furthermore, not only was Dan exhibiting the characteristics of a man in emotional turmoil—he appeared in something of a flat spin—he also seemed keen to get plastered. Rob had had his own first homosexual encounter under the influence of copious quantities of Bacardi many years before— and was growing increasingly convinced if anything was ever going to happen between them, tonight was the night.

As Dan stood poised to sit back down beside him, slopping beer unsteadily as he did so, Rob decided to up the ante. After all, he'd been patiently listening to Dan tell him how much he loved Orianna, yet when Rob tried to get him to clarify *precisely* why things had gone irretrievably wrong, Dan couldn't begin to explain. He was simply insistent that they couldn't communicate properly, didn't understand each other, and were on different planes. If this wasn't a euphemism for diverging sexual paths, what was? To Rob, who'd had a few affairs with women as a teenager that had been similarly confusing and dissatisfactory, it was obvious. Orianna wouldn't ever satisfy Dan. Not only emotionally, but physically.

"Shall we go downstairs?" he ventured.

"Why? I'm alright here, aren't you?" It was true they had a table to themselves.

"Have a dance?"

Dan frowned. "I don't—er—like dancing."

"Really?" Rob was bewildered. Hadn't Ivy said Dan had been seen at G-A-Y? If he didn't like dancing, why go?

But then Dan elaborated, "I love dance music—just not dancing."

"They play better music downstairs. We can sit and listen, if you prefer."

Dan appeared happier. "OK," he said amiably. "Let's go."

Rob led the way down the spiral staircase. The basement was red-lit, smoky, and the sound system pulsed heavily and hard.

The beat subtly shifted, and Dan bellowed, "I love this one!" over the laid-back intro. He stood gulping his beer, taking in the surroundings. Shortly, as a catchy keyboard melody segued into the mix, he started tapping his foot.

Good, Rob thought, he's relaxing. And he knew a surefire way to speed that up: "Fancy a chaser?"

"Oh, um, yeah, why not?" Dan grinned, and followed Rob over to the bar.

As they leaned their elbows against the cool surface, Rob was acutely conscious of the proximity of Dan's forearms to his own. Aah, he sighed to himself. When we were roommates, Chloë and I spent many a happy hour contemplating the unique appeal of male forearms. And whether it was the dark hairs that promised an equally hirsute chest, the thick wrists that hinted at real muscular strength, the understated watch, or the uncannily beautiful hands, didn't matter. Dan had a fine physique all around, and it was everything Rob could do to restrain himself from reaching out and touching him.

With a stroke of luck, at that moment the bartender came to take their order, and as Rob leaned forward to ask for two tequilas, his forearm brushed against Dan's, almost of its own accord. It was a way of gauging things without seeming too obvious, and Dan didn't flinch or try to pull away.

Exhilarated, Rob led them to an alcove and sat down. Dan plonked himself next to him and—to Rob's delight—drained his tequila in one gulp. Rob did the same. His ability to rationalize was now reduced further; his actions governed by lust, not reason.

Rob edged closer to Dan so that his thigh was ever so slightly pressed up against his. He slipped his arm around the back of the sofa—not so close that it was in contact with Dan—but close enough so other punters would realize Dan was his territory. Steer clear, the gesture indicated.

"Tell me," he said, with more than a touch of flirtation in his voice, "has it made you think again about women at all, this stuff with Orianna?"

"What do you mean?" Dan furrowed his brow.

"I just wondered . . ." Rob ran his finger suggestively around the top of his tequila glass, "whether it's made you, well, think . . . that they're more trouble than they're worth?"

Dan snorted. "Too bloody right."

Rob nodded in sympathy.

"Keep this to yourself, obviously, but I'm probably going to look for another job."

"Really?"

"Yeah. Get out of Green. It's all too heavy for me, frankly. Too much gossip; too many people knowing my business."

Hmm, thought Rob. I wonder if you're frightened someone's going to blow the lid on your sexuality. Sounds that way to me. But he realized Dan might not be ready to admit as much without some gentle guidance. "I mean forgive me for saying so—I'm sure Orianna's a very nice girl and everything, when I met her I *really* liked her—but nevertheless, you could say . . . her behavior as you're describing it, all these neuroses about other girls and so forth—it does seem a mite, well, irrational . . ."

"You're telling me." Dan nodded vigorously. "I really don't get it."

"That's women for you," said Rob. He felt slightly guilty at condemning an entire sex but his focus was not on fair play.

"You think?"

"Sure." Rob took a large gulp of beer. "They're from Venus, remember?"

"Different species," agreed Dan.

"Prefer Martians myself." Rob laughed, and Dan laughed with him, loud and long.

This is my sign, Rob decided. He leaned forward, and before he had the chance to reconsider, kissed Dan full on the lips. Dan's mouth was wonderfully warm and soft, a sensation made more erotic by the way his stubble rubbed against Rob's skin.

As Rob sat back, it took him a second to gauge Dan's reaction. Dan hadn't recoiled, so at first Rob was sure he'd done the right thing. Although Dan looked faintly surprised, Rob was convinced this must be because he was anticipating another more intimate and exciting move. After all, Dan's mouth was open.

But as Dan's expression took shape, Rob realized with mounting horror, that the look on his face wasn't one of pleasure, or anything approaching it. His gaping jaw was the result of speechlessness. Oh Lord, thought Rob. For he could tell this was the aghast response of a totally straight boy when confronted by the utterly unexpected—a thoroughly unwelcome pass from someone of his own gender.

Hell, thought Ivy, sneaking into the loo for another little snifter, so what if I've got work tomorrow? I know I promised to call Ed when I got home, but it'll keep. It *is* my birthday, after all.

She inhaled, first up one nostril, then the other. Yes! Who needed alcohol, when there was cocaine? The night was young. She'd an urge to text Russell. He'd turned down the invitation to join them all at Cassio's after work, explaining he had an agency project he wanted to finish off at home. Earlier Ivy had been content to leave him to it, but the cocaine high meant the need to fulfill her dominatrix fantasy was more urgent. Still, however keen she was for speedy gratification, she couldn't resist a witty text, so tapped:

> On my birthday I like to tie up my own presents . . . Thought I'd make my way over to yours so we can see in All Hallows Eve in X-rated style together. OK?

Then she quickly replenished her lipstick and went back upstairs, where Orianna was waiting on a stool pulled up at the bar. The rest of their colleagues had gone home long since, protesting they didn't have the stamina for late-night drinking.

"Isn't it funny," Ivy mused, confidence increased by the drug, "to think of the last time we came here together?"

Orianna looked doubtful. "I'm not sure *funny* is exactly the word I'd use."

"Oh, OK, not *funny* then," said Ivy lightly. "Interesting."

"Mm." Orianna nodded.

"We've come a long way since, though, haven't we?" Ivy smiled.

"Er . . . yes," said Orianna. "A lot's happened . . ." Her voice trailed off, and she looked away. Ivy knew she was thinking about Dan, and how they'd still been together then. Ivy had believed Orianna was getting over him, but this was a clear indication that she wasn't. That Orianna continued to view events in terms of how they related to her relationship with Dan, rather than to their friendship, upset Ivy, and from her upset sprang malice. A touch of spite was all she needed to lose her restraint; combined with cocaine confidence, it gave her the incentive to reveal the fact that she'd been withholding the entire evening.

"Cassie's pregnant," she said.

The color drained from Orianna's cheeks. "What?"

"Cassie's pregnant," Ivy repeated.

"*No!*" A howl of intense anguish, then Orianna's face crumpled and she fell silent.

Ivy felt remorse. She and Orianna had become much closer again; she was even beginning to believe she might be able to forgive her at some point—not yet, but one day. Seeing Orianna's face contorted like this, she had an impulse to reveal the baby wasn't Dan's, but Leon's. But she pulled herself up short. What a *stupid* idea! Of course she couldn't. Such a confession would only expose not just all the lies she'd told regarding Dan and his supposed affairs, but also the information she'd withheld about who Cassie was really sleeping with. No, she was in too deep to start being honest. And although Ivy had a nagging doubt this fabrication might backfire on her, at this point the only way forward was to continue. "Yes, indeed."

Eventually Orianna regained her voice. "How do you know? Did she tell you?"

"Not yet she hasn't, no."

"Oh?" Orianna looked hopeful for a second. "So she might not be, then?"

If Ivy couldn't alter her tactics, at least she could adopt a kind manner to alleviate her guilt. "I'm afraid, sweetheart, that I'm pretty sure she is. Sorry."

Orianna was crestfallen. "Honestly?"

"Yeah. I didn't want to tell you until I was positive."

"Oh."

Ivy noticed Orianna's hands had started to shake. Oh dear, she thought, conscience pricked further. She took hold of one of Orianna's hands and squeezed it; whether to make herself or Orianna feel better she didn't quite know.

"What makes you certain?"

Orianna was speaking so softly that Ivy had to lean closer to hear her. Ivy took a deep breath. Here at least she could be truthful. "Well, the first thing I noticed was several weeks ago. She seemed to be spending *hours* in the loo."

"But she's always done that," protested Orianna, hope rising in her voice.

"I know, I know," agreed Ivy patiently. "So I wanted to be sure, and I am—she's had morning sickness. In fact, not merely morning sickness, but afternoon sickness too. Even Cassie couldn't spend *that* much time repairing her makeup."

"I suppose she has been looking a bit rough recently. I just assumed that was because she and Dan were . . . well, that she wasn't getting much sleep."

"Anyway, I think she's over the worst of that now."

"You do? Perhaps it was nothing, then. Although . . ."

Ivy detected that she was bracing herself. "Mm?"

"You could be right . . ."

Ivy chivvied, "Don't you think she might be a bit plumper, too?"

"Again, I thought that was going out with Dan." Orianna's voice was small. "He likes his food so much. I suppose I didn't like to look at her too closely—I've been avoiding her."

She glanced up and smiled at Ivy, weakly. "You've helped me manage that by getting her off my back. Thanks."

"That's OK." There was a long silence.

"And it's hard to tell exactly what she's been wearing lately."

"Precisely. All that loose flowing stuff—ghastly! We should christen her the bag lady!" Ivy laughed, attempting to lighten the conversation. "And tonight she refused a glass of champagne, whereas normally she'd happily have at least one."

Orianna narrowed her eyes, recollecting. "Oh, now that you mention it, she did. Dan got her that juice, didn't he?"

"Yes." There was another silence. Ivy waited, conscious Orianna had a lot to assimilate.

At last Orianna said, "Christ, how awful. Awful." Her eyes filled with tears. "So how many months do you think she is?"

"I don't know." Ivy shrugged. "Four? Something like that?"

"But Dan and I broke up less than eight weeks ago! That must mean she got pregnant while Dan was going out with me!"

Lord, thought Ivy, imagine working out the sums that quickly. She knows when she and Dan split to the actual day. "Er . . . maybe . . ." she muttered.

"Oh, Ivy! I don't know if I can handle all this. I really don't." Tears streamed down Orianna's cheeks.

"Of course you can!" said Ivy, suddenly stricken that Orianna would be the colleague she'd lose, not Cassie. Although she still resented Orianna's professional supremacy intensely, she didn't necessarily want her to leave the agency.

Who knows what will happen then, she thought, who might be brought in to replace her? Whereas Orianna and I have been doing lots of nice work together recently and if things carry on the way they are, Orianna could even see to it that I get promoted to creative director too. Either that or Trixie will find *me* a job—she's only put a couple of suggestions my way so far but obviously it takes time when you're at my level of seniority—and then I'll be the one to move somewhere new.

Orianna sighed. "Honestly, I'm not sure I can. Lord knows, it's been tough enough already. But seeing Cassie getting bigger and bigger before my eyes, and what will everyone at Green say?"

"I'll take care of that," said Ivy, matter-of-factly.

"How?"

"I'll tell Cassie she'd better keep quiet about who the father is," said Ivy. "If she wants to keep her job. Put up and shut up, I'll say. You know I'm good at getting people to do that."

"Thanks," said Orianna quietly. "That would make life a bit easier." She stopped, then added, "Jesus, Ivy, you don't think he'll *marry* her, do you?" And at this thought, she couldn't hold back any longer, and began to wail.

For a brief moment Ivy could see the humor in it all; here they were causing a scene in Cassio's *again*. But she could hardly point this out, and instead said vehemently, "God, no! I'm sure he won't." Then she reached across the bar for a napkin and handed it to Orianna.

Orianna wiped her eyes. "You never know . . . what with their both being Jewish, and all."

Ivy shook her head. "You know me, honey, my instinct is usually pretty good. I *truly* don't think he'll marry her." Ivy remained niggled by guilt, so at least could reassure her on this front. "Let's face it, if he was seriously into her he'd be more public about their affair, wouldn't he? He'd think bugger the consequences?"

"He might just be doing that to be kinder to me."

This is unbelievable, thought Ivy. She's still potty about him! Will Orianna never learn? Once more she felt a mite spiteful. "Or not wanting everyone in the agency to think he's a prick."

But Orianna's mournfulness continued unabated. "I suppose a part of me hoped . . ." Her voice dropped to a whisper, as if she could barely face saying it. "Well, that it would be me, having children with Dan."

"Of course." Although this was the first Ivy had heard of it directly, she wasn't surprised Orianna felt this way. Unlike Ivy, who didn't concede to a maternal bone in her body, Orianna had made no secret of the fact she wanted children. They never talked about it, but it was an unspoken understanding. But at least, thought Ivy, Orianna wasn't one of those desperate women so broody they'd use a turkey baster to impregnate themselves. A born romantic, Orianna believed children should be the result of a happy union, preferably a marital one—she'd always said so.

Orianna sniffed. "I'm sorry. You must be sick of me crying."

"No, no, not at all."

"But I'm ruining your birthday."

"Don't be silly!"

"You know what? I think I'd like to go home."

"Really?"

"Yeah. I just want to be on my own for a bit. If we go now"—Orianna checked her watch—"I can still catch my train."

"True." Ivy nodded, thinking *and I can get laid.*

While they were waiting for the bill, Ivy dashed to the loo for another quick snort, purely to ensure she maximized her stamina for Russell. At the train station she gave her friend a hug. Orianna had momentarily stopped weeping.

"Will you be OK?"

"Yeah, I'll be fine." Orianna forced a faint smile. "You gonna get a cab?"

"Mm." Ivy was elusive.

"I'll see you in the morning then." She disappeared into the crowd.

Just then Ivy's mobile beeped to indicate a message. Ah, good, it must be Russell. She opened the text.

> Still tied up in work matters. No can do to the X-rated version. Catch up with you tomorrow.

Ivy was incredulous. Russell—refusing a shag? In order to *work*? It was totally out of character. And it was her birthday! As his words sank in, she grew more enraged. The tone was so insouciant, it was downright insulting. And now, thanks to him, she was wide awake at midnight in the middle of Soho, with no one to hang out with and nowhere to go.

33. I must leave her company

To: Everyone
From: Dan Cohen
Date: Monday, November 24, 11:15
Subj: Fond farewell

This may come as something of a surprise to some of you, but I will get straight to the point. I'm leaving Green. I am taking vacation time in lieu of notice, so will depart at the end of next week.

After much deliberation, I have decided to go freelance to give myself time to consider what my next permanent move should be.

Lastly, owing to the personal nature of my departure, I won't be having a farewell drink.

May I take this opportunity to say how much I have enjoyed
working with everyone.

All the best,
Dan

Well, that's it, thought Orianna. He's leaving and I find out through an
e-mail. He might have had the guts to tell me himself. It sounds so formal, not like Dan remotely. "The personal nature of my departure" indeed! It's me and Cassie he's talking about! Why doesn't he have the balls
to say so? I could have helped him phrase it: "I've fucked around with
women, perhaps even the occasional man, and I've fucked up" would be
more appropriate.

At that moment the internal phone rang.

"Hi," said a familiar voice.

"Oh, hi," she said, caught short. It was Dan, but she didn't recognize
the extension number. "Where are you calling from?"

"The boardroom. I didn't think you'd answer if you knew it was me."

"I wouldn't have," said Orianna bluntly. She was still trying to gather
her thoughts about his departure.

"I wanted a private word."

"I see."

"Er, I wondered, did you get my e-mail?"

"Yes, why?"

"Bollocks," said Dan. "I wanted to tell you first."

"Shouldn't have pressed *Send* then, should you?"

"I guess not." His voice was quiet, subdued. As it should be. Though
it was a bit late to be sheepish.

"So," said Orianna. "You couldn't cut it." She knew she sounded
aggressive, but that was how she felt.

Dan sighed. "Guess not."

"Don't know what you're expecting me to say about it."

"I thought perhaps we could talk."

"What about? So I could wish you bon voyage? Good luck? No Dan."

"Oh."

"Look, it just didn't work out. You're leaving. In some ways I'm glad."

"You are?"

Although a voice inside her head was screaming otherwise, she said, "Yes. It'll make things easier for everyone. Let's drop it there, shall we?"

"Are you absolutely sure that's what you want?"

Orianna wasn't, remotely. Then she pictured Cassie, growing contentedly bigger only yards from her, and Dan close by, tactfully playing it down, but all the while becoming increasingly attached to both Cassie and the baby.

They won't be able to keep their relationship secret much longer, she thought, and when the truth comes out, it will be more than I can stand. Yes, if Cassie isn't going to resign, I suppose Dan leaving is the best option.

"I'm sure," she said, trying not to let her voice betray her upset and anger, and put down the phone.

34. What's the business?

To: Everyone
From: Russell North
Date: Monday, December 10, 9:15
Subj: Keeping Green in the black this Christmas

It may or may not have escaped your notice, but the world is currently in the midst of a global recession, and unfortunately Green Integrated has not avoided its impact. As a result things are tight, budget-wise. I'm hoping we can make it to New Year unscathed in terms of layoffs but this requires your help. Some general pointers follow.

1. I'm sorry to have to inform you that bonuses will be suspended until further notice. For precise details, speak to your line manager, though I'm sure you appreciate it's better to curtail these than have to lose staff.

2. I'd also venture to suggest now is not the time for extravagance in terms of expenses. I'll be keeping a close eye on your applications for reimbursement over the Christmas period. I am sure you will appreciate this is not just for your sake but for the sake of the agency as a whole.

3. Finally, although it pains me to announce this, we will not be able to hold the annual party at the Groucho Club this year. Because we on the board believe we should practice what we preach, Stephen has gallantly forgone his company membership (thereby saving a tidy sum) and we will be holding the party on January 3, when it's more cost-effective, at Kettner's. Also, the party will start at 6 p.m., not lunchtime, so we can continue to service our clients fully during the day.

Thank you for your understanding and patience.

And Happy Christmas!
Russell

To: Orianna Bianchi
From: Ivy Fraser
Date: Monday, December 10, 9:23
Subj: Re: Keeping Green in the black this Christmas

Tight git.

Oh well. Orianna couldn't say she was sorry. She'd been dreading the party and it was a relief it wasn't going to echo the evening she'd got together with Dan.

What a year it's been, she thought, glorious and torturous in equal measure. If spring and summer were the happiest months of my life, the three months since have been surely the most miserable.

At that moment there was a knock at her door.

"Come in," she said.

She looked up from her screen to see Cassie, who said, "I wonder if I can have a word? There's something I'd like to talk to you about."

Taking in her expression of apprehension, Orianna steeled herself. If Cassie's going to confide in me about Dan, I don't want to hear, she thought.

She'd been managing to conceal her hurt as best she could; she hoped most of her colleagues were unaware how much she was smarting inside. She'd resisted confronting Cassie and borne the situation with a fortitude she didn't believe she had, but was unsure she could handle it were she faced with the relationship directly.

Cassie shut the door and stood before her, shifting from foot to foot. Then she blurted, "I'm pregnant."

Sure enough, it stabbed Orianna like a spear to the heart. But perhaps she really was becoming tougher; certainly it seemed to help she'd prepared herself for the news. It took only a few seconds for her to feign surprise—after all, she'd better not betray she'd already been told by Ivy. "Oh?"

Cassie nodded. "I thought you had a right to know."

That's an understatement, observed Orianna, but simply said, "I guess I do."

"As you're my boss and all."

Orianna fought the urge to be scathing. Instead she forced a smile. "When's it due?"

"April."

Another spear. This confirmed that Dan had been sleeping with the two of them concurrently. She concealed a shudder and asked, "So you're nearly five months?"

"Yes. I wanted to hold off as much as possible before telling you. I'm aware I've not been here that long."

It was all Orianna could do not to lean across her desk, grab her by the throat, and yell, *"Hold off on telling me that you're pregnant because you've not been at the agency that long? Stuff your maternity rights, screw formalities—isn't the point that you're pregnant by my ex-boyfriend? The man I hoped I might have children with, until you came here!"* Yet she was rapidly learning to think one thing and say another. Still— damn it; she was sick of letting Cassie get away with such shameful behavior, and there was no one else within earshot. She was going to make Cassie squirm. She asked point-blank, "Who's the father then?"

Cassie went scarlet.

Rather than let her off the hook, Orianna prompted, "Someone I know?" Her sarcasm could not be more overt.

To her amazement, Cassie replied, "I'm not sure it's any of your business." If this elusiveness was an attempt at diplomacy, it was so awkward that Orianna was startled into silence. This gave Cassie time to illuminate: "I think it's best that you and I don't talk about it. I just wanted you to know that I plan on working right up to my due date—or as close to that as I may, all being well. And, if it's OK with you, I'd like to come back to work as soon as possible after the baby is born. I really enjoy it here at Green."

I bet you do, thought Orianna. What cheek! But she only permitted herself to raise her eyebrows. "Oh?"

Cassie continued, "I'll need the money."

"I see."

"Anyway, that's all I wanted to say. I don't want you to worry it'll interfere with my art direction, because I'll do my utmost to make sure it doesn't."

"Mm."

"I'll get back to my work."

"Fine."

Not for the first time, it occurred to Orianna what an enormous relief it would be to get rid of Cassie as well as Dan, but she was aware that firing someone—especially a pregnant woman—was a legal minefield. With any luck Cassie wouldn't want to return to such a stressful job once the baby was actually born.

Alone again, she sat back in her chair and exhaled heavily. After a few minutes, to take her mind off the encounter, she leaned forward and re-read Russell's e-mail.

I'm sure Ivy won't be the only one griping, she thought. Goddamn it, now I'll have all my staff berating me about their bonuses and panicking they're going to be made redundant, along with everything else. And I guess I shouldn't be surprised the forecast sounds so bleak profit-wise with the economy in its present state, but I do find it frustrating that the company finances seem to be getting worse when we've won a lot of business since I took over. To be bringing in new clients is a rare accomplishment, so why is the agency still struggling?

Orianna wasn't suspicious by nature, but she was seriously beginning to wonder. Every time she asked Russell to clarify why they were taking such a huge loss and requested precise figures, he shirked the issue.

Bugger it, she thought. The tone of Russell's e-mail is annoying and if I can't confront Cassie, at least I can confront him. She hit *Reply*.

To: Russell North
From: Orianna Bianchi
Date: Monday, December 10, 10:20
Subj: Re: Keeping Green in the black this Christmas

I'm sure you're busy but I really would like to discuss this with you in more detail. It is still not clear to me why the agency took a loss in November, when we have won several substantial pieces of new business from Bellings Scott, not to mention a considerable amount from existing clients.

I have requested clarification before but now this is urgent. Not just because the majority of the creative department will be beating a path to my door within the next few hours as a result of your e-mail, and I would like to be able to answer their questions, but also because, as financial

director, it's your job to keep me informed about monetary
issues. So far I've been kept in the dark.

Thank you.
Orianna

While Cassie was in with Orianna, Ivy was sitting at her desk several
yards away, watching.

This is a test, she thought. Cassie might let slip that Dan's not the
father.

But over the last few weeks, Ivy had done her utmost to secure the
baby's paternity would be remain secret. "Remember the company
policy about in-agency relationships," she'd warned, when Cassie had finally confided that she was pregnant. And when Cassie had muttered she
wasn't sure she wanted to settle down with Leon, although Ivy was surprised, it gave her exactly the fuel she needed. "Quite right: far better not
to mix business and pleasure. Keep your private life to yourself for as long
as you can—it'll be much easier. Then you can see how things pan out
with Leon and make your own decision, rather than have agency tattle-
tale make it for you." Cassie seemed content to go along with this, so her
meeting Orianna in private didn't cause Ivy undue alarm. Anyway, there
wasn't much opportunity for concern, for presently her phone rang.

"Ivy?" It was Russell.

"Yeah?"

"Can you spare a minute?"

"Sure."

"My office?"

"Fine. Be with you in a sec." She pressed *Save* and got to her feet. Once
in Russell's room, she shut the door and took a seat opposite.

"Did you see my memo?"

She laughed. "Yeah, nice one."

He looked at her, straight. "I'm serious, Ivy."

"Oh?"

"The agency's not doing that well."

"Really?" Ivy knew how much new business they'd won; she assumed he was making a needless fuss.

"No."

"Oh."

"I won't beat around the bush. Some of the points in question apply as much to you as anyone. Frankly, more."

Ivy frowned. "Huh?"

"I've asked everyone to mind their extravagance, Ivy, and I'm asking you to do the same."

"Me?"

"Yes, you."

"What?" Given her special relationship with Russell, Ivy had taken it for granted she would be exempt.

"Your annual bonus, Ivy. It'll have to stop."

She needed to be certain she understood him correctly. "Come again?"

"You heard me. Your bonus. We can't afford it anymore. Not for a while, anyway."

He couldn't be serious! Without her bonus she'd be earning *much* less! How on earth was she going to be able to afford her car? Her apartment? Buy designer clothes? Drugs? She sensed her mouth opening and shutting like a goldfish, but before she had time to formulate a response, Russell continued, "And that's not all. There are also your credit cards."

"What about them?"

"Your company Visa is one thing; but in particular, your Harvey Nichols charge card, Ivy."

"So?"

"I can't keep hiding these sorts of expenses." He picked up a statement. "Women's wear, three hundred and fifty pounds . . ."

"Mm." Ivy fingered her cashmere cardigan.

He pressed on. "Accessories, beauty. I mean, honestly, Ivy. The fifth-floor food hall? Over a hundred pounds? Get real."

" 'Get real'?!" This wasn't the kind of language she was used to from Russell.

"Yes. The agency can't afford to feed you on champagne and caviar. This is the twenty-first century."

He was being so patronizing! "If I'm so out of date," she quipped, "how come you've never said anything before?"

"Because I've let it go for as long as I can."

"Oh." She looked him in the eye, to check he meant it. Unfortunately she knew Russell well enough to know that expression. Firm and unyielding. Possibly even—when it came to money—power-crazed. Often she found it erotic. Though it indicated he wouldn't budge, however hard she pleaded.

"OK." She got to her feet. "I get the message." And she stomped back to her desk, filled with indignation.

All day Orianna waited for a reply from Russell. She made sure he was in the agency throughout the afternoon, and checked her e-mail at regular intervals. OK, so he appeared to be immersed in papers or focused on his screen, but that was no excuse for not responding. If he's hoping I'll let it go he's much mistaken, she thought.

By six o'clock she'd gone beyond curiosity, or even understanding. She was fuming. No doubt her rage was compounded by having repressed her resentment of Cassie, but still she had every right to be furious. Didn't Russell owe her some civility? He might not be her number one fan, nevertheless she had worked damn hard over the last year, put her heart and soul into her job, and in the face of the most grueling personal challenges, had not allowed her work, or the agency, to suffer.

How dare he cut me out of the loop? she thought. Does he think because I'm creative, that understanding facts and figures is beyond me?

"Condescending prick," she muttered. Screw him. I've spent the best part of my life being innocent, and look where it's gotten me: shafted by the man I loved and the woman I hired. Well, I'm not going to let it happen again.

Her colleagues seemed more anxious than ever to been seen working all hours in the wake of Russell's e-mail. It was 9:45 p.m. before the last of her coworkers tapped on the glass of her office on his way out.

"I'll lock up," she mouthed.

Finally she was on her own in the department. She could hear a vacuum on the floor below; she didn't have long before the cleaner reached the top floor, so she hotfooted it across to Russell's office.

His door was unlocked; to bolt it would have seemed odd in a chiefly open-plan environment. Best not turn on the main light; instead she went to his desk and switched on his lamp. Orianna wasn't sure what precisely she was seeking, but she'd a hunch she was onto something.

Firstly, she tried his desk drawers. Locked, every one of them. And his filing cabinet: the same. Still, Russell kept the company petty cash there, it was to be expected. No point even attempting to open his computer—it was sure to be password-protected, and Russell was not someone whose code she would crack. No, what she was looking for was probably something he'd accidentally left out, the significance of which might not be immediately obvious. She began to riffle through his in-box, when she thought she heard the sound of the vacuum on the stairs. While the cleaner might not be aware who Orianna was, being caught searching the office of the financial director late at night was not worth risking. If Russell noticed anything was amiss the next day, she didn't want anyone to be able to point the finger at her.

Rummage, rummage. A load of invoices—mainly from suppliers, she knew most of their names. There were a couple she didn't recognize on cream-colored paper, but she wasn't aware of every single company the agency dealt with and they all seemed legitimate—stationery, photographic development, office furniture . . . More rummaging. Her fingers flicked sheet after sheet, like a bank teller counting bills. A few receipts—again they appeared to be in order; parking receipts, train fares, magazines. Then, right at the bottom of what she took to be the paperwork Russell had been handling that day, a familiar logo caught her eye.

Harvey Nichols.

She pulled out the piece of paper—it was some kind of a statement.

But *Harvey Nichols*? She frowned. This wasn't a credit card statement, as she might have expected. Orianna had a company credit card—a Visa—as did many of the senior suits. But this was for an account card; furthermore, it bore the name . . . *Ivy Fraser.* That in itself was strange, but it might not have been that strange had it not also borne the Soho Square address of Green Integrated where Orianna would have expected to see Ivy's home address in Hoxton. What on earth had Ivy bought at Harvey Nichols that could possibly be chargeable to the company?

Just then Orianna heard the thump of the vacuum being lugged up the stairs. Quick as a flash, before she had a chance to read the statement in any more detail, she ran out of Russell's office, heading for the photocopier. She lifted the lid, placed the statement on the glass, and hit the green button.

Damn!

The machine hadn't been used for an hour or so, and had gone to sleep. It was vast, and always took several minutes to warm up. She could hear the sound of the vacuum cleaner even closer now, on the landing outside.

Ah! That was it—the fax machine. Ancient technology, barely used these days, but some printers still preferred orders faxed through, so there was one in production. It made photocopies too, and was left on 24/7. She ran over to Dan's desk, and fingers trembling, shoved the statement into the document feeder. She pressed the *Copy* button and it whirred into action, sucking the sheet of paper into its roller. For a dreadful moment Orianna thought it was going to chew it up, but no, slowly, slowly, it fed the page through, and, *beep beep beep,* spewed it onto the top of the machine. Simultaneously, a copy popped out the other side.

Orianna grabbed both items, ran back to Russell's office, shoved the original statement back in the bottom of his in-box, turned off the desk lamp, and scooted out again, shutting the door swiftly behind her. She was just heading back to her desk across the open-plan department, clutching the copy, her heart racing, when the cleaner wheeled the vacuum into view.

35. These may be counterfeits

Ten minutes later, Orianna was on the subway home. It was between rush hour and pub closing, so she managed to find a seat. Before the train had reached the first stop, she'd yanked the photocopy from her bag and scanned the contents. It didn't take long to get the measure of it.

```
November     Women's wear: £350.00
November     Accessories: £199.00
November     Beauty: £109.00
```

That was just the start. It was a list that would have made Victoria Beckham proud. The previous month's balance appeared to have been cleared in full, but the outstanding amount due was still in excess of £1500. Moreover, not one of the items appeared to be a legitimate work expense.

As the train hurtled from Covent Garden to Holborn, Orianna's thoughts shot ahead. Why is this statement being sent to Green? she wondered. Far as I know, Ivy doesn't even have a company credit card.

Creatives are mainly office-based and deal with clients via account handlers—no copywriter has a call for one. I never had one till I was made CD, let alone a Harvey Nichols charge card.

It didn't look good, but Orianna was reluctant to jump to the wrong conclusion.

I suppose, she justified, it's possible there's a reason for Ivy to have details of her personal store card sent to the agency—perhaps she doesn't want Ed to see how much she's spending on clothes.

If Orianna had found the statement among Ivy's papers, she'd have been convinced this was the case. Though why was it at the bottom of *Russell's* in-box? Not only that, but his e-mail warning he'd be keeping a tighter rein on expenses showed the issue had been on his mind.

Orianna was totally honest when it came to claiming money back from the agency—and her instinct was to assume no one else would dare take liberties, especially given the firm's finances were so stretched. If Ivy had been surreptitiously spending company money, it explained a lot. The sums weren't enough to make or break the agency—whose turnover went into seven figures annually—but the expenditure wouldn't help, as it came straight off the bottom line. It didn't take an Einstein to calculate that if Ivy was going through this much on a monthly basis, it added up to a junior's salary—and thus a potential lay-off if she carried on. It also helped to explain how Ivy always looked so fantastic, dressed from head to toe in designer gear. Orianna knew Ivy was paid well—she'd been shocked to learn how well—but her official income still didn't seem high enough to fund her near-legendary wardrobe. And whereas Orianna had previously assumed Ed shelled out for the extras, now she was wondering if that was only half the story.

Could Ivy be the chief culprit Russell was referring to in his e-mail? she thought. Although why would he be prepared to let her expenses slip through unquestioned—what's so special about her? And if he's willing to sign off on someone else's illegitimate purchases, who's to say he won't be prepared to claim huge sums on his own behalf, too? After all, if the rumors are true, Russell doesn't only have a huge house in the country; he has an amazing penthouse in Chelsea Harbour, too.

Jesus, these are big accusations, Orianna realized. Yet it did make sense. For months she'd been thinking the money coming into the agency didn't equate with its profits. Perhaps this was why. But would Ivy really be involved in something so ugly?

I'm sure she doesn't realize how serious this is, she thought. Though it would be odd; Ivy's the last person I imagine would get involved in anything unwittingly. Then again, perhaps she's all too aware of the trouble she could get into and how her actions could affect the agency and its staff, but is prepared to risk it for her own ends . . . Wise up, she told herself. If Dan can lie to me and Cassie can be altogether blasé about my feelings—isn't it possible Ivy could be equally self-seeking too?

At once she pushed the idea aside.

Ivy is my friend, she protested inwardly. I know her better than any-one. She's far from altruistic, true, but don't forget how kind she's been in the last few months. Think how she supported you though your breakup with Dan—remember that night with the pizzas and wine? And didn't she swallow her pride and push aside her grievances about the promotion so you could both carry on working together? Hasn't she been a model of professionalism when it comes to teaming with Cassie, yet also gone out of her way to forewarn you about the pregnancy, so you were forearmed when confronted with it face-to-face? Surely this speaks volumes about your friend.

Deep in her heart I'm sure she cares for other people, Orianna con-cluded. I reckon she's been hoodwinked by Russell. Her insatiable desire for the latest clothes has prevented her from seeing things clearly.

However . . .

If there was a stronger force that drove Orianna than loyalty, it was honesty. And no matter how much she'd sharpened up her act and learned to mask feelings of late, and no matter how much she loved her friend, Orianna had integrity. She was determined to seek out the truth. To add fuel to this, Orianna was also driven by ambition. And when it came to her career, heaven defend those who threatened it. The well-being of the agency—and her livelihood—was at stake. If she had to go out on a limb to fight for them, then she would.

The train took several minutes to get to Caledonian Road, and Orianna began to formulate a plan. One lone charge card statement was not enough to hang anyone by. She had a suspicion Ivy's expenses were the tip of the iceberg and more financial irregularities lurked beneath. If Russell was stealing from the company on a grand scale, she'd need better evidence. It would be easy for Ivy and Russell to come up with some excuse about the store card; for two such swift thinkers, justifying relatively small-time filching would be child's play. And she really wanted to expose Russell, not Ivy. Yet if she was going to gather enough proof to accuse Russell of full-blown fraud, she wasn't sure she could handle it on her own. She'd need help. Someone who knew the company; someone with a head for figures.

Obviously she couldn't involve Ivy, and she didn't want to involve anyone else who was on the board until she was sure.

She needed someone relatively impartial, but experienced with purchase orders and invoicing. A person with knowledge of agency profits and loss, who knew the company inside out and who Orianna could trust; an ally who was quick, shrewd, direct, and as plain-speaking as she was.

As the train drew into Caledonian Road, it came to her.

Ursula.

Ursula was away till after Christmas—her sister lived in Australia and she'd taken three weeks off to visit her—but once she was back, Orianna would turn to her for help.

36. She was too fond of her most filthy bargain

Usually Ivy took pleasure from the walk down the street toward her apartment on a winter evening. The building, an old garment factory, was an impressive five-story, redbrick block built at the turn of the century. There was nothing quaint about its imposing silhouette against the night sky, and its huge bulk served as a welcome reminder of how well she'd done. But tonight she looked up at the windows to her loft apartment and her heart sank.

The lights were on.

It couldn't be the cleaner: she came on Mondays. Ed was home.

First Russell, now Ed, she growled to herself. Today is not a good day.

She turned the key in the lock and pushed open the door. Thanks to several cumbersome shopping bags and her Louis Vuitton purse, she had to edge her way through sideways. She'd been late-night shopping— needing a spree after Russell's sharp words, though she knew better than to risk his wrath by doing so at Green's expense. Instead she'd gone to Selfridges and used the account card she shared with Ed. From there she'd headed to the gym to pump out any remaining resentment, and by the end of her workout it was so late she'd decided to get a taxi back and bathe at home. Here she was, at nearly ten thirty, tired and sweaty from exercise, not to mention hungry. All she wanted to do was pop a snack in the microwave, have a nice deep bath, and tumble into bed.

Yet there he was—her husband—shoes off and feet curled up comfortably beneath him on the sofa, looking to all intents and purposes as if he lived there.

"Hello," he said.

"Hi. Didn't think I'd find you here."

"Thought I'd surprise you."

"You have." Ivy knew she sounded curt, but couldn't be bothered to conceal it. His beard has grown even more, she observed. How repulsive!

"I got some unexpected leave."

"That's nice." Ivy hadn't expected to see Ed till Christmas Eve; for a dreadful moment she thought maybe he was going to stay until then and beyond. Involuntarily, she shuddered. "How long you off for?"

"Just a couple of days." Ed took a sip of his usual whisky and soda. "Going back Saturday."

"Oh."

"So, how are you?"

"Me?" It was a long time since anyone had asked Ivy how she was. Even Orianna, who'd been relatively interested in her welfare before Dan came along, seemed to have too much else on her mind at present to inquire. Not that it bothered Ivy; she'd not necessarily have told the truth anyway. Indeed, she didn't really know what the truth was anymore, or how she was, deep inside. She was at a loss as to how to respond.

"Yes, you?"

"I'm fine, I guess."

"Fine?"

"Mm." She nodded. She was, wasn't she?

" 'Fine,' Ivy?"

"Yeah." She scowled. What was he driving at?

"Is that all you can say?"

"Yes." Her anger mounted. "Why?"

"Because I haven't seen you for nearly two months, Ivy, or spoken to you at any length for weeks. You even cut me short on your birthday, for Christ's sake."

Hadn't they talked more recently than that? Ivy cast her mind back. It was true. She'd been just about to go to Cassio's with her colleagues when he'd phoned her at work. On her mobile it was easy to vet his calls, but the receptionist at Green had blithely put him through so she'd been caught short.

I promised I'd call him later, she remembered. Then I had some coke and got pissed off with Russell . . .

She felt a second's remorse.

"And now all you can say is that you're 'fine,'" he finished.

She grimaced. It's not much in the way of communication, is it? she thought. But I can't face a confrontation with Ed, not now. "I need to have a bath," she said, hoping to change the subject. "And eat."

"*Fine.*" Ed emphasized the word. "Perhaps we can have a chat when you've finished you ablutions. Over some dinner."

"I was just going to have something from the freezer."

"Believe me, I wasn't offering to cook you a three-course meal. Let alone take you out."

Ivy was stung. Although miffed by Ed's presence, she liked to be the indifferent one. If anyone was going to be rude, tradition held it was usually her.

She went into the bathroom and turned on the hot water. It was her custom to air the room while she was at work, so the ventilator window was still open, and it was chilly. She closed the catch, stripped off her clothes, and pulled on her dressing gown, which she kept on a hook at the back of the door. Then she scooped her hair up into a bathing cap; hardly her sexiest look, but sex was rarely on the agenda these days where she and Ed were concerned.

One drawback to living in a building that hadn't been purposely built for habitation was the water system left a lot to be desired. If another tenant chose to bathe simultaneously—as they must be doing now—it affected the pressure, and the hot tap took ages to run. Oh well, she thought, if Ed's going to have a go at me, better sooner than later. She stepped back into the living room.

"I guess it's been a while since we've talked," she conceded.

"Mm." Ed grunted.

"I said I'd call you back, didn't I?"

"Yes, Ivy, you did."

"I'm sorry."

He was silent, obviously waiting for her to continue.

"We've been ever so busy at work."

"Me too." His tone was dry.

"Though I suppose that's not much of an excuse, is it?"

"No. Not when it comes to your husband, I don't believe it is." He drew in his breath. "That's the million-dollar question, isn't it, Ivy?"

"What do you mean?" She had a creeping suspicion she knew where this was headed.

"I thought you wanted to have a bath."

"I do."

"Well, this might take a bit longer than the time it takes to run the water."

"Oh."

"D'you want to turn it off? Or talk after?"

"I'll turn it off," she yielded, and went and did so.

She took a seat on one of the arms of the sofa. Not so near to him as to be overtly intimate; nor so far as to preclude reaching out to him if it might help sway things her way.

"I want a divorce," he said, without a word of warning.

It was all Ivy could do to remain seated. He'd intimated he wasn't happy before, but never this. Eventually, she stuttered, "Why?"

"*Why?*" He hooted. "Because I live at one end of the country and you at another, we don't see each other for weeks on end and when we do we don't have sex because you never want to. Plus it seems you're happy not to speak to me from one month to the next."

For once Ivy felt herself flush. "I guess I have been a bit remiss," she admitted. Russell's words still rang in her ears. I'm about to lose my bonus, my account card, and from now on I'll be on a regular salary . . . She panicked. What a dreadful time to split with Ed. I must be able to get him to rethink matters. "I'm sure we don't need to do anything quite so rash . . ."

"I'd hardly call it rash," Ed corrected. "This has been going on for months, years. It's not the first time I've tried to talk to you about it."

Better try harder, thought Ivy. She reached out a bare foot and gently began stroking her husband's thigh. "I can make it up to you, I promise."

To her surprise, he took hold of her foot and stopped her. "That's just it, Ivy. You don't get it, do you?"

Her lips pursed. This was proving tougher than she thought. "Get what?"

"I don't *want* you to make it up to me."

"Why not?"

He sighed. "Do me a favor. Let's stop pretending. You don't love me anymore, do you? You haven't loved me for years." He took a sip of whisky. "Sometimes I'm not sure you ever did."

Ivy recoiled. There was truth in his words, but she couldn't bring herself to acknowledge it. Much as she appreciated the validity of his remarks, she was more appreciative of what her marriage provided in terms of domestic security. Ed had bought the apartment several years back, and she doubted very much he'd let her keep it should they decide to separate. Although Ivy would be entitled to some of the capital if they sold it, between them it was the only major collateral they had.

Eventually he prompted: "Say something."

"I don't know what to say."

I should tell him I love him, she thought, it would help. But I don't love him, and I can't bring myself to. There's something about that beard . . . It's so repulsive, I can't feign interest. The idea of sleeping with him is nauseating.

"Well, if you won't, I will," Ed continued. "Are you having an affair, Ivy?"

She was flabbergasted, but instinctively rushed to defend herself. "What on earth makes you think that?"

"Because I know you, Ivy, although you might not reckon I do. However much of a cold fish you sometimes seem, I know you can't last long without sex; so if we're not doing it, you must be getting laid somewhere else." He looked at her; she sensed he was searching for an indication of her feelings.

She turned her head away. She could see steam billowing in the bathroom—the air would soon chill the water if she didn't get a move on. How she yearned to run in, bolt the door, and shut out Ed and his accusations!

"On second thoughts," he reconsidered, "I'm sure you wouldn't tell me, even if you were. It's not escaped my notice that you can be the most terrific prevaricator when it suits you, so there's not much point in asking. Perhaps it doesn't really matter."

"*Doesn't matter?!*" Ivy couldn't keep the indignation out of her voice. How could it not matter that I'm sleeping with someone else? What on earth has got into him that he can be so cool and uncaring?

"No. Not really."

"Why not?"

"Because whether you're having an affair or not, I'm not prepared to be your meal ticket any longer."

"Huh?"

"Oh, come on, Ivy. We both appreciate that's pretty much all I am to you these days." For the second time that day, Ivy's mouth opened and shut like a goldfish. "And whether you're having an affair or not, it's irrelevant to me. Because I am." Her jaw dropped wider still, and stayed wide. "I've started seeing someone else. It's only been a couple of months or so—since I was last here. I attempted to talk to you then—I even tried you at the office as you ignored my other calls, but you promised to call me back later and didn't and I suppose"—he rubbed his beard as he contemplated, ugh—"that's when I gave up on you and me once and for all. It wasn't long after that that things took off between the two of us, though I've known Mary a while . . ."

Ivy had no wish to hear all this, but she was too astounded to stop him.

Ed continued, almost as if he was enjoying being cruel, "Anyway, she's called Mary, as I say; she lives in Aberdeen. You may as well know the truth. We seem to have fallen for each other. I think I might love her, and I believe she feels the same."

Again all Ivy could say was, "Oh."

It's one thing for me not to love him, she thought. It's quite another for him not to love me.

She was hurt, insulted. Ivy was so used to being adored by Ed, albeit from afar, and supported by him, having him do exactly what she wanted, buy her whatever she desired whenever she asked, that jealousy seared through her: she hated Mary at once, purely on principle. And as Ed sat there looking at her, unwavering, Ivy was forced to stretch her powers of analysis to the hilt.

He tried to talk to me that night I rushed off to Orianna's too, she remembered. Is this why he's not called me lately? The reason he's grown a beard? Because he knew I'd hate it? I should have read the signs—what a fool I've been!

Ivy could have kicked herself, yet Ed hadn't finished. "Frankly, if I'm going to be anyone's meal ticket, I want to be Mary's. Though funnily enough, I'm not sure she's that interested in my money."

"I wouldn't bet on it," snapped Ivy.

"Not all women are like you." Ivy could have sworn she heard Ed mutter "Thank God" under his breath. "She's not the materialistic type, and anyway, she's a head teacher—she's got a fairly reasonable income of her own."

"Can't be much if she's only a teacher."

"Whatever. There's not much point in arguing. In short, I want a divorce, Ivy. I want a divorce as soon as possible because Mary and I plan on moving in together."

"But you've only just met—surely you barely know her!"

"No, Ivy. If there's anyone I barely know, it's you."

Ivy shuddered. There it went: her domestic security, crumbling again, just as it had nearly three decades ago.

37. Keep our counsel

As luck would have it, Orianna was sitting a few places from Ursula at the Kettner's office party on January 3. The room was lit by candles, the air thick with chatter—it was the perfect opportunity. Once they'd finished eating she picked up her wineglass and headed over.

"Swap with me, Leon?" she said. "I want to hear all about Australia." Leon did as he was bid and she lowered herself into his vacant seat. "So how was your trip?"

"Great!" enthused Ursula. "It's a fantastic place. I loved Sydney—and my sister's having an absolute ball. She's not working that hard, I must say, but not everyone's a workaholic like me. You can have such a wonderful standard of living. Personally," she lowered her voice and leaned near, "I can't understand why anyone would want to leave the place." She jerked her head in Cassie's direction. "Can you?"

Orianna winced. Contemplating Cassie was hardly where she wished to take the conversation. "I wouldn't know."

"So what d'ya reckon about . . . ?" Again a flick of eyes toward Cassie. "*Her.*"

"What about her?"

"Being knocked up."

Orianna started. This was the first time anyone other than Ivy and Cassie had openly spoken of the pregnancy.

"She must be . . . six, seven months now?"

"Mm." Caught short, Orianna admitted, "Cassie and I have discussed it, obviously, because her maternity leave will affect the department. The baby's due at the beginning of April."

"Ahem. Ladies?" It was Gavin, a bottle of red in one hand, white in the other.

Orianna covered the top of her glass. "I won't, thank you." She wanted to remain sober—she'd been waiting weeks for this.

"Very noble." Ursula held out her own for a refill. Once Gavin had moved away, she pulled her chair up to Orianna's so the legs were touching. "Though what *really* interests me"—she leaned close; Orianna could feel her breath on her cheek—"is who the father might be."

Well I never, thought Orianna. Does Ursula truly not know? Ivy's done a great job of keeping it all hush-hush. Bless her.

"Cassie won't say," lied Orianna. She was too proud to let on she knew herself.

"No, I appreciate *that*. She's being *ever* so secretive about it."

That's because of me, thought Orianna, but simply said, "I gathered."

"You must have some idea," coaxed Ursula.

Orianna felt the sharp dart of pain she suffered every time she thought of Dan. "No, not really . . ."

"Well, *I* have."

"What do you mean?"

"I've a *suspicion*," continued Ursula, her tone betraying shameless delight in discussing someone else's business, "that it could be Leon."

"LEON?" Such was Orianna's shock like a jack-in-the-box out it popped. Her voice was way too loud.

"Shh." Ursula put her finger to her lips. "Don't tell the whole agency."

"Gosh." Orianna sat back, winded.

"I might be wrong," acknowledged Ursula, but with the assurance of one who believed she wasn't.

"Gosh," Orianna repeated. She reached over to the table and poured herself a mineral water to buy a moment to think. She said bluntly, wanting clarification, "She was shagging him, then?"

"Darling Orianna." Ursula patted her knee. "I know you can be a little naïve, but didn't your mother tell you that's how conception usually occurs?"

Orianna ignored the dig, digesting Ursula's hypothesis. For a brief moment she believed the baby might not be Dan's after all. Indeed, it *would* explain why Cassie had been so reticent to divulge who the father was. "I didn't even know they were seeing each other."

"I don't know for *definite*," confessed Ursula, and Orianna's heart sank. It was just hearsay, then. Ursula continued, "It's only that once, when I was in the agency late working downstairs, I went up to the studio to amend some artwork. And I saw them together—I guess they thought they were on their own. Put it this way, it didn't seem very *platonic* to me."

Orianna had a sudden vision of them caught in flagrante on Leon's desk. "What were they doing?"

Ursula read her mind. "Nothing *that* extreme, and I couldn't be sure, because they were hidden from the doorway by his Mac. As I came into the room they sprang apart, and she pretended to be looking at his screen, but they appeared *ever* so embarrassed. And you know I wouldn't say this if I wasn't positive—it did seem that they'd been snogging."

"No!"

"And you know what made me doubly certain?" She nudged Orianna conspiratorially. "What *really* gave it away?"

"What?"

"He had lipstick all around his mouth!" she exclaimed in as loud a whisper as she could get away with. "I mean *lipstick*—how tacky is that!"

"Very," Orianna agreed, thinking: Cassie, a surfeit of makeup, how true to form.

"Though one thing I don't get"—Ursula furrowed her brow—"is why she should be so secretive. If they're going out, what's the big deal?"

"Maybe she doesn't want everyone to know he's the father," said Orianna.

"Could be." Ursula nodded. "I wonder why not?" Then she answered her own question. "Maybe when she said she was pregnant, he didn't want to know."

Yet instinct told Orianna Leon was the honorable type. "Doesn't sound like Leon to me."

"No, nor me."

"Mm." They looked at each other, both frowning now.

After a while . . . "I've got it!" Ursula clapped her hands.

"What?"

"Maybe . . ." She took a sip of her wine, taking pleasure in prolonging the expectation. "She doesn't know *who* the father is."

How *awful,* thought Orianna, struck by misery again. To think that Dan dumped me for this mess. Ugh. She shivered.

"After all, she puts it about a bit." Unaware of Orianna's distress, Ursula laughed once more. "Still, when it's born we'll know soon enough!"

"Know what?" Both women jumped apart simultaneously as Russell came up behind them and forced his face between theirs. "What are you two chin-wagging about so intensely?"

"Nothing." Orianna blushed.

"None of your business," said Ursula curtly.

"You seem thick as thieves."

"Well, we're not." Ursula smiled, sarcasm barely veiled. "It's only girls' talk."

"I can take a hint when I'm not wanted." And he wandered off.

"Twat." Clearly Ursula was in the mood to be candid. Great—it was the lead Orianna was looking for.

"Actually, Urs, I didn't come over here to talk to you about Cassie."

"What then?"

"There's someone else I wanted to ask you about. But it'll look a bit dodgy if we carry on sitting here like this." She glanced about her, and, sure enough, there was Russell, eyes narrowed, watching them across the table. He might not be able to hear them, although it wouldn't surprise Orianna to learn he had lip-reading down to a fine art.

"Oh?"

"Russell," she murmured. "But it's something pretty serious."

"How serious?"

"Serious, serious. Serious enough to get me in big trouble if he gets wind of what I'm telling you, but equally serious enough to get the agency into even bigger trouble if I don't confide in someone."

Ursula sussed the situation with typical efficiency. "How about we take a little walk?"

"Excellent idea."

Ursula got to her feet. "Better not be seen leaving together. Follow me in a bit. I'll meet you outside the Curzon on Shaftesbury Avenue in five."

38. Villainy, villainy, villainy!

The Saturday after the Kettner's party, Orianna met Ursula again, on a bench in Soho Square. If they were going to snoop around the agency as agreed, they'd decided it was best done over the weekend, when the likelihood of discovery was remote, and Saturday was better than Sunday—recession or no recession, even the most diligent employees rarely darkened the doors of Green on weekends. More to the point, they could be almost certain Russell wouldn't show. No matter how much he pressured others to work all hours, it was well-known the weekend was when he returned to his wife and family in the country.

Orianna was a few minutes early, but Ursula was already waiting.

"Got your keys?" asked Ursula.

Orianna jangled her pocket—as creative director, she was privy to a set.

"Let's go then." Ursula jumped up and hugged her overcoat to her skinny frame. "It's bloody freezing." Their breath steamed in the icy air.

Once inside, they headed straight up to the top floor. As usual, Russell's door was open.

"His cabinets will be locked," whispered Orianna. It was as if she could feel their financial director's presence even though he was miles away.

Ursula tugged at the drawers regardless. "Bugger."

"Now what?"

"We could try his PC." Ursula bent to flick on the hard drive. But Orianna didn't hold much hope of cracking Russell's password even with two of them, and ten minutes and a great deal of cursing later, she was proven right.

"Next?"

Ursula scanned the office. "You found this Harvey Nichols statement in his in-box?"

"Yes."

"Perhaps we should go through that again." She reached for the three-tier stack and took a seat. "One of us better keep watch. Why don't you wait by the door of the department—let me know if someone's coming? Only don't be too obvious."

"Sure." Some found Ursula's stridency overbearing, yet it had never bothered Orianna. And now, despite her nerves, she had to smile. It's because Ursula's this capable I sought her help, she thought.

As she sat waiting on one of the communal sofas thumbing her way through a directory of illustrators, it seemed Ursula was taking forever to inspect Russell's papers, but eventually she came bounding over.

"Look." She plonked herself next to Orianna. "It's just a hunch . . ."

"So was my theory about that statement," reminded Orianna.

"Yeah, exactly. But—see all these invoices?" She checked the door then proudly brandished a stack of papers.

"Yes." They looked exactly like the ones Orianna had seen in Russell's in-box a few weeks earlier. "They're from suppliers. Nothing untoward there, surely?"

"I reckon they could be fake."

"Fake?"

"Yes. Who *are* these suppliers? I don't recognize them, do you?"

Orianna peered closely at the cream-colored paper. MONTANO & SONS, PRINTING & REPROGRAPHICS.

"No," she admitted.

"Me neither." Ursula's voice accelerated in excitement. "And-I-would-have-thought-wouldn't-you?-that-one-or-the-other-of-us-would-have-heard-of-a-printer-that-the-agency-was-using-this-much?" She paused for breath and slowed herself. "I haven't heard of them either, and trust me, I know most of the printers in London. So I searched on Yell-dot-com, and there's no record of Montano and Sons at this address."

"Are you sure they weren't just ex-directory?"

"Why would a printer be ex-directory? I've Googled them too—there's no printer with that name anywhere. Which is odd, don't you think?" She didn't wait for a reply and her voice sped up again. "Yet-according-to-these-invoices-we're-putting-tens-of-thousands-of-pounds'-worth-of-business-their-way."

Orianna frowned. "But what's the point of doing that?" Then it dawned on her. *"You're saying he's forging invoices so he can pay himself?"*

"Precisely." Ursula sat back on the sofa, smugly.

"Wow," said Orianna.

"Wow indeed. I don't know exactly how he's doing it, but it's my guess he's paying the money—"

"—into his own bank account."

"Yup. And I bet it's not an account anyone else in the agency knows about. It wouldn't surprise me if it's even offshore."

Orianna examined the invoices again. "This is all very well, but how can we prove it?"

Ursula scratched her head. "That's where you've got me."

"Tell you what. We need to copy these invoices before we put them back. You stay here and do that; keep an eye on the door. I'll go and give Russell's office one last look." And before Ursula had time to come up with a better suggestion, she was off.

Once again Orianna went through the in-box. Nothing. Through the packets of paper he kept by his printer. Every single sheet was blank.

Through his wastepaper basket. Nothing. She even inspected the family photos he had lining his windowsill.

Then, just as she was about to give up and leave the office, she stopped. Could it be . . . ? Hmm, possibly . . . She went back to the paper by the printer. Yes, sure enough, one of the packs contained paper that wasn't white, but cream. A coincidence?

She cantered out to Ursula, a sheet in her hand, grabbed once of the invoices, and held it up to the light. "See this?"

"What?"

"Same paper."

Ursula squinted. "Mm?"

"Here." Orianna pointed. "It says 'Conqueror.'"

"So?"

"It was by his printer. His personal printer—Russell's."

"Ah." Ursula raised her eyebrows, impressed. Then she looked doubtful. "I'm sure you're right—this is the same paper he's using to print off these invoices. Though I doubt it's enough evidence for the fraud squad, don't you?"

Orianna was deflated.

"It's just cream paper. Conqueror—it's not that uncommon, is it?"

"I guess not."

"You can buy it in most branches of Smiths."

Orianna sighed. "So now what?"

"We need to prove this is the *actual* paper he's using . . ."

In a split second it came to Orianna. "I've got it!" she exclaimed. Not for nothing was she an art director, her knowledge of markers and pens first-rate.

"Yes?"

"I've got one of those UV pens in my drawer."

"A what?"

"Remember? Russell gave us them months ago, asked us to mark our Macs and PCs with the agency postcode. The ink's invisible, but it shows up under ultraviolet or something. So the police can trace your stuff should it get stolen."

"Oh yeah, I do remember. How brilliant! And it'd be easy to detect if it's been printed on afterward, over the top."

"Too bloody right. You wait here," Orianna bossed her colleague, "and I'll go and mark every sheet of that cream paper."

"How are-you-going-to-mark-it?"

Orianna grinned, tickled by the divine justice. "I reckon '*forgery*' will suffice, don't you?"

39. Hell and night must bring this monstrous birth to the world's light

It took weeks for Orianna and Ursula to gather evidence. Throughout the rest of January and February they had no joy at all.

"It's nearly the financial year end," Ursula pointed out. "I reckon he's concerned he's overdone it. Our figures are grim, but still, he doesn't want the company to go under. Where would his income be then? What do you bet he waits till we're a little closer to April fifth before counterfeiting some more."

Sure enough, come March, when Orianna made her regular Saturday checkup at the agency, she discovered three invoices in the tray which added up to several thousand dollars.

Carefully, she slid them from the in-box—noting which papers they sat between. Then she went to her office, unlocked her filing cabinet, and removed a handful of the cream Conqueror paper she had stored there. She'd bought a packet from W. H. Smiths weeks earlier, and put it by in preparation for this moment.

Next, she went to the photocopier, loaded the paper, laid the first invoice on the glass, and pressed *Copy*. Eventually it churned out—darker than the original so she adjusted the settings. It took a few attempts, but soon she had it perfect. She repeated the process for the remaining two invoices, and then she carried both sets over to the window and compared her copies with Russell's originals.

Well done, she said to herself. The difference is almost impossible to detect.

She removed the remaining Conqueror from the copier and tucked it under her arm. Then, with her copies in one hand and the originals in the other, she headed to Russell's office. She slotted the copies into the exact spot she'd found the originals. Finally, she returned to her own office, put the Conqueror back in her cabinet, found a large envelope for the originals, and popped them inside.

That evening, several pivotal events took place.

In Battersea, thanks to a phone call from Chloë urging him to give it a go, Rob discovered Internet dating. "It's only a small step on from those chat rooms you love," she said. "And what have you got to lose? If you don't mind me being frank, I reckon it's high time you stopped hankering after straight boys. Surely Dan was one disaster too many?" It was true his experience with Dan made Rob cringe whenever he thought of it, so, grudgingly, he checked out a couple of sites she recommended. He opted for the one with the tastiest selection—reasoning there was little point in sharing interests if you didn't fancy one another—and it rapidly proved the ideal vent for his e-mail addiction. By midnight he'd completed his personal profile in glorious detail, scanned in a flattering shot from the wedding the previous summer, and fired off witty responses to a number of promising-looking gentlemen. Then he sat back, fingers metaphorically crossed, and waited for their answers.

In Hoxton, Ivy perched on the sofa, bracing herself to read her divorce papers. They'd arrived by courier at the agency, but she'd not wanted to open them in public. Now, cigarette in hand and a gin and diet tonic by her side, she was as prepared to examine the contents of the large manila envelope as she'd ever be.

She ripped it open and pulled out several sheets of paper.

It transpired they weren't actual divorce papers as such; a cover letter from Ed's lawyer explained these would follow at a later date. This was simply the announcement of an official separation.

Nevertheless, it was the first stage of untying the knot, and a sure sign that their marriage was over.

Ivy took a drag on her cigarette and inhaled the smoke deep, deep into her lungs.

Meanwhile, in Camden, Dan was watching one of his all-time-favorite movies, *Predator 2*. He'd spent countless Saturdays since his split with Orianna in front of the TV, though it seemed no amount of gunfire and explosions could blast away his misery.

He'd tried phoning Orianna a few times since he'd left the agency, but she had never returned his calls. Even freelancing didn't take his mind off his troubles, so he'd decided to look for a full-time job again, hoping a fresh challenge might help him get over his heartbreak. The day before he'd been to consult the well known headhunter, Trixie Fox, about finding a permanent position.

"I don't hold out much hope," she'd said at the end of their meeting. "We're in the middle of the most ghastly recession, and there's not a lot around. Obviously I mustn't tell you who, but I've had a senior creative from your agency on my books for several months—she's *very* senior— and I can't find her anything for love nor money. She's even prepared to look abroad, though I've had no joy there either."

Dan's stomach had turned over at the news. It sounds like Orianna is thinking of leaving Green as well, he thought. What a pity that would be. I've left—surely there's no need for her to go too? And if she leaves the country there'll be no chance of us getting back together. How horribly depressing.

As the final credits of the video rolled, he made a vow.

I'll give it one last shot at talking to her, he decided, before she disappears from Green forever.

A couple of miles northeast, in Holloway, Orianna was indulging in one of her favorite pastimes: sharing a pizza and bottle of wine with a girlfriend. But on this occasion the girlfriend wasn't Ivy. She'd not confronted Ivy directly lest it hamper the case they were putting together, nevertheless, Orianna was disinclined to spend time with her erstwhile writer since discovering she was colluding with Russell. Instead she was with Ursula, and on the coffee table before them lay a brown envelope containing Russell's invoices.

"Reckon we've nailed him," said Ursula, and they clinked glasses.

Finally, in Hammersmith, Cassie was lying on the sofa. Despite all of Leon's assurances that he thought she appeared beautiful no matter what, she'd never felt so horribly huge and uncomfortable, so whalelike, in her life.

Suddenly she reached for his wrist and squeezed it as she grimaced in pain. "Oh fuck!"

Leon, who'd been feeling laid-back because he was a trifle stoned, sat bolt upright. "What?"

"That was a contraction."

"You're not due for three weeks!"

"I know." Cassie winced again. "But I'm telling you—it was. This is it, Leon."

40. Confess a truth

Orianna and Ivy were thrashing out some urgent concepts for Bellings Scott when there was a swift tap at the door and Ursula stepped into Orianna's office without waiting for an invitation.

"Everything OK?" she said.

Orianna knew what she was driving at. Earlier that day she'd made a call to the criminal investigation division.

"Yes, fine. We're to go in tomorrow morning at ten."

"Right. I'll have to shift something, but no worries."

"Go where?" Ivy sounded intrigued.

"We're just checking out a potential new client." Orianna was elusive. "Nothing that need concern you at this stage."

"Oh," said Ivy. "Be like that then."

Too right I will, thought Orianna. If Ivy's pissed off, I'd rather she came out with it straight. She was increasingly aware gripes of this nature were designed to manipulate her emotions, and it riled her.

But before she could get really irked, Ursula continued, "I presume you heard about Cassie?"

Orianna's heart began thumping fast. "No."

"She's had the baby."

"I thought it wasn't due until April," said Ivy.

"It arrived three weeks early."

"Is it alright?" asked Orianna.

"Yes," said Ursula. "He weighed over six pounds."

"So it's a boy?" said Ivy and Orianna in unison.

"Yup." Ursula beamed, not bothering to hide her relish at being the one to impart the news. "Leon tells me Cassie went into labor on Saturday."

"*Leon?*" Again in unison.

"Apparently he was with her."

"No!" exclaimed Orianna, heart lifting. "Is he the father then?"

"Not sure," said Ursula.

"Not sure?" Clearly Ivy was as keen to know as they were.

Ursula shook her head. "He didn't say specifically. Anyway, I've had an idea, as I will confess I'm frightfully curious . . ."

"Yeah?" from Ivy.

"She's at Queen Charlotte's, I'm told."

"Oh?"

"In Hammersmith. So I don't know what you reckon, girls, but I thought it would be nice if we paid her a visit. Perhaps later, after work. After all, I'm dying to see the baby, aren't you?"

Hitherto, Ivy would have resisted when Orianna and Ursula insisted on going by subway to West London, but these days she was more money conscious, so she concurred without fuss. This very week Ed had insisted they put the apartment on the market.

"We'll get flowers at the other end," ordered Ursula as she set a brisk pace toward Leicester Square, and again Ivy demurred without argument.

What if the truth about the baby's father comes out? she worried, and for a second was tempted to make an excuse not to go. Yet for all her anxiety, Ivy was no coward, and she wanted to be present to deal with any revelations head-on. Moreover, she was growing increasingly wary of Orianna's friendship with Ursula. Orianna had become strangely distant over the last few weeks, and at the same time she and Ursula seemed to be getting exceptionally close. Ivy was more than a mite jealous. No, she decided, I'm damned if they're going to see Cassie without me.

The Piccadilly line was packed all the way; from the station they had a ten-minute walk to Queen Charlotte's.

What a bore public transport is, observed Ivy. I do hope I don't have to use it for long.

At the entrance to the hospital was a flower stall, and, at Ursula's insistence, they had a large, hand-tied bouquet made up specially. "We can't give Cassie any old prearranged bunch," she insisted. "We'll spend what we saved on fares."

Clearly she's got different priorities, thought Ivy.

It all served to delay the moment of truth, and, as she stood waiting for the florist to tie the cellophane wrapper, Ivy became increasingly apprehensive. Locating the right ward involved yet more hassle; they took a wrong turn and ended up wandering around in confusion. Eventually, they found Cassie.

Ursula led the way, bearing the bouquet before her like a flag.

"Hello." She beamed. "We thought we'd surprise you."

Ivy wasn't sure, but it seemed that Cassie blanched at the sight of them, although because she was paler than usual it was hard to tell. Ivy gave her a rapid once-over. Devoid of all makeup, blond hair bedraggled and in need of a wash, she appeared a different person entirely.

If I didn't dislike her so much, I might feel sorry for her, thought Ivy. She looks so young, almost vulnerable. I suppose she is thousands of miles from her home and family.

"Hi," whispered Cassie, weakly. Whether the weakness sprang from shock or physical exhaustion was difficult to ascertain.

"He-ello," said Orianna.

Hmm, thought Ivy. She sounds on edge too.

"Hey," she said, not sure of an appropriate greeting.

Ursula seemed determined to make up for the rest of their hesitancy. "Where's the baby? Can we have a look?"

"The nurse has him. She's taken him away for some measurements. She'll bring him back in a sec."

"Oh," said Ursula, deflated. "Never mind, we'll wait a bit, won't we?"

Ivy and Orianna nodded.

"So," she continued breezily. "Shall I get a vase for these?"

"They're lovely." Cassie smiled. "Thank you."

"They don't really need a vase," observed Orianna. The bouquet had its own globe of water. "I guess you're going home soon, aren't you? They'll be easier to carry tied up like that."

"You're right," said Cassie. "We're out of here tomorrow."

"Oh, OK." Ursula propped them on top of Cassie's bedside cabinet and she pulled up a battered plastic chair. Ivy and Orianna followed her cue; Orianna sat on the one armchair, Ivy perched on the edge of the bed.

Perhaps I can steer the subject away from the baby's paternity, thought Ivy. "How was the labor?" she asked.

Cassie grimaced. "Grim. Don't let anyone ever tell you otherwise— it's bloody agony."

"I gather Leon was with you," said Ursula.

"Yes, he was." Again, was it Ivy's imagination, or was Cassie avoiding Ursula's gaze?

"Must have been a bit of a hero."

"You could say so. He's been very good to me lately."

To Ivy's complete surprise, Orianna piped up, "Have you been seeing him then?"

Now there was no question—Cassie was fazed.

A long silence followed.

At last Cassie said, "Kind of."

Well that doesn't help at all, thought Ivy.

At that moment the nurse returned, wheeling the baby in a clear plastic crib.

"Here he is," she said.

Ursula shifted her chair, Orianna jumped up, Ivy got to her feet; all so the nurse could edge the cot in alongside Cassie's bed. It also meant they could peer at its contents.

And there, wrapped up in a pale blue blanket, face scrunched up like a little old man, was the baby.

Make no mistake: he was white.

"Oooh he's lovely," cooed Ursula.

"Isn't he?" echoed Ivy.

Orianna couldn't think of what to say. She was devastated. For a while she'd been praying the baby would turn out not to be Dan's. Now, though she was no expert in ethnology, she knew there was no way this child could be Leon's.

She peered down at the tiny bundle; his hair all dark and matted, his face wrinkled and pink as he slept. She felt like weeping. What an awful mistake to have come—a crazy idea. It was only because she'd hoped— though the chance was very slim—she might discover the baby wasn't Dan's that she'd agreed to visit. And here she was, looking at Dan's child, the little boy part of her still felt should be hers.

Yet Orianna wasn't the only one finding the situation hard to handle; she could sense Ursula brimming with curiosity beside her. Orianna knew she'd been far more convinced the baby was Leon's than anyone, and eventually she couldn't contain herself any longer.

"Cassie," she said, with the same authoritarian tone she used when briefing a crucial piece of work, "I thought the baby was Leon's, but it's obvious he's not." Orianna's heart was thumping faster than ever now, her palms were sweaty, she could scarcely believe what she was hearing. "So tell me, please. Just *who* is the father of this child?"

Again there was a long silence.

Cassie looked around at the three of them, evidently trying to decide whether or not to confess. Finally, exhaustion seemed to get the better of her; after all the physical and mental exertion of the last few days, she could bear keeping the secret no longer.

"Russell," she said.

41. Heaven truly knows thou art as false as hell

"But I thought it was Leon's!" cried Ursula.

"But I thought it was Dan's!" cried Orianna.

"But it can't *possibly* be Russell's!" cried Ivy.

They all spoke at once, so only the end of Ivy's sentence was audible.

"Shh." Cassie put her finger to her lips. "You'll wake the baby." She turned to Ivy. "What do you mean it can't possibly be Russell's?" She stared at her, hard. "I think I should know."

Such was Ivy's astonishment that she started to shake from head to foot. Luckily she was sitting down already, or she'd have had to anyway. Then, as she absorbed what Cassie was saying, jealousy surged through her like an electric shock, a jealousy more intense than she'd ever felt before. It jolted her entire nervous system, striking at her very sense of self, calling everything into question.

Cassie's slept with Russell? she thought. How can that be? Russell is sleeping with me! It surpasses belief!

It was impossible to get her head around it. She was going to faint. Be sick. Or both. Everything was swimming in front of her—Orianna, Ursula, Cassie; their faces anxious, quizzical, defiant . . .

Like pennies dropping in a slot machine, the realizations tumbled thick and fast.

Woah, she thought. I saw Russell eyeing Cassie up, didn't I? On Cassie's first day, all that time ago. So there was no doubt he was attracted to her from the outset. Plus, come to think of it, I've been the one to initiate our clandestine liaisons over recent months. Take my birthday in October—and it wasn't the only time . . .

Ivy had assumed she was the strong one in the relationship, so—as with Ed—had been slow to pick up on the signs. And what about the lecture he'd given on her expenses? How typical that he should feel he could shaft her financially—the moment screwing her no longer paid!

Before she could finish unscrambling it all, her thoughts were broken by Ursula. "So you've not been seeing Leon?" she said to Cassie.

"I had been, yes," Cassie answered, with surprising directness. "So I did think the baby might be his. But now—why lie? It's obvious that's not the case."

Tentatively, Ursula probed. "So—er—let me get this straight. You've been having a thing with *Russell* then?"

"I suppose you could put it like that." She paused. "We slept together a few times, if you must know."

"*Before* Leon?"

Cassie looked sheepish. "I was—er—sleeping with them both, just for a while."

Hence the confusion, concluded Ivy. It confirmed what she'd figured, still, it pained her greatly. She'd been cheated on not just by Ed, but Russell too. She'd been made to look a fool. Maybe not deliberately by Cassie, yet she was certain Russell had known exactly what he was playing at. Doubtless he'd gotten off on the duplicity.

"Oh." Ursula sat back in the plastic chair, winded. Then she added, "But you realize Russell's *married*?"

Cassie snorted. "I'm not stupid."

"Ah. Right." There was a moment's silence. "That didn't stop you?"

"He came on to me," explained Cassie, with a shrug of her shoulders.

Ivy shuddered. The idea that he was seducing Cassie while giving her the brush-off!

"I think it's his responsibility to be faithful, not mine," said Cassie.

Ivy struggled to work it out. *I wonder if she fancied Russell at all?* she spat inwardly. *I bet she thought he might help her career.*

"Anyway, whatever . . ." Cassie leaned over to check the baby again; he appeared to be sleeping on, oblivious. "Being hitched doesn't stop Russell."

"You mean he's done this before?"

"Before?! Aw, come on. Don't tell me you didn't suspect as much—he's scarcely the faithful type."

Despite her private tumult, Ivy couldn't help note Cassie's true colors seemed to be emerging. How forthright she was being, pugnacious, almost. And to think she thought she looked vulnerable, sitting there without a scrap of makeup, hair disheveled! Ivy was witnessing a side to Cassie she hadn't known existed; like a lioness protecting her newborn cub, her aggression seemed to stem from self-preservation, or anger, or both. Still, however primal, Ivy didn't like it. This posed a new threat.

Ursula restated, "Let me be absolutely clear: you were seeing them simultaneously?"

"Leon and I were hardly full-on initially," said Cassie. "He knew I was seeing other guys. For a while last summer, I thought I'd have some fun—I'd just arrived here, remember. Men do it all the time."

"Then you got pregnant."

"Yes."

"Strikes me as a trifle careless."

Cassie blushed. "I appreciate that now."

"And you told them both?"

"I did." Cassie nodded. "I believe in being honest."

Ivy writhed in discomfort. Cassie seemed to be looking intensely at her.

"Wow." Ursula shook her head, incredulous. "Rather you than me."

"I realized I'd been pretty irresponsible." Cassie sighed. "So I believed that was the least I could do. And once I'd decided to keep it, I told them both that too. Leon was very understanding, all things considered. He's been a good friend to me recently. Whereas Russell refused to even acknowledge the child might be his. Dropped me, like a proverbial hot potato. No support. No interest. Nothing."

There was another few seconds' silence.

"I think Russell's a prick," said Ursula. "For what it's worth."

"I found that out a bit late," said Cassie. "Found out a *lot* a bit late, come to that." Again her eyes bored into Ivy.

Shit, Ivy panicked, finding it virtually impossible to keep pace. Was it possible Cassie knew about *her* and Russell? And it wasn't over yet . . .

Orianna had been silent for the entire proceedings. Now she interjected, "But what about Dan?"

Cassie turned to her and frowned. "What about Dan?"

"I understood you were seeing him?"

"You what?"

"I thought the baby was his," said Orianna.

Cassie snorted again, this time with laughter. Then, glancing at Orianna's face, she paused, and said more sympathetically, "What on earth gave you that idea?"

"Ivy told me," said Orianna.

Now all three of them turned to Ivy.

"Seems like you've got some explaining to do," said Cassie.

"What do you mean?" asked Ursula.

"I've never shagged Dan in my life," said Cassie, simply.

Orianna gasped. "You haven't?"

Cassie shook her head. "No way."

"Oh!"

"I wouldn't dream of doing such a thing. You hired me, you're my boss. You've always been really nice to me. Whereas she"—Cassie glared at Ivy—"*she's* been shagging Russell, not merely for a few weeks in the summer like me, but for *years*."

"RUSSELL!" from Orianna and Ursula. This time the baby stirred.

Yet another long silence.

"Who told you that?" asked Ursula, eventually.

"Russell did." Cassie shrugged her shoulders again. "I went over one night—to tell him I was pregnant, in fact. He responded by saying it was pathetic of me—stupid—to get myself in such a mess. Said he was hardly the commitment type. And then, when I was getting ready to leave, *she* texted him." She spat the words at Ivy. "It was your birthday, and he was so angry with me that he showed me your message; said your ongoing affair was evidence of his inability to commit— not just to me, or his wife, but to you, or anyone. That's when I realized what a total dick he is. I'll have no qualms about suing *him* for child support. Quite frankly, you deserve each other."

Ivy started to shake all over again.

Cassie knew about me and Russell for months without breathing a word! she thought. The sneaky little cow!

"You and Russell . . ." said Orianna, slowly. "So that explains the expense account."

Expense account?! How the fuck did Orianna find out about that?

"And why you didn't want me to reveal who the father was." Again Cassie scowled at Ivy. "So you could dupe Orianna."

"So you could dupe us all," said Ursula. "I bet she started those rumors about Dan being bisexual too. Tell me, did he even ever go to G-A-Y, Ivy?"

The silence seemed to fill the entire ward; the sense of expectation was huge.

Ivy's head was spinning. So here it was.

Revelation. Confrontation.

She was beyond excuses, beyond quips, beyond anything. She felt sick, wanted the ground to swallow her up; to be anywhere other than here.

Eventually, at a loss as to any other course of action, shakily, she got to her feet, and, precipitated by adrenaline, fled as fast as she could from the scene.

———

The doors of the ward swung closed.

Before Orianna had the chance to think, she was standing. "Excuse me, I need to sort this—now." And she sprinted after Ivy.

Ivy might be fitter than Orianna, and she might have longer legs—but she couldn't control the traffic. It was still rush hour, the main road outside the hospital was packed, and, as cars whizzed by with barely feet between them, Ivy was forced to come to a halt on the edge of the pavement.

"STOP!" Breathless, Orianna caught up with her.

Seeing a potential gap in the nearest lane, Ivy tried to make a dart for it across the street, but Orianna grabbed her by the hair.

"No you don't!"

"OW!" Ivy struggled to pull her tresses from Orianna's hands. Orianna held on tight.

"Just what the *fuck* do you think you're playing at?" yelled Orianna, heedless of passersby. Fortunately there was another stream of traffic, and Ivy was forced to remain where she was. Orianna kept tight hold of her hair, in case.

"Ow!" Ivy repeated.

If she was in pain, Orianna didn't care. "You told me Dan was going out with Cassie!"

"So?" Ivy jerked up her chin.

"They never even slept together!"

"No." Ivy smiled now, sarcastically, and Orianna saw a cruelty in her face she'd not acknowledged before. It was a shock to see it directed pointedly at her.

"You led me to believe they had."

"And you're more the fool for believing it." Ivy snorted, then laughed. "You even thought he might swing both ways, didn't you?" Orianna caught her checking the road out of the corner of her eye. It remained impossible to cross.

"But why all the lies, Ivy?"

"Why?" There was no mistaking Ivy's tone now: it was so full of venom it seemed to contaminate the air. "Let go of my fucking hair," she commanded. "And I'll tell you."

Rapidly, Orianna assessed Ivy's predicament. Would she make another bolt for it? Somehow Orianna doubted it. If she did, Orianna would only follow her, so it was worth the risk to get some answers. She relaxed her grip.

Ivy stood up straight, smoothed her hair, and turned to face Orianna. "I put Dan's watch in Cassie's handbag."

"You did what?"

"You heard me." Again Ivy smiled maliciously.

"But why? Why bother?"

"You *really* have no idea?" she asked, venom now mixed with incredulity.

"Not really, no."

Ivy shook her head. "You truly are too *nice* for your own good." She made the word sound like the worst possible attribute.

"How d'you mean?"

"You're so pissing naïve, Orianna."

"Oh?"

"I hate you."

For all her shock, the words pierced Orianna with the sharpness of a dagger. "But I thought we were friends?"

"Friends? *Friends?!*" Now Ivy was shouting. A couple of pedestrians turned to stare; neither Ivy nor Orianna cared. "Friends don't betray each other, Orianna."

"How did I betray you?"

Ivy held her palms up to communicate how obvious she felt it was. "For starters, you kept me in the dark about Dan."

Orianna was aghast. "Because of *that*? But I thought you understood why I didn't tell you—after what happened with Clive."

"You used to tell me everything. And suddenly you stopped."

"That's hardly fair," protested Orianna. Although perhaps there is a grain of truth in it, she realized. Maybe I did exclude Ivy, when I first met

Dan. But that's normal, isn't it? I can't read Ivy's mind; I had no clue she was still seething. "You seemed to forget all about it."

"Just because I *seemed* to, didn't mean I had."

"Oh." Orianna remained confounded. I suppose I was rather self-absorbed, she recalled, though it doesn't seem reason for Ivy to *hate* me. Not only that, when Ivy is so private herself, she seems to be exhibiting dreadful double standards.

"*And* you took that promotion," sneered Ivy.

"Ah." Now it was becoming clear.

"You deserted me, professionally, without so much as a hesitation."

She knew there was some truth in this too. Though again she'd assumed Ivy had forgiven her.

"And then you employed Cassie, a junior, to work with me without involving me at all."

"I'm sorry," said Orianna. "I honestly thought you'd like her—we always liked the same people before."

"When we interviewed them *together*."

"But *I* was the creative director. It's quite normal for the head of department to hire people without consulting anyone else. Neil used to."

"*She's fifteen years younger!*"

"She was all we could afford. I was going to carry on working with you too."

"It was insulting!"

"It wasn't meant to be. I was trying to do my best."

"*Your* best! Exactly! Always looking out for yourself, never looking out for me!"

"I tried to look out for you as best I could."

"Like hell you did!"

"I'd love to know if you'd have done it any differently, given the circumstances," said Orianna. "I'm not sure you would."

"Who cares, frankly, what I *might* have done. You were the one who got promoted. You were the one who fucked me over, OK?" Orianna sensed loathing emanating from Ivy's every pore.

Orianna mulled it over for a few seconds. Ivy appears convinced she holds the moral high ground, she thought, but surely my misdemeanors are nothing compared to the games she's played? Ivy's behavior was malicious, evil; she set out to hurt people, cause harm right from the start. Whereas I was just trying to walk the tightrope between looking after my own interests and caring for others.

The more Orianna thought it through, the more unjust it seemed, and the more her anger grew. She faced Ivy square on. "I'm not as naïve as you think."

"And what do you mean by that?"

"Oh, you'll find out soon enough." Orianna recalled the phone call she'd made earlier. "Put it like this: if you'd played less dirty yourself, there might have been the money at Green to hire someone on your level—a proper partner, to work with you full-time."

Ivy said nothing.

"And if *you'd* been straight—honest, loyal—you might have a right to have a go at me."

Further silence.

"But you weren't." Now Orianna was spitting too. "You've been playing it dirty for years, Ivy. Before I even started seeing Dan, let alone got promoted."

Ivy paled. "I don't know what you're talking about."

"I believe you do. And if you're in any doubt, it'll become clear very soon. So, frankly, if you know what's good for you, I wouldn't show your face in Green again, not just for a while, but ever. And in the meantime, don't you dare lecture me on betrayal." She was at that point where anger and adrenaline had taken over and she felt articulate, clear-thinking, and totally impetuous. "You've betrayed Ed. You've betrayed Cassie. You've betrayed Dan. You've betrayed the agency and your colleagues. And you've betrayed me. You're an adulterous, scheming, thieving, lying bitch."

She raised her hand, and, with all the force she could muster, slapped Ivy across the face.

42. A word or two

Maybe it was fate or simply a fluke, but when Orianna stepped through her front door later that evening, the phone was ringing.

"Hello?"

"Orianna?"

"Dan!" She didn't bother to conceal her delight. "How weird—I was just going to call you."

"You were?" He sounded a little wary.

"Yes!"

"Oh."

"We need to talk."

"We do." She heard him sigh. Was it relief? She wasn't sure.

She'd better make herself clear. "I owe you an apology."

"Why?"

"It's a long story. Too long for the phone. Suffice to say, I found out a whole load of things this evening, about Ivy. Among them the fact that she lied to me about you."

"Me?"

"Yeah—she hinted months ago you might be bisexual."

"Really? And you believed her?"

"Not completely, no, I wasn't sure. But then she told me you were seeing Cassie."

"Ah. Ri-ight." Yet he didn't sound as shocked as she'd expected him to be.

"Did you know she'd done that?"

"Not exactly. Though I thought she was up to something."

"Why didn't you say?"

"I wasn't sure, so I didn't know what precisely to accuse her of. And when I tried to speak to you about her—"

"I didn't listen," said Orianna, flatly. "No, you're right, I didn't." I wish I'd trusted him, she thought, instead of trusting Ivy. "And that's why I need to apologize."

"I see."

"I'm sorry. I feel terrible about it. It's my fault, in some ways. I should have been surer of you. Not jumped to conclusions." After so much muddle and so many months, Orianna was desperate to clear everything up as fast as possible. "Listen, I appreciate it's getting late, but, er, are you busy, now?"

Dan only hesitated for a split second. "No, I'm free."

"Can I come over?"

"I'll come to you," he offered.

"Are you sure?"

"Of course I'm sure—that's why I was calling, in fact."

"Really?"

"Yeah. I wanted to talk—I was worried you were looking for another job, leaving the country."

"What on earth gave you that idea? Not Ivy, by any chance?"

"No, not Ivy. So you're not?"

"No."

"Ah, right. I must have got the wrong end of the stick." He gave another sigh; this time she was certain it was relief. "Anyway." Another momentary hesitation. "It would be nice to see you."

"It would be nice to see you too."

In all the months that he and Orianna had been dating, Dan had never got from Camden to Holloway so fast. He checked himself in the mirror—yeah, he looked fine—grabbed his car keys and his wallet, and within less than two minutes was behind the wheel. He found a space right outside Orianna's apartment.

It felt strange, going back after so many months apart. It was so familiar, yet different. When he'd last been there, the window box had been jaded, its geraniums blooming one last time. But now it was spring, the box was filled with daffodils.

"Hi," said Orianna as she opened the door. She smiled.

She looks different, he thought. Her hair's longer, but that's not the only thing. She seems older, wiser somehow; it suits her.

"Hi." He smiled back. *I think it's going to be all right, he thought.*

"I believe I've got some explaining to do."

"Me too." *But first, forget talking.* He held out his arms.

Orianna stepped forward, and embraced him. "I've missed you," she said.

To: Everyone
From: Orianna Bianchi
Date: Wednesday, March 24, 8:47
Subj: Changes

It may have escaped your notice that Ivy Fraser hasn't been in the office for over a week. It's my understanding that rumors are rife, and I wish to be straight with you all: Ivy will not be returning to Green. She was found guilty of serious professional misconduct, not to mention various other,

more personal transgressions which make it no longer
viable to continue her working relationship with the agency.

It has also come to my attention that a few of you saw our
financial director, Russell North, leaving yesterday afternoon
alongside two police officers. He too will not be returning to
the agency in the foreseeable future.

Unfortunately we have discovered major fiscal irregularities
over the last few weeks and these implicate certain
employees at the deepest and most serious level. The
matter is currently at the hands of the fraud squad and
under investigation. I am asking you all to keep this
confidential while they do so, and we will let you know
the outcome of their findings when full details emerge.

Finally, and on a more positive note, without wishing to
embroil you all in my private life, a number of you have
recently noted the ring on my left hand. I am delighted
to announce that yes, indeed, Dan Cohen and I did get
engaged over the weekend.

All the best,
Orianna

43. Great of heart

To: Chloë Appleton
From: Rob Rowland
Date: Sunday, August 31, 11:47
Subj: Happy endings

I know you love a good wedding nearly as much as I do, so I thought I'd drop you a line about the one I went to yesterday, especially as you've met the couple—remember Orianna and Dan, that night in Blacks?

Chelsea Registry Office isn't quite as romantic as the church your brother was married in last summer. Dan's Jewish, if you didn't realize, and Orianna's Catholic, so they opted for neutral territory to ensure no one would get miffed. And it worked—apparently everyone was cool about the ceremony, as Orianna's parents love Dan, and Dan's parents adore Orianna. Anyway, the venue is quite glam in its way, given its rock star heritage—and the weather was fantastic—warm and sunny. Typical, it rains for weeks, then just as summer ends, it turns gorgeous.

Orianna looked divine—she's been working out with me since May to get into shape for the big day—but I suspect she was born to be curvy, and we only succeeded in toning her up ever so slightly. Still, her dress was stunning, and she glowed with happiness.

There was a small part of me that wondered if Ivy might show up, but she didn't. Sometimes I wonder what's happened to her; one minute I was seeing her every week, then a message saying she'd no longer be able to come to the gym. I appreciate that she and Orianna had that big falling out—remember all that palaver about the watch I mentioned? Apparently the agency is doing great now, and you never know, sometimes the strangest things happen at weddings. It's only that in a funny way I kind of liked Ivy and am sorry not to have heard from her again.

Instead another colleague of Orianna's, Ursula, made a speech after the dinner. She had Orianna sussed—it was all about what a talent she is, how kindhearted and generous. But I swear to God, Chloë, you've never heard anyone talk so fast in your life!

As for Dan, he was every inch the dashing groom. He and I did, eventually, succeed in getting rid of the paunch he was always so self-conscious of, although it took a huge effort and I reckon the chances of it remaining that way are slim. But Dan looked so proud, he couldn't stop grinning all day, and he gave the most touching, honest speech—it made Orianna cry—and it's clear he truly cares for her.

It's hard to imagine how I could have ever thought he was gay—I do feel silly about that now. But then I had Pierre on my arm on Saturday, and it's amazing what a different perspective a new man gives a guy. Things with him continue to go *brilliantly*—it's been four months now, can you believe? We've even been talking about moving in together. It would mean we could stop spending our lives schlepping from one side of London to the other, because I find not being able to be with him as much as I'd like frustrating. Who'd have believed Rob, settling down, eh? And all through the Internet?! I've got you to thank, my girl, for introducing me to that, and believe me, I do, every day.

In the meantime, I'm glad to hear you've decided to stop dating several men at once and settle for the banker. I always thought he sounded too good to waste.

Lots of love,
Your dear friend,
Rob
xxxx

44. Here is my journey's end

Several months later, Ivy was just back from a run when the phone rang. She'd had to forfeit her gym membership along with her salary and apartment, and now she had to make do with the local park in West London as a backdrop for exercise. Still, she'd been lucky that the directors at Green had simply insisted she pay back the money she'd claimed as illegitimate expenses, thus avoiding a humiliating court case, unlike Russell. Anyway, she was getting pretty good at the living-on-a-shoestring lark; it tested her ingenuity, and as for a personal trainer—well, with her amount of self-discipline, who needed one?

She grabbed the receiver seconds before the answering machine clicked on. "Hello?"

"Ivy? It's Cherie Gurley-Morgan here." A clipped, well-spoken, older woman's voice.

"Oh!"

"Just to say that I got your manuscript yesterday . . ."

Ivy took most conversations in her stride, but this made her heart race.

". . . and I *love* it!"

"Really?"

"I think it's great. Absolutely great. And any friend of Trixie's is a friend of mine—we go back years, you know. Did she tell you we used to be a team together before I went into publishing? All that stuff about advertising—*so* accurate. Must be autobiographical—is it?" She didn't pause for an answer. "Anyway, I hope you can fill me in face-to-face, because I'd be delighted to represent you. It's a difficult market at the moment, but your style is so commercial, I'm sure we'll get publishers interested, just the same. Who knows, if we play it well, we might even get an auction going, swing you a nice hefty advance."

Ivy beamed, and steadied her voice. "Oh, right." She mustn't sound too excited, yet she was thrilled.

"Though first I think we should meet up, give you the chance to check if you like me, the way I work."

Like her? thought Ivy. As if I wouldn't!

"So I was wondering, would you be free for dinner sometime this week?"

"Er . . ."

"How about Wednesday?"

Ivy hadn't been out for weeks. "I'll, um, check my diary." She fumbled with some spare paper lying on the table. Seconds later: "Yes, that looks fine."

"If you're not sick of it, I thought we should go to your namesake, in Covent Garden."

Ivy had hardly dined out since she'd left Green, let alone eaten anywhere worth being seen in. "That would be lovely."

"Eight thirty then," said Cherie. "I'll book a table. What do you look like, so I know who to expect?"

"I've got bobbed red hair," said Ivy. She'd had it cut to mark she was moving on. "And I'm, er"—she coughed—"in my early thirties."

"Super. Publishers prefer a nice young writer. I'll come back to you if there's any problem, otherwise, see you there."

There was a click and Ivy was alone again in her little studio apartment.

Well I never, she thought. Cherie Gurley-Morgan is just about the most powerful literary agent there is. Trixie has come up trumps after all.

Ivy picked up her copy of the manuscript. She'd altered actual events, changed characters, and painted herself far blacker (and slimmer) than she really was. But how much more fun it was to make herself the dark one, and she reveled in the idea that only she would know where the truth ended and fiction began. In essence, the story remained true to the realm of advertising as she saw it, and there was something deeply satisfying about being able to exploit her experiences, profit from what had happened, and twist the plot to suit her own ends.

Bugger copywriting, thought Ivy. I don't need any of those idiots to make me successful—and rich. I'm going to be a novelist—a *bestselling* novelist—and show the world a thing or two. What better way to get even?

Acknowledgments

2002: There are numerous people who helped me with *Getting Even*. On the professional front, I would like to thank my editor at Orion, Kirsty Fowkes, who was able to see both the big picture and the fine detail; my agent, Vivien Green, whose TLC went way beyond the call of duty, and Amelia Cummins too; and my publisher, Jane Wood and Rachel Leyshon.

On the personal front, amongst those friends deserving special mention are Patrick Fitzgerald, Bill Graber, Jenny Lingrell, Karl Miller, John Scott, and Carolyn MacQuaide.

There have been my advertising cohorts: Stephen Andrews, Polly Beale, Ursula Benson, Sally Elms, Debbie Fagan, Jasper Garland, Carla Greco, Jackie Donnellan, and Diane Messidoro.

Then, as ever, there's my mother, Mary Rayner, whose input I could not do without, and Jonathan Richards.

Last but not least, my cat Othello, who jumped on my bed at an opportune moment one night and inspired me; and William Shakespeare, to whom I owe a plot device or two.

2012: I'd also like to add thanks to my editor at Picador, Francesca Main, who helped sharpen up this revised version; and all the lovely people at St. Martin's Press, especially Sara Goodman.